THE UNKNOWN DEVIL

A C.T. FERGUSON PRIVATE INVESTIGATOR MYSTERY (#2)

TOM FOWLER

WIDENING GYRE MEDIA

Do you like free books? You can get the prequel novella to the C.T. Ferguson mystery series for free. This is exclusive to my VIP readers. Just go here to get your book!

Editing by Chase Nottingham

Cover design by 100 Covers

 Created with Vellum

For Lisa and Isabel.

This book is dedicated to the memory of Lisa Mainolfi. She battled brain cancer on and off (mostly on) for eight years, and while it claimed her health and, eventually, her life, it never dimmed her spirit and joie de vivre. She brightened and bettered the lives of all who were fortunate enough to know her. Santayana said, "There is no cure for birth and death save to enjoy the interval." Lisa enjoyed it like few others, and the world is poorer for her passing. She leaves behind a husband and a son (my godson). May she rest in peace.

CHAPTER 1

Some people accept things easily, and others need a great deal of convincing. It has nothing to do with skepticism—which I have in droves and support in others—but a stubborn disbelief someone could possibly deny you something. The woman on the phone with me personified this trait.

"I don't do domestic cases," I said for at least the third time.

"But I'm sure my husband is cheating on me!" I heard crying at the edges of her voice. The tears may have been sincere, or they could have been a play for sympathy. Either way, I resolved to hang up on her if she started bawling. I have my limits.

"Then you don't need me, do you?"

My question gave her pause. It took her a few seconds to devise a comeback. "I'll need to prove it in court," she said.

As comebacks went, it wasn't one for the ages. "Do you have a smartphone?" I said.

"Yes, an iPhone."

"Do you know how to work the camera?"

"Of course I do."

"Then I have to reiterate you don't need me," I said.

"But I do," she said. "You do this for a living."

"That doesn't mean I take better pictures than the average

person. If you want to give a photo essay to a lawyer, call a photographer."

"But—"

I cut her off. "I don't do domestic cases. There are plenty of people who do."

"But I can't afford to pay them." Now the tears came. I remembered my resolution.

"Then I suggest you practice with your iPhone," I said, and hung up before she could implore me again. My first case started out as a domestic situation and turned into much more. In my illustrious eight-month career as a pro-bono private investigator, it had been my only domestic case. I resolved to keep it that way.

The woman who was sure she had a cheating husband called back. Some people just can't take no for an answer. I ignored the call and did the same when she tried two more times. The fourth time must have driven the point home. All this client-dodging made me hungry. After a few minutes of deleting junk emails, I got up, locked my house, and ventured out into Federal Hill for lunch.

I bought the house a little more than a month ago. The Fells Point apartment was fine, but I didn't like the idea of running a business out of there. The management company concurred. They allowed me to break my lease five months early without paying their usurious fee. I liked Fells Point enough to stay, but I found a great house in the Federal Hill area of Baltimore. It was an end rowhouse, and the previous owner had been a doctor of some sort, so the house came with an office.

Living in Federal Hill meant no shortage of food options. During the workday, Baltimore is a city of people stuffed into buildings. The exception is lunchtime, when the huddled masses yearn to breathe and eat freely, and the streets are awash with people walking to or from a lunch spot. I lived a few blocks from the Cross Street Market and headed there.

The Cross Street Market is a long building packed with food vendors and sellers of various tchotchkes. In the areas between the vendors are a few places to sit and eat. It was a warm mid-July day, and a lot of people milled about, straining the air conditioning and making me hope I could get in and out quickly. I grabbed a salmon burger and sweet potato fries from Frank's and walked back to my house. Total time gone: twenty-five minutes.

The food made it worth the walk and the crowd. Like I usually did, I ate at my office desk, reading about the Orioles and baseball in general as I lunched. The Orioles won a tense extra-inning road game in Boston the previous night. I tried to watch the entire game but fell asleep in the twelfth inning as midnight loomed. I felt old at twenty-eight and a half.

I was busy watching the highlights when my doorbell rang. Because of the home office, a ringing doorbell doesn't mean a potential client. Sometimes, it's my daily delivery from Amazon. This time, a young man who looked about seventeen peered back at me from the other side of the peephole. He didn't seem like a delivery driver. Process of elimination made him a potential client. If so, he would be my youngest. I opened the door.

"C.T. Ferguson?" he said.

"The one and only."

"I want to . . . I might need your help."

"Let's talk about it." I invited him inside and led him down the hall to my office. It was about eleven feet square with hardwood floors and plain walls I needed to do something with. A large desk with three monitors connected to a powerful custom-built laptop consumed most of the room. If I sat behind the desk just right, the screens blocked my view of potential clients. This was by design. My young visitor took one of my guest chairs as I sat in my leather executive model. The boy looked at the remaining sweet potato fries on the desk and frowned.

"I didn't mean to interrupt your lunch," he said.

"Don't worry about it," I said. "If I feel hungry, I'll eat in front of you." He didn't know what to say, so he opted for nothing. True to my word, I munched on a couple of fries. He continued not knowing how to begin. I helped. "I presume you didn't come here to watch me eat."

"No," he said, coming out of his reverie. "I think I need your help."

"I'm listening."

"My name is Brian, Brian Sellers. I'm worried about my older brother, Chris. I haven't seen him for a couple days."

"Is his absence unusual?" I said.

"I live with him. I usually see him every day."

"You live with your older brother?"

He nodded. "Our dad split not long after I was born. I don't even remember him. Our mom . . . died a few months ago."

"I'm sorry."

Brian gave a small smile and took a deep breath before continuing. "Chris and I have always been close, so he invited me to live with him and his girlfriend."

"Is she gone, too?"

"Yeah," he said after pondering it for a second. "I guess I didn't think about it, but I haven't seen her for a couple days, either."

"Maybe they took a vacation," I said.

"No, he would tell me."

"Maybe they went to Vegas to get married."

"He'd tell me something like that," Brian said, shaking his head. "It's why I'm concerned."

I took a notebook from my top desk drawer and jotted down a few details, mostly about the names Brian threw at me. "What's the girlfriend's name?" I said.

"Anna. Anna Blair."

I jotted it down. "Oh, and I have to ask—do you spell Brian with an I or a Y?"

"An I."

"Thank goodness."

My fake relief got him to grin. "I've never liked the Y, either," he said.

"I need a timeline," I said, refocusing us back to why Brian came to see me. "Today is Tuesday. When's the last time you saw your brother?"

Brian thought about timeframes for a second. "Saturday night," he said.

"You're sure?"

"Yes. He was awake and doing something on his computer when I went to bed. He seemed pretty engrossed in it. Probably another raid or something. I could never get into those games. Anyway, when I got up Sunday, he and Anna were gone. I haven't seen them since."

"I presume you've tried to reach him."

"He doesn't answer his cell. No response to texts or emails."

"What's his cell number?"

"410-555-9190."

I tried it from my office phone and put the call on speaker. After five rings, we got a voicemail. I ended the call without leaving a message.

"You've been home alone the last two days, then," I said.

"Yes."

"How old are you?"

"Sixteen," said Brian.

"You go to school?"

"Of course."

"Where?"

"Kenwood."

"In the county?"

"Yeah, we live in Rosedale."

I looked at my clock. "So you got from Kenwood to Federal Hill around lunchtime on a school day."

"Tuesday's a light day for me."

"And now you're home alone," I said.

"I can take care of myself."

"Maybe you can, but you can see how this is concerning."

Brian rolled his eyes. "What are you going to do, tell the county I'm living by myself for now? Find my brother and it all changes."

"I'm not going to dime you out," I said. "I simply want you to be aware of your situation."

"What do you mean?"

"Your brother and his girlfriend have been gone for two days. You can't reach them. We have to consider the possibility this wasn't of his own accord."

Brian frowned and nodded. I could tell he'd already considered it. How could he not, having lost both parents already? "I know," he said. "I thought about it."

"Have you also considered whoever made him disappear now knows you're home by yourself?"

I watched the rosy color flee Brian's cheeks. "No," he said, confirming the obvious. "What should I do?"

"First, you should call the county police and file a missing persons report. Two days is enough time for them to start looking into things. Do you have anyone else you can stay with?"

He shook his head. "I don't think so."

"No other family?" I said.

"Not locally."

"Friends?"

"I could ask."

"Ask. It might be overcautious, but we don't know at this point."

"All right. Does all of this advice mean you're going to help me?"

"I'd be kind of a dick if I said no at this point, wouldn't I?" I said.

"Totally," he said.

"Well, I guess I can't be a dick," I said.

* * *

I HOPED I didn't need a new car. My Lexus sedan threw about every warning light possible a couple days ago. The dealer told me it would be a while and also be expensive. I loved my car, but good sense required me to consider a new one. For now, I drove a blue Chevy Caprice Classic I acquired a couple months ago. In exchange for not ratting him out, the chop shop owner gave me a good deal. The car would win no prizes for aesthetics, but its V8 engine came from a Corvette and still responded with alacrity when I stepped on the gas. It also blended in with other cars better than a silver Lexus.

The Caprice came with an automatic transmission. I loathed automatics. My Lexus was one of the few sedans made with a manual. It was now an endangered creature. The new luxury sport sedans didn't have the option, and I wasn't paying Lexus prices for a coupe. Acura and Infiniti suffered from the same problems.

This combination of factors led me to a BMW dealership. The salesman looked askance at my Caprice as I got out. "My other car is a Lexus," I said.

"And now you're ready for German luxury?" he said.

"I'm ready for a test drive."

He brought around a black 340i with the M sport package. "I don't have one in a manual," he said. "People just don't get them as often anymore."

"Most people are missing out," I said.

"You know it. I know it. They don't know it."

He fetched a license plate, and we got into the car. I liked the feel of the seats. The steering wheel felt good in my hands. If I liked the way the car drove, it would make a fine replacement for the Lexus. I took it out on the road. Towson in the afternoon does not allow many opportunities to open the throttle. I wanted to gauge how the turbocharged inline-6 responded but had no such opportunities. The car drove well. I managed not to hate the automatic, though I noted when I would have held a gear longer or downshifted at a different time.

After about a half-hour of listening to a sales pitch while negotiating Towson traffic, I turned back into the dealer's lot. The salesman reminded me he didn't have my phone number. I told him he was correct and left. Once I was back in the Caprice, I tried calling Chris Sellers again. No answer.

I thought about Brian Sellers on the drive back to Federal Hill. His father left when he was young. I could probably find the dad, but would it do any good? He didn't want to be involved with his sons then; why should now be any different? With his mother also gone, Chris may have been Brian's last living relative, and now Chris was missing, too. Brian was a bright teenager who just lost the most important person in his world.

My sister died when I was sixteen. I knew how he felt.

CHAPTER 2

I called Kenwood High School and got Brian's schedule. All it took was me saying I was Chris Sellers and could you send it to this other email address instead? I seem to have been locked out of my primary one. You can? Thanks. People want to be helpful, which makes social engineering so much easier.

I continued my run of low-tech hacking by getting Chris and Brian's address from the phone book. If this continued, I'd have to cancel my Internet service and go into hiding. I settled for going to Rosedale and sitting on the house. Brian attended a study group and band practice after school. He wouldn't be home for a few hours yet. I hoped Chris would show up and solve my case for me. It would keep the lack of technology going, if nothing else.

Looking at Brian's schedule passed a little time. High school schedules changed a lot since I was sixteen. Brian enjoyed more free time and more classes to prepare him for college. How did high school—and a public high school, no less—manage to become so much more efficient in the last dozen years? Brian took a good course load, with AP classes in math and history. I noticed the lack of any computer science class. Perhaps secondary education failed to make the quantum leap I first thought.

After about an hour, I got the suspicion Chris Sellers may not be coming home. Another hour cemented my hunch. It's important for detectives to develop keen intuition. I then developed my observation skills by watching a woman in a sports bra and tiny shorts jog down the street. You never know who might be packing a concealed weapon. My observations left me confident the jogger was clean.

Once the jogger left the street, I called Sergeant Gonzalez with the Baltimore County Police. He and I had worked together a couple times, and I knew he'd be delighted to hear from me. "What now?" he said.

"I was just thinking how happy you'd be to hear my voice," I said.

"We aim to please. What's up?"

"Anyone file a missing persons report on a Chris Sellers?"

"What am I, the information desk?"

"You keep working with me, and you'll make lieutenant."

"Whatever. Hold on." Elevator music played in my ear. Even the BCPD went the mellow mood music route. I expected crime-stopper tips, some boring public service announcement, or at least better music. I thought about telling Gonzalez, but he would tell me he wasn't the complaints department. Then I wondered if businesses actually used complaints departments, and how hellish it would be to work in one. Elevator music has an effect on me.

"Had a report filed a couple hours ago," Gonzalez said as he came back on the line. "You find the guy already?"

"Little too quick, even for me," I said. "His brother came to me earlier today. I told him to file a report."

"Brian his brother?"

"The young man would be he."

"He? Listen to you."

"I have to show off my private school education when I can," I said.

"You know anything about this missing guy?"

"I know about as much as you."

"When it changes, you tell me," Gonzalez said.

"You, too."

"Sure," he said and hung up.

I went back to developing my intuition. No more comely joggers came by and allowed me to practice my powers of observation. I lamented their absence as I drove away about a half-hour later.

AFTER I GOT HOME, I surveyed the state of my refrigerator. Its state was not good. My pantry proved little better. I saw a few options for cooking, but nothing struck me as good. A perk to living in Federal Hill was the abundance of restaurants and bars. Anything I wanted to eat could be gotten within a few blocks. The tradeoff was living around so many hipsters and yuppies—I could get whatever food I desired, but I rarely wanted to stay and eat it.

I set off from my house to get dinner. By the end of the block, the combination of heat and humidity already set me to sweating. There are four seasons of equal length on the calendar. There are also four seasons on the Maryland calendar, but their lengths are far from equal. Spring starts sometime around late March and gets chased out by summer six weeks later. Memorial Day, theoretically in the spring, comes with temperatures near ninety and humidity to match. Welcome to Baltimore, where the summer air is so thick it could double as a soup.

A few minutes later, the blessed coolness of The Abbey's air conditioning washed over me. I ordered a Santa Fe burger and fries and enjoyed a craft beer of difficult pronunciation while I waited. It tasted good, even if I would have trouble ordering it again without pointing at the beer list. After ten more minutes, armed with dinner in a plastic bag, I braved the hot, humid air and walked back to my house.

I just finished eating when my doorbell rang. No one called first. Clients, current or prospective, rarely dropped in on me. Maybe I would need to get a real office if I wanted those visits. What's the point of putting your feet up on your desk if no one can see you do it? I went to the front door and looked through the peephole. A tall, thin man in a decent gray suit stood on my stoop. Behind him, a Town Car sat double-parked. I opened the door. "Yes?"

"Mr. E would like to speak with you," the man said.

Obviously, the identity of Mr. E was supposed to be clear to me. "Who the hell is Mr. E?" I said.

"Do you have a few minutes?" he said in a non-answer.

"Sure."

"Thank you, sir." He turned and started toward the Lincoln.

"Call me Mr. F," I said to his back.

* * *

I SAT BEHIND MY DESK. Mr. E and his driver, who found a parking spot, sat in my guest chairs. The driver pulled a small, rectangular device out of his pants pocket and pressed a button. I heard a faint buzzing sound. I glanced at my phone. No signal. I reached down and eased the second drawer of my desk open. If these guys brought a cell phone jammer, I wanted a gun in easy reach.

"Mr. E doesn't like electronics," the driver said.

"What does Mr. E think is inside your little box?" I said.

The driver smiled. Mr. E smiled. I smiled, too. Smiles all

around. "I presume Mr. E will replace my phone if your fucking gadget destroys it."

"It won't," Mr. E said.

"I'm so relieved." They didn't say anything else. I didn't feel like carrying the conversation, so I fell silent, too. Let them break it.

After a minute, Mr. E did. "You remember me?" he said.

I looked closer. His suit was a few shades darker and a few hundred dollars more expensive than his driver's. He possessed the classic Italian complexion along with dark eyes and black hair. I guessed him to be about forty-five and wondered if the black came from a bottle. Stubble covered a face which would look the same if he shaved every hour. A few bits of gray dotted his five o'clock shadow. When he had been standing, I pegged Mr. E for five-ten, giving me four inches on him. He had an average build—not fat, not skinny, and not muscular. His voice sounded familiar, but I couldn't place it. "No," I said after a moment of thought.

"I remember you," he said. "You used to play in Tony's poker games. Hell, you were the only one there under twenty-one."

Tony Rizzo, the head of organized crime in Baltimore, once hosted poker games at his restaurant in Little Italy. Tony had been a friend of my parents forever. I started playing in the poker games when I was in high school and played right on through my college years. I was no threat to turn pro, but I could hold my own at the table. Within the remembered context, I remembered seeing a younger version of Mr. E's face and hearing his voice. "I can place you now," I said.

"Always good to be remembered. Alberto Esposito." He extended his hand. I shook it.

"Now I know what the E stands for. At least I've solved one mystery today."

"I think I solved that one for you."

"I'm taking credit for it," I said. "What can I do for you?"

"I want to tell you a story," he said. "I was in Tony's crew. We were pretty tight. In a few years, I was basically his right-hand guy. I figure he's gonna groom me to take over for him one day."

"Tony has a daughter."

"A daughter . . . but not a son. What? You think some broad is gonna run things when Tony's gone?"

"I'm pretty sure Gabriella isn't 'some broad,'" I said.

"Sure," Esposito said with a wave of his hand. I could forgive his casual sexism, but I knew Gabriella. We were the same age. "Anyway, Tony was acting like he wanted to hand it over to me someday. Turns out, not so much."

"What happened?"

"Four years ago, he tells me I can't learn anymore from him. He sends me to Cleveland." Esposito scoffed and shook his head. "Fucking Cleveland. You ever been?"

"No."

"Don't. It sucks."

"I'll cross it off my bucket list," I said.

"Make sure you do."

"So you were in Cleveland. Did you have to stay there?"

"It's where Tony sent me," he said. "The guy in Cleveland is an asshole. Younger than Tony and a little more modern but without the old-school business sense Tony has, you know? He and Tony are friends, so he agreed to show me around and teach me what he could. I spent four years there. I learned everything the dumb shit knew in a month."

"Why did you stay?" I said.

"Tony wanted me there. I wanted to come back. Even told Tony, but he wanted me to stay and learn. I says I learned all I could. Tony says I don't know shit, then. So I tell Tony to go to hell."

"You're still alive, so I guess he didn't take it too personally."

"Nah. I'd been gone about a year by then."

"You hated Cleveland, you'd stopped learning from the guy there, and you quit Tony," I said. "I'm still wondering why you stayed."

"Money," Esposito said. "Mr. C wasn't the sharpest knife in the drawer, but he knew how to make money. His hands were in a lot of pots. Had a lot of cops and lawyers looking the other way. He knew how to run things."

"You think Tony doesn't?"

"I think Tony's old. What is he now, seventy?"

I shrugged. "Sounds about right."

"He's still living off the old rackets. He doesn't want to get involved in drugs. Fucking blacks and Mexicans make a killing selling drugs. There's no reason Tony shouldn't get a cut."

"Look," I said, "I don't really care how Tony makes his money, and I don't care about untapped markets."

Esposito smiled again. It looked sincere. "Of course you don't. You can't help me with something like a cut of drug money."

"And I wouldn't, regardless of my ability to."

"But there is something you can help me with," Esposito said. "There's a killing to be made online. Mobs overseas are doing it. The smart ones here are getting into it. Tony's a dinosaur; he ain't gonna touch it."

I thought about how this situation might relate to me. I still didn't care how Tony made his money or how much he left on the table by not being the modern mob boss Esposito wanted him to be. Esposito remembered me from Tony's poker games. He was back in town and sought me out. I doubt he came here for Texas hold-'em tips. "You want me to help you find ransomware?" I said.

He smiled again. This one broadcasted full wattage. "Better," he said, "I want you to write it for me."

"Come again?"

"You ran your mouth back in the day how good you were with computers." Esposito nodded at my office setup. "You got three screens here and at least as many computers, I'll bet. You could write it."

"You could download it," I said. "A few good ransomware products are out there."

"I don't want what everyone else uses. I want something new. Something ain't getting caught by Norton or whatever."

"Most ransomware doesn't get caught by those programs," I said. "You can download some good ones to give you what you want."

"You could write me better stuff."

"Maybe, but I won't."

"Think about it. Some poor bastard goes to use his computer one day and all his files are encrypted. He can't get anything back unless he pays two hundred. He's paying the two hundred."

"You can almost get a new computer for as much," I said.

"But you can't get your files," he said.

There were ways around it. I figured Esposito knew, so I didn't bother pointing it out. It wouldn't have dissuaded him anyway. "Even if you get this ransomware," I said, "what are you going to do with it? Tony's still in charge."

"Tony's old," Esposito repeated. "He ain't changing with the times. He ain't keeping up. It's time for some new blood."

I shook my head. "Let me get this straight," I said. "You want me to write you a new piece of crimeware, even though you can download your choice of the best."

"Uh-huh."

"And you intend to use the proceeds from it to fund some kind of takeover of the Baltimore mob."

"Uh-huh."

"And I presume your plan ends with Tony dead. Tony, whom

I've known my whole life. You basically want me to help you kill Tony Rizzo and take over for him."

"Pretty much," Esposito said with a nod.

"Get out of my house," I said.

"Mr. E does not get refused often," the driver said, reminding me he was still in the room, wasting his portion of the oxygen.

"He's getting refused today," I said. "Get out. Both of you. Don't come back."

"You need some time to think about it," Esposito said. "It's a lot to take in." He stood. The driver did, too. "I'll give you some time. But remember, I came to you. I know you could do this. And you're used to Tony, so I know you ain't gonna cheat me."

"I also *ain't* writing you a piece of ransomware."

Esposito smiled again. This time, it reminded me of a predator. "One way or the other . . . with or without you, I'm taking over for Tony. It'd be a lot better for you to count me as a friend than an enemy."

"I'll take my chances," I said.

"You think about it," he said. Esposito and the driver walked back to my foyer, then outside. I left the door open and watched. The driver opened the right rear car door for Esposito, then closed it once the boss was settled. He got in, started the Town Car, and pulled away. I took note of the license plate as the car passed my house: MISTER E.

What an asshole. And I knew I hadn't seen the last of him.

CHAPTER 3

I didn't like having Esposito come to my house and threaten me in so many words. I also didn't relish the idea of a jackass like him taking over for Tony. Tony was old and set in his ways, and I figured he had sent as many men to their graves as some tinpot dictators. Still, I had known him my whole life and could work with him. I couldn't see myself getting along with Esposito. Better the devil you know.

Besides, with Tony dead, where would I get good Italian meals for free? The case against Esposito mounted.

Having to deal with Esposito sapped my desire to work my current case. I made up for it by going to the gym. I'm not much of a weight lifter, but I throw up some iron here and there to keep my strength above par. After a half-hour of free weights, I got on the treadmill for three miles. An hour on the go tired me, but I strapped on some MMA gloves and went after the heavy bag. Punches, elbows, and knees. Twenty minutes later, sucking wind, I finished my second bottle of water and hit the showers.

Smelling clean and feeling refreshed, I left the gym. Two women dressed like they wanted to be seen working out headed toward the front door. Despite my fresh workout scent and vibe, they kept talking to each other and walked right on past me. Perhaps I needed to flex as I walked to the car.

Behind the wheel, I thought about the case for the first time in a couple hours. In some ways, two days was a long time to be missing, and in other ways, it was no time at all. I called Joey Trovato and told him I wanted his professional opinion. Conveniently for him—and unfortunately for my wallet—he hadn't had dinner yet. We agreed to meet at Della Notte.

When I arrived fifteen minutes later, Joey was there, and the bread basket was already empty. I took my time walking to the table, enjoying the smells of the restaurant. Pasta, meat, and tomatoes hit my nostrils in equal amounts. Sometimes, the aroma of the place was just as good as the food.

Joey was a black Sicilian of good demeanor and boundless appetite. I slid into the booth opposite him and looked at the barren basket. "You give 'fast food' a whole new meaning," I said.

"This was the second one," Joey said.

"Jesus. I never would have agreed to this if you'd told me you hadn't eaten today."

Joey smiled. "I had a light lunch."

"Just one pizza?"

"You're hilarious."

A waitress showed up and dropped off another basket of bread and another dish of oil and spices. She asked if we wanted appetizers. We did. Joey ordered mozzarella sticks. I opted for garlic bread with cheese.

"No more than shitty pizza," Joey said as the waitress left.

"I just worked out for an hour and a half," I said. "I need shitty pizza right now."

Before Joey could scarf down the third basket of bread, I broke off a couple pieces and put them on my appetizer plate. I thought the spice array in the oil looked lacking, but it tasted good. It didn't seem to stop Joey. He finished his two pieces before I did and polished off the rest of the basket in short order. Joey always possessed an appetite and had forever been over-weight, but he wasn't obese and surprised people with his athleticism. At every occasion, he ate well on my dime.

The waitress dropped off our appetizers and freshened our drinks. We ordered entrees—chicken parmesan for Joey and whole wheat linguine with meat sauce for me. The waitress walked away. Her tight black pants were more interesting than any of the décor. Exposed brick added a nice touch, but the rest looked like most Italian restaurants. Joey and I both watched the waitress disappear into the kitchen.

"Whole wheat pasta?" Joey said.

"Does it offend your heritage?" I said.

"And my palate."

I took out my phone and called up a picture of Chris Sellers. "This guy has been missing for a couple days." I slid it screen-up across the table. "His younger brother hired me to find him. Has he been to see you?"

Joey shook his head. Like me, he had always been good with computers. He used his skills to create new identities for people. It allowed him to do well for himself, but he also got to see a lot of people at their worst. "Haven't seen him," said Joey.

I flipped to the next photo. Anna Blair smiled up at us. "Seen her?"

"I wish," Joey said.

I shrugged and put my phone away. "I figured it was unlikely."

"They been gone two days?"

"Yeah. No word anywhere."

"I'll keep an eye out," Joey said.

"Thanks. I think Chris would want to take Brian with him if it got to the point they came to see you. They're all the family they have."

"You think the brother is dead?"

I pondered his question for a second. "I don't know," I said. "I don't have a great intuition for this sort of thing."

"What does your gut tell you?"

"He's alive," I said after a moment of thought.

"Listen to your gut."

"It's done wonders for you," I said.

Joey patted his stomach. "Damn right."

* * *

CHRIS SELLERS, like most people a few years younger than I, maintained a sprawling social media presence. I wanted to find places he might have been. His uploaded pictures—and there were a lot of them—could have geolocation data in them. For now, I settled for his LinkedIn page. It listed the company he worked for, a small government contractor I never heard of. They kept an office in Aberdeen, just off the proving ground. I found a couple of his coworkers who were closer. One of them agreed to meet me.

I met Bobbi Lane in the Barnes and Noble Café in White Marsh. Like most people who meet me, she arrived first. I ordered an iced chai and met her at her table. Bobbi was a tall and slender light-skinned black woman with delicate features. I might have called her exotic looking if I hadn't spent over three years in Hong Kong. She wore an outfit suggesting she was going for an evening run after our meeting. I approved of both the clothes and the exercise.

"You're the detective," she said as I sat opposite her at the small table.

"I am," I said. I showed her my ID. She looked at it and nodded.

"I don't think I've ever talked to a private detective before," she said.

"I'll try to set a high bar."

She smiled. "You carry a gun?"

"Yes."

"Ever shoot someone?"

"Not yet."

She smiled briefly before returning to business. "You said this is about Chris."

"His brother came to me. No one's seen him or his girlfriend for two days."

"We were wondering about him."

"I take it he hasn't been to work?" She shook her head. "No calls?"

"No," Bobbi Lane said. She took a small drink from something resembling a smoothie. "He always calls if he's running late or anything like that."

"Is he running late often?"

"No more than anyone else, I guess. He's just better at letting us know."

"How closely do you work with him?"

"We're on the same team."

"What is it you do?"

She cast a glance around the room. "You know we work for a contractor."

"I do," I said.

"OK. I can't tell you a lot of specifics. We're both researchers. Chris is a postdoc. I'm a grad student."

"What do you research?"

She smiled again. It was a good one. Gloria's was better, but a man could get used to seeing Bobbi's. "That's one of the things I can't tell you."

I thought about a better tack to approach this. "Open source research?"

"For the most part," she said.

"On the Internet."

"Yes."

"The Internet isn't classified," I said.

"I guess you have me there." Bobbi took another sip of her smoothie. I smiled in encouragement. It wasn't my full-power version. I didn't need her disrobing in the café. Fewer lumens would still have a good effect.

"Computer stuff," she said after a moment. "We're both computer scientists. The government is . . . always looking for an edge when it comes to technology."

"Exploitation?"

"Now we're getting into I-can't-tell-you territory again."

"Can you let me know how Chris's research was going?" I said. I sipped my chai while she thought about her response. It wasn't coffee, but it came pretty close.

"Promising," she said. "He did a lot on his own, too. I know he built a test lab in his apartment."

"He did a lot of research off-hours?"

"Yes," she said. "He definitely enjoyed it."

"Did he work at home?"

"For practical stuff, he'd use his lab. He put some virtual machines together." She paused. "You know much about computers?"

"Your company would be desperate to hire me if I hit the open market," I said.

She eyed me up and nodded. Maybe I passed some kind of trial. "OK. He had a VM lab where he would . . . test out his research and document his findings. That kind of stuff he did at home. Most of the time, if he wasn't at work or home, he was in a coffee shop somewhere."

"So the government's future computer exploits could have

originated in a Starbucks?"

"I never said exploits." Bobbi grinned and sipped her smoothie.

"No, you didn't," I said. "But you didn't have to."

We sat in silence for a minute. I doubted she had much else to tell me, at least anything she'd be willing to share here. While Bobbi glanced around the café, I took the chance to admire her legs. She had toned runner's legs, matching the rest of her body. I wondered how many miles she did in a week. "You think you can find him?" Bobbi said.

"I'm good at finding people," I said, "so I think so."

"I hope you can. Chris is a good guy."

"You ever meet his brother?"

"Yeah, the Christmas party last year," she said. "Chris brought his girlfriend and Brian."

I didn't know much about her yet besides a name. "What'd you think of her?"

Bobbi shrugged. "I only met her twice. Never got much of a chance to talk to her, so I can't say what she was like."

"Did you like her?"

"She was fine, I guess."

"But?" I coaxed.

"But I'm not sure she's right for Chris. They're really different."

"You know what she does?"

"I think she told me once, but I don't remember."

"Must not have been interesting," I said with another encouraging smile. The wattage might have increased. If I were forced to encourage Bobbi to keep her clothes on, I doubted I was up to the task.

"It wasn't." She gave a non-collegial smile back at me.

I took out a business card and slid it across the table. "If you hear from him or think of anything to help me find him, let me know."

Bobbi took the card and looked at it. "One of these is your cell?" she said.

"The 410 number."

"What if I want a running partner one day?" She showed me a quick, almost shy grin. I might need to be careful how much I put into my smiles when attractive women were involved.

"You can call me for anything," I said.

* * *

COUNTING national places like Panera and Starbucks, plus smaller local joints, there were eight coffee shops near his apartment where Chris Sellers could have done his work. The one I was about to leave would be one of them, if farther than the rest. I showed his picture to the baristas, but none remembered seeing him. Ditto at the proper Starbucks a few doors away. Yes, there's really a Starbucks a few doors down from the Barnes and Noble Café, which is a rebranded Starbucks. It didn't make sense to me, but both were always crowded, so it worked out.

I started circling back toward Chris Sellers's apartment. The first two places were swings and misses, but I found someone at the third place who recognized him. "I see him in here about once a week or so," she said. Lucy was a cute barista who looked like she just finished high school.

"How often are you here?" I said.

"Four nights a week, usually."

"When was the last time you saw him?"

She thought about it as she worked on someone's order. "I guess about a week ago? I mean, I don't try to keep track of customers. Unless they're cute." She grinned.

"I guess Chris didn't meet your cuteness standards?"

"Gross . . . he's way too old."

I decided not to ask about myself. Kids these days.

* * *

THE NEXT PLACE I tried was the same: someone saw Chris Sellers about once a week and hadn't seen him in approximately the same timeframe. The next coffee shop was a local place called The Great Bean. I parked around the side and went in. It featured brick walls, postmodern art, and furniture I took for reclaimed wood. I always wondered why no one claimed it the first time. The manager recognized Chris's picture. He might have been a year out of college. I lamented the standards for management in the coffee shop industry as I talked to him.

"You see him often?"

"Couple nights a week," he said as he checked off a couple things on an inventory list.

"When was the last time?"

He looked up at me and frowned. "Don't you all talk to each other?"

Uh-oh. "What do you mean?" I said.

"Someone was just in here asking about him," he said.

"A cop?"

"I don't know."

I looked out front. A car's headlights switched on. I dashed out the door. A black Town Car sped away from the curb. As I watched it drive away, I saw the rear license plate.

MISTER E.

Well, shit. What the hell was going on?

CHAPTER 4

THE NEXT MORNING, I HAD COFFEE WITH MY COUSIN RICH and Detective Paul King at The Daily Grind in Fells Point. I met King through Rich for a case I wrapped up a month or so ago. Rich showed the short hair and general neatness he learned in the Army and maintained since. He looked like a cop. King looked like an artsy rock singer who couldn't decide on a way to dress. His blond hair was shaggy and generally looked like a straw mop placed atop his head. He wore a neat goatee framed by a perpetual five-o'clock shadow begging for a razor.

This was only my second cup of coffee for the day, so I opted for a strong light roast. Rich and King already started in on theirs. "Can't get enough of me?" King said as I slid onto the chair opposite them.

"I'm desperate for fashion and grooming tips," I said.

Rich snorted. King looked at me for a second and grinned. "You've come to the right place, then." He jerked his thumb at Rich. "This fucker dresses too much like a square."

"A square?" Rich said. "What is this, 1965?"

I steered us back toward the task at hand. "Rich tells me you've enjoyed a varied career," I said to King.

"Little of this, little of that," he said.

"How about organized crime?"

"I was on a task force for a while."

I sipped some coffee. Its strength impressed me. I should have added a little more creamer. I couldn't get any now, though. Rich always chided me for not drinking my coffee black, and he wouldn't let me live it down for weeks. Pride goeth before the coffee.

"Couldn't get Tony?"

King let out a chuckle, but I couldn't hear any humor in it. "I don't think we could have gotten him even if it was the goal."

"Too connected?" I said.

"Tony's old school," said King, "and he's been in charge for-fucking-ever. Yeah, he has cops in his pocket." Rich frowned at the remark but didn't say anything. "I'm sure he's got people in the state's attorney's office. Judges, too, if push ever came to shove. Tony knows the wheels to grease. He's probably taken more pictures with mayors than their wives have."

"So what happened?"

King sampled his coffee. "Tony doesn't have everything on lockdown," he said. "You'd think he might. Baltimore ain't the size of New York or anything. But you see some . . . pockets of resistance pop up every now and then. Someone tries to grab a piece of something."

"What does Tony do?"

"Sometimes nothing. Sometimes, he does what you might expect."

"So your task force took care of those . . . pockets of resistance, as you put it."

"Basically, yeah. If you take a cynical look at it, we did Tony's dirty work for him. We took down the people who were making money he could have been making."

"Seems like a shitty outcome," I said.

"The task force can say it did something," Rich said. "They

made arrests. They got criminals off the street. Mission accomplished."

I shook my head. "You ever hear of Alberto Esposito?"

"Name's familiar," King said. He frowned and drank some coffee to fuel his thoughts. I liked his plan so much, I had some coffee too. "He was with Tony a few years ago, right? Then he left."

"About four years ago, he went to Cleveland."

"What the fuck is in Cleveland?" King said.

I filled them in on Esposito's story. "I'd never heard of him before he came to my office," I said. "He wants me to write some malware for him."

"Like a virus?" Rich said.

"More or less."

"Are you going to do it?"

"Of course not."

"Guys like Esposito ain't used to being refused," King said.

We watched a couple of college girls come in. They wore tank tops and spandex shorts. There were few things to love about summers in Baltimore. Once you tossed out the heat and humidity, the list consisted of girls in summer clothes and Orioles games. Pretty girls in small clothes topped the list. "I don't think they have any concealed weapons," King said after a minute.

"You can never be too vigilant," Rich said.

"I need the practice," I said. "You two are more experienced detectives than I am."

The girls got their coffees and left. Reality resumed.

"So Esposito is interested in a virus?" King said.

"Sounds like it. When I told him no, he said he'd give me time to think about it."

"Could you write him what he wants?"

"Sure."

"I'm glad you're not going to," Rich said, frowning at King.

"He shouldn't need me to," I said. "He could find what he wants online and download it."

"Why come to you, then?" King said.

I sipped some more java. Now I wished I had a pastry to go with it. I eyed the last quarter of Rich's danish with envy. "He said he remembered me from Tony's poker games," I said. "And he remembered I was good with computers."

"It ain't always nice to be remembered," King said.

"Now I've told him no, I'm worried he's going to find someone else. There are less principled people out there who could do what I could do."

"Even less principled than you?" Rich said with a grin.

"Hard as it is to believe, yes," I said. "I think he's already looking for one." I told him about Chris Sellers and the Town Car leaving the coffee shop.

"Is there a missing persons report?" Rich said.

"Yeah, but he lives in the county."

"You working with Gonzalez?"

"So far."

Rich finished his pastry. I might need to get one to go. "What are you going to do now?" King said.

"I was thinking about getting a danish," I said.

"Good plan. Maybe you can buy one for Esposito and get him to leave you alone."

"Right now, my plan is to keep telling him no," I said.

"What if he insists?" Rich said.

"Then I guess I'll have to insist, too," I said.

* * *

Bobbi Lane told me some interesting things about Chris Sellers. I looked into him with more depth once I got back home and finished the danish I took with me from the Daily Grind. He submitted his doctoral dissertation at Johns Hopkins. The subject? The increasing modernization of Eastern European crime syndicates and its potential effects on organized crime in America. His thesis might as well have served him up on a plate for someone like Esposito.

I found his dissertation was under consideration, but I couldn't find the text of it anywhere. It may have been for the best: I would have been tempted to read it and didn't want to get wrapped up in a long paper. If Esposito were looking for Chris Sellers, I couldn't afford to waste much time.

Like most computer science people, Chris Sellers wrote his own code. And like most computer science people, he posted it online. His handle on repository websites matched the one on his Gmail account. I wondered if Esposito found any of the code this way. It didn't take any special knowledge of anything related to computers. Sometimes, the easiest hacks are the best ones to use.

I wanted to look at the programs Chris Sellers wrote. Considering their nature, I built a new virtual machine just for this purpose. It's the same thing I did when working on my own code. Over the years, malware has gotten smarter and some can tell when it's being run in a VM; it will disable many of its features to make evaluation harder. I didn't want the program to execute, however.

I downloaded a bunch of Chris Sellers' code and looked at it. He wrote all of it in the C programming language. A man after my own heart. He made copious comments in it, as well, which was another thing I liked about him. The specific piece I looked at was a basic backdoor, designed to maintain access to someone's computer. From what I could tell, it would be very effective and impossible to detect.

From there, I looked at more of what Chris Sellers had written. Some of his programs did simple things like email automation. Spammers had similar tools available, but this would be a good one to have in their back pockets. It would make a great platform from which to launch a large phishing attack. After a couple hours, I hit the mother lode. Chris Sellers started working on a new piece of ransomware. His comments mentioned analyzing samples from Russia, Ukraine, and other places in Eastern Europe. He made some impressive innovations with the code, making it much harder for traditional anti-malware and anti-exploit tools to stop. He hadn't finished it. By my guess, he had about half of it written. Then there would be more time for testing, development, and refinement. It would require weeks, but at the end, this would be an impressive piece of ransomware.

This would be something Alberto Esposito would want. No wonder he had taken an interest in Chris. I would need to find him and keep him away from Esposito. With a tool like this, Esposito could raise a lot of money quickly and try to usurp control of the city from Tony. And then he could do something about yours truly who spurned his request for ransomware.

I couldn't let it happen.

* * *

COMPARED TO CHRIS SELLERS, Alberto Esposito had a minimal online presence. He was one of about nine people in America who still had a MySpace page, but he hadn't updated since early in Obama's first term. His Facebook page looked equally old and was also locked down to the point I couldn't see any pictures. Given time, I could get around his settings, but I doubted it would be worth it. LinkedIn listed Esposito as a "self-employed business consultant." His profile there remained reasonably current with over 200 connections. I wondered if anyone like Esposito had ever been busted or gotten anyone else busted just from social media profiles.

I took some screenshots and notes based on the connections,

especially the ones added recently. Maybe Esposito would turn to someone else to write his ransomware for him. Maybe I would find a "self-employed persuasion consultant" who would work over Chris Sellers until he did what was asked of him. Regardless, I found some names to run through the BPD's databases.

During my first case, Rich left me alone with his work computer for a few minutes. Since then, I've maintained an easy way into their network. Every now and then, they try something new to secure things, but those measures never deter me for long. I fed the fifteen names I wrote down into the BPD's database. Ten came back with criminal records, mostly for crimes in the assault family. Add in a few gun felonies and the occasional sexual assault, and you had a bushel of real peaches.

I looked at the list I made and found the one Esposito had known the longest: Raymond Delcoro. There was another Delcoro on Esposito's contacts list as well, Michael. The BPD told me they were brothers with Michael being the older, and both showed similar criminal records. I also learned they shared a house in Gardenville, a neighborhood in northeast Baltimore. For lack of any other avenue to explore, I got in the Caprice and headed for Gardenville.

* * *

The Brothers Delcoro lived on Mayview Avenue near the bottom of the hill where Mayview dead-ended at Todd. I could see their house from Todd, so I sat and waited for something to happen. No cars were in their driveway or in front of the house. I waited some more. I drank some water. No activity near the house. I found a zombie-killing game for my phone and butchered some undead while I staked out the place. If this PI thing bored me into quitting, maybe I could reinvent myself as a zombie hunter. All I'd have to do first would be invent zombies.

I got hungry about an hour in. Water wasn't cutting it. Just as I looked for nearby convenience stores on my phone, a car came down Mayview and pulled into the Delcoros' driveway. One man got out and went into the house. The car, a silver Accord resembling a million other cars on the road, backed out of the driveway a few minutes later, continued along Mayview and made a right on Todd. As it went past, I got a look at the driver: Michael Delcoro. When he drove away, I fired up the Caprice, used Mayview to help my U-turn, and followed him.

Michael Delcoro wormed his way through some depressing neighborhoods. For all the gentrification happening in some parts of Baltimore, neighborhoods like Gardenville still had the interrelated problems of poverty and crime. Apartment complexes were full of people who wanted something better and were too beaten down to hope it would ever happen. I was guiltily relieved when we got onto Moravia Road and more businesses and industrial areas sprang up.

He got onto 95 South. Hanging back so as to not tip Michael Delcoro off, I got onto 95 South, too. Ahead, I saw two silver Accords. One of these days, I would have to get more observant of things like tag numbers. Both Accords exited at Boston Street because of course they did. From there, they went in different directions. I picked one to follow, hoping my mental coin flip came up correct.

I soon discovered it had not. The Accord I followed pulled into the parking lot of a large Best Western hotel. A slender, attractive Asian woman got out and walked toward the hotel. I would much prefer following her to following Michael Delcoro. She, however, was not useful for my case. I had no idea where Delcoro had gone once he exited at Boston Street. I didn't have anyone else to follow at this point, so I headed back to 95 and went home.

* * *

ON A LARK, I decided to look at Chris Sellers' incomplete ransomware again. I created a new virtual machine and uploaded the code. About a third of the way into it, I found what I had been looking for.

Ransomware holds a computer and its files hostage via encryption but is easier to defeat than many people think. Reimaging the hard drive or using system restore is often enough. Of course, you have to be able to boot to a CD or USB drive to do it. If you can, the ransomware can't stop you from reimaging or restoring and getting rid of it.

Chris Sellers' could.

One of the first things his program did was delete any system restore points, taking the easy option off the table. Next, the program corrupted the partition table and master boot record. This meant even redoing the hard drive wouldn't get rid of the ransomware; with its hooks in everything, it would just show up again. Replacing the hard drive would be a solution, but by the time users thought of it, they might have simply paid the ransom and cut their losses.

I was impressed. More importantly, Alberto Esposito had been impressed. I wondered how he ever heard of Chris Sellers and his work. Esposito was a more modern thinker than Tony Rizzo and maybe more modern than a lot of guys in Tony's position. He could have been savvy when it came to programming, though nothing in his history suggested such aptitude. I was curious if someone put him on to Chris Sellers. And now with Chris disappearing, I wondered what Esposito had to do with it and what his next move would be.

CHAPTER 5

I WOKE UP THE NEXT MORNING HUNGRY FOR INFORMATION
and thirsty for justice. In addition, I was hungry for breakfast and
thirsty for coffee. Resolving the second set first, I whipped up a
quick omelet with wheat toast and a local dark roast. While I ate,
I pondered how Chris Sellers found himself on Alberto Esposito's radar. Chris seemed like an upstanding guy, and I couldn't
imagine them moving in the same circles, which meant Esposito
had to cast a net. I wondered who besides Chris Sellers swam
into it.

After breakfast, I looked at Esposito's LinkedIn page again.
This time, I wasn't interested in gangsters hiding amid clever
euphemisms. I wanted someone at Hopkins or at the contracting
company where Chris Sellers worked. I hoped it wasn't Bobbi
Lane. She'd make a good running partner and interrogating her
about Esposito afterward would be a downer. A name jumped
out at me: Danny Esposito worked at Hopkins as an admissions
officer for graduate and doctorate programs.

I went back to the BPD's system. Danny was Alberto's
youngest brother. He showed one DUI but otherwise lived a
clean life, apart from feeding his brother information. He had to
know what his brother did for a living, even if he may not have

known why Alberto wanted someone like Chris Sellers. At some point, I would need to talk to Danny.

Right now, I wanted to exercise. I hit the dojo, where I worked over a bag for twenty minutes and sparred for about as long. Then I went home and ran two miles around Federal Hill Park. Only completing the testosterone trifecta with a trip to the shooting range would have left me feeling manlier. I thought about building something with power tools when I got home but settled for taking a shower.

I needed to see someone.

* * *

FOR AS LONG AS I had known Tony Rizzo—which would be over half of my coming-up-on-29 years—I knew he was a gangster. I watched too many movies, and stereotypes get to be stereotypical for a reason. Tony had been in charge of organized crime in Baltimore for decades, probably the duration of my life. On top of it all, he and my parents were friends forever, and he always let me eat for free in his restaurant. I harbored many reasons for wanting to keep him around and in charge.

I parked near *Il Buon Cibo*, Tony's restaurant, and walked in. The lunch crowd filled about a third of the first-floor dining room. As usual, Tony sat alone near the fireplace, which held no fire during summer lunches. Tony's table sat apart from the others, save two placed nearby, each occupied by one of Tony's goons. They were used to me by now, so they merely practiced their glares as I approached. Tony looked up from his cup of coffee and local section of the *Sun*. He smiled and nodded at the chair opposite his. I sat.

"C.T., good to see you," Tony said. I believed him. The smile reached his eyes. Tony hadn't been happy to learn I worked as a

PI, but none of my cases conflicted with his interests. I hoped to stay on his good side.

"You too, Tony," I said.

"You come hungry?"

"Starving, actually."

"If I didn't know better, I'd think you came to see me for free food." Tony snapped his fingers, and a waitress appeared. She was a pretty college girl and wore the white shirt unbuttoned precisely enough to be interesting.

"Yes, sir?" she said.

"Give my friend whatever he wants," Tony said, inclining his head toward me.

The perks of sitting at The Man's table. "Do you need a menu, sir?" she said to me.

"I've been here enough," I said. "Veal parmesan, whole wheat pasta, side salad, unsweetened iced tea. Please."

"Certainly, sir," she said, taking notes on her pad and vanishing as quickly as she materialized.

"Whole wheat pasta?" Tony said. "You becoming a fucking health nut?"

"I've been a health nut for years," I said.

Tony laughed. "So you have."

"If you offer it, I'm going to eat it." I looked around the restaurant. The décor conjured images of a ristorante in Italy, or so the decorator wanted us to believe. It looked authentic enough to me, but I had never been to Italy. Tony's resembled many in Brooklyn, which I guessed was authentic enough for most people. "How's the lunch crowd?" I said.

"Not bad," said Tony. "We do better at dinner. Lots of places aren't closing between lunch and dinner anymore. Pisses me off."

"You still close?"

"Yeah, from three to five. Used to be two-thirty until a bunch of people bitched about it." He paused. "How come I can't get a steak at two-thirty?" Tony said in a higher, mocking tone. "Because it's two-thirty, you asshole."

"Ah, the demands of a younger clientele," I said.

"It ain't the same neighborhood anymore. We all gotta change with the times."

The waitress returned with my lunch. Another perk to sitting at Tony's table was the ginormous portions of food I got. The large plate struggled to hold the side of veal set atop it. Cheese bubbled and fragrant steam rose from everything. The salad came in a bowl befitting a full-sized offering. The greens and reds popped. A cup of the house creamy Italian dressing sat off to the side.

I put some on my salad and cut about half the veal to let it cool. Tony sat in silence while I ate the greens. He and his goons shared a few looks. One came up, whispered something in Tony's ear, and left when Tony nodded. I wouldn't ask, and Tony knew it. After a moment, he said, "I know you didn't come here for the food and company. What's on your mind?"

"Alberto Esposito," I said after taking the first bite of my veal parmesan. It almost cooled enough.

Tony kept his expression neutral. "Who?"

"Tony. Really?"

It took a minute, during which I kept eating, but Tony smirked. "Fine. I guess I can't play dumb with you. What about him?"

"You sent him away."

"Yeah. To Cleveland. He had stuff to learn that he couldn't learn from me. And I had stuff to teach him he didn't want to learn." Tony shook his head at the memory. "So I sent him to Cleveland. He could learn there. Besides, it's fucking Cleveland. Maybe it'll teach him a little respect."

"I don't think it worked."

It took Tony a second, but he caught the meaning. "What? He's back in town?"

"I'm guessing he didn't come by and say hello," I said.

"Not exactly," Tony said. "Ain't heard a peep from him for months. I figured he was working."

"He probably was. Now he wants to work on taking your job."

My remark made Tony chuckle. I didn't expect his reaction. I anticipated seething anger and maybe a minor outburst to make all his lunch patrons remember just who owned this restaurant. He kept chuckling as I ate another bite.

"I didn't know I brought jokes," I said.

"That dumbass . . . taking over for me?" Tony said. "Shit. Better people than him have tried. I'm still here. Wanna guess where they are?"

"I have a good idea."

"Of course you do. You're a smart kid, C.T. I thought Esposito was smart, too. Thought he had potential. I guess not." He paused. "Wait, how do you know this asshole?"

"He came to see me."

"Why?"

"Said he remembered me from your poker games," I said.

"What did he want?" said Tony.

"I think he wants to modernize things. He asked me to write some ransomware for him." I wondered if Tony knew what ransomware was.

"What'd you say?"

"What do you think? I told him no."

"Did he take no for an answer?"

I shrugged. "He said he'd let me think on it. My answer isn't changing."

"You need help with Esposito?" Tony said.

"I can handle him," I said. "My concern is I think he's still looking for someone to write his ransomware." I told Tony a little about Brian and Chris Sellers. "I saw Esposito's car speeding away from a coffee shop the guy frequented. Our former friend is definitely on the hunt."

"You think the kid wrote the malware for him?"

"I'm not sure. Esposito wants to find him. I have to think it has something to do with the ransomware."

Tony frowned in thought. I took another bite of the veal. It would be my last after eating just over half of it. It probably constituted the normal dinner portion. I signaled the waitress and told her I would need a box. Only after I packed up my lunch for tomorrow did Tony say anything. "You think he's coming for me?" he said.

"You know how these things work better than I do," I said. "But if I had to guess, I would say he wants the ransomware to raise some quick cash. He'll use the funds to get some men . . . and then he'll come for you."

"I want your support," Tony said.

I frowned. "Meaning what?"

"What do you mean?"

"We're friends, Tony. Have been for years. I like you, and I want you to stick around. But I'm not one of your soldiers."

"Fair enough." Tony nodded. "Then I'd like you to stay out of it."

"Exactly what I'd like to do."

"But you came here today," Tony said.

"I wanted to warn you. I'm sure people have gone after you before. It must come with the job. This is the first one I've seen, though. Esposito is determined, and if he gets the right ransomware, he can pay enough people to come after you."

Tony nodded and looked at something in the middle distance. I finished my tea. "Thanks, C.T.," he said.

"Sure, Tony," I said.

"Keep me updated on Esposito. If you see him, if he calls you, whatever."

"Not what I'd call staying out of it."

Tony smiled. It didn't reach his eyes. "I don't want you to do anything you don't want to do."

"I don't mind."

"Good. Thanks for coming in. Always good to see you." This time, Tony's smile included his eyes.

"You too, Tony." We shook hands.

I left.

* * *

I ARRIVED home to find Gloria Reading waiting. Like me, Gloria hails from a wealthy family. Unlike me, she never learned to mingle with people outside her tax bracket. Despite this, I found Gloria endearing in her own way. We enjoyed a relationship of convenience. My last case had been a tough one, and Gloria confessed to being worried about me. I gave her a key in case she needed it and never got it back. One of these days, I would ask for it Today, however, a beautiful woman in a small tennis outfit sat on my couch. There were worse fates.

Gloria grinned at me. "You need a shower?" she said.

"I'm good," I said.

"I just came from practice. I definitely need a shower." Gloria stood. "I guess I'm taking one alone." She started for the stairs.

"No need to waste water," I said, following her. "I'm sure I sweated a few drops somewhere."

"That's why you want to shower with me?"

"It's on the list somewhere, I'm sure."

It didn't take long for her to remind me of the other reasons.

* * *

LATER, I sat in my office, nursing a decaf coffee and looking for any recent online activity from Chris Sellers. I could find none. He hadn't posted code in any of the usual online haunts. All his social media pages remained dormant. His cell phone hadn't been used or even talked to a tower in days. I didn't want to speculate about his well-being—it wouldn't do his brother any good—but if Chris were still alive, he took care not to be found.

I noticed a change in the light from the hallway. Gloria stood in the doorway. "What are you working on?" she said. She walked into the office and sat in one of my client chairs. Gloria never made it past the doorway before. I figured her allergy to working kept her at bay.

"My most recent case. A guy has gone missing. His brother hired me to find him."

"How old is the brother?"

"Sixteen," I said.

Gloria winced. "That's young to lose a brother."

"Or a sister."

She gave me a delicate smile. "You saw something of yourself in this kid?"

I nodded. "Unlike me, their parents are dead. They have each other. I'm trying to make sure they still do."

"You think the missing brother is alive?"

While I thought about my answer, I watched Gloria. She could feign interest well, and she did for a while whenever we talked about my cases. She would look away here and there and twirl her chestnut hair around a finger. This time, she sat and looked at me. No fidgeting. No distractions. No faking. She was actually interested this time. "I hope he is," I said. "No one's seen him for a few days. No sign of him online." I told her the basics about the code repositories and how he'd gone dark even there.

"What about offline?" she said.

"I've checked out his usual haunts." I left out the parts about

Alberto Esposito and seeing his car speeding away from the coffee shop.

"How old is this guy?"

"Twenty-four, I think."

"He has to be more plugged in than you think. You talked about his code thingies. Don't people talk about stuff like that anywhere?"

Of course they did. And I hadn't looked there. I smiled. "I didn't check yet," I said. "Thanks."

Gloria smiled, too. "I hope that helped."

"Me, too. You seem way more interested than usual in my case."

"You do good work," she said. "For a while, I kept waiting for you to ditch the job, but that's not you. You're good at this, and you're helping people. That's important."

"Have you seen *Invasion of the Body Snatchers*?" I said.

Gloria chuckled. "I'm not a pod person."

"I don't know," I said. "Might require some close inspection later."

"Closer inspection than the shower?" she asked.

"Water makes a proper inspection impossible."

"Is that a fact?"

"It is."

"Well," she said, "right now, this pod person is hungry. I don't think I could be inspected on an empty stomach."

"We'll have to eat, then," I said.

* * *

THE CONTENTS of my refrigerator and pantry would not combine into an adequate dinner, so we went out. Gloria had a jones for Italian. I ate it for lunch but didn't mind having it again. I didn't need a repeat of seeing Tony, however, so we chose one of his competitors in Little Italy: Della Notte. Even though I had been there with Joey, I didn't mind going back. Because Gloria's ghost would haunt me if she were seen dead in the Caprice, she drove her Mercedes coupe. The valet accepted it with a wide smile. It wasn't often a college kid got to drive a car shaped and colored like a rocket.

We got a table and perused the menu. Gloria ordered a bottle of wine I sampled once and found decent but not great. I ordered a Caesar salad appetizer and salmon linguine for dinner; Gloria opted for veal parmesan. "You're going to have to play a lot of tennis to work it off," I said when the waiter left with our menus.

She grinned. "I figure we'll work off some of the calories later."

"Maybe I'll order dessert, then."

"Maybe I'll help you eat it," Gloria said.

The waiter dropped off my salad. Like a proper Caesar should, it came with anchovies. Gloria picked up her fork and eyed my salad, then frowned when she saw one of the tiny fish. "It's authentic," I said.

"It's gross," she countered.

I found anchovies on pizza gross—one anchovy was sufficient to ruin an entire pie—but in a Caesar salad, they were quite good. I drank mostly water with the greens, wishing I had a better wine to wash it down with. Gloria showed a greater interest in my work. Maybe we could improve her wine label snobbery next. Of course, like me, she enjoyed several kinds of snobbery. It must have helped us get along so well: on some level, we understood each other.

"You're going to look for this guy online?" said Gloria as the waiter cleared my small plate and freshened our waters.

I nodded. "I got a good suggestion."

It made Gloria smile. "I'm glad I could help."

If she'd said those words a couple months ago, I would have

chalked it up as a trite remark. Today, I believed her. "I'll start tonight," I said.

"Tonight?" Gloria said. Her eyes shone, and the corner of her mouth turned up.

"Schedule permitting," I said. "There's always the morning."

"You think you'll be able to find him?"

"I hope so. I'm sure he has a large presence. When I did a lot of coding at his age, I was all over the Internet." I kicked myself again for not thinking of this. Because I identified with Brian Sellers, I overlooked the fact Chris Sellers and I had quite a bit in common. He might even be as good a coder as I.

"Will all of that help you find him?" Gloria said.

"Someone has to know something about him."

"And they'll talk to you?"

"I might have to show off my coding bona fides," I said. "If they think I'm one of them, they'll talk to me."

The waiter returned with our dinners. Steam rose from both plates. I took a deep breath and inhaled the wonderful aromas of salmon, pasta, tomato sauce, garlic, and spices. Gloria and I scrapped conversation and ate. We drank some more wine—it proved to be a decent pairing with my meal, at least—and scarfed down our dinners.

So far, Gloria knew I was looking for a missing fellow with a younger brother. She didn't know about Alberto Esposito and his interest in Chris Sellers. I debated telling her as the waiter took our plates away and promised to return with a dessert menu. While Gloria and I had grown closer, we still didn't have a traditional relationship. The evening we spent together involved a meal, conversation, and sex. During a recent case, however, I needed to stay at Gloria's house for a few nights. I think the occasion made us closer. We hadn't talked about it, however. Maybe one of these days, we would.

I ordered two cannoli for dessert. Gloria looked at me over her wineglass. "There's a complicating factor in the case," I said.

She put her glass down. "What's that?"

"Someone else seems to have an interest in the missing brother."

Gloria frowned. "Who?"

I lowered my voice and gave her an abbreviated version of the Alberto Esposito story. "I don't know how he fits in," I said, "but I know he's involved, and I'm sure I'll see him again."

"Be careful," Gloria said. She grabbed my hand. I didn't resist. When she looked down and saw what she had done, however, Gloria pulled her hand back and hurried it into her lap. The waiter spared us any further awkwardness by bringing out our cannoli. The shell was light and flaky, with fresh, sweet ricotta inside, and a sprinkling of chocolate chips on top. I ate mine in a few bites. Gloria nursed hers. I didn't know if she wanted to savor it or if the recent tenor of our conversation made her concerned.

Even after she finished her cannoli, Gloria remained quiet. I spooked her by mentioning Esposito. She downed her remaining wine in a single swig and added the last couple ounces from the bottle to her glass. I paid the check. When we got outside, Gloria handed me her keys. "I drank more wine than you did," she said. I loved the pickup and sportiness of her car but didn't care for the smallish driver's seat. If I wanted to drive something shaped like a rocket, I would have been an astronaut.

I tipped the valet and adjusted the seat and steering wheel. Before I could take off, Gloria grabbed my face and kissed me hard. "Drive fast," she said.

The Benz complied.

CHAPTER 6

BACK AT MY HOUSE, I INTENDED TO WORK ON THE CASE. Gloria, however, had other plans. I no sooner closed and locked the front door when she shoved me against it and kissed me. "So aggressive," I said when I got a chance.

"You mind?" she said in a breathless tone.

"Nope."

I tried steering Gloria toward the stairs, just inside the front door. She had other ideas again, instead steering me into the living room. She shoved me onto the couch and slid on top of me. I didn't resist.

LATER, Gloria padded upstairs while I tossed some clothes back on and went to work in the office. In my college days, both under-grad and grad, I availed myself of forums where coders of all skill levels would come together, talk about their programs, solicit help, and sometimes carry on about life. One of the people I met there ended up as a colleague in Hong Kong. I hoped Chris Sellers made at least one such e-friend, and I hoped I could find him or her—I knew a lot of girls who were great coders—and get the person to talk to me. If I got lucky, I might even find Chris himself.

I looked up the most popular online hangouts for coders. To my non-surprise, they'd changed since the days I posted my Python ramblings for the world to see. None featured an easy way to search for a member without knowing the user name. I signed up for the most popular three and looked for Chris Sellers under any handles he might use. I found him on all three.

Did I reach out to him directly? What if his accounts were inactive? I checked his profile on one of the sites.

He logged in three days ago.

He was alive then.

I had to contact him. His profile on codingchat.com showed him to be an active user with more posts and more recent activity than on the other sites. I opened a new message. Now I only needed to figure out what to say. Other than this blip of online presence, Chris Sellers disappeared. He had to have a reason for doing so. I couldn't come on too strong, or he'd blow me off. While I'm often a fan of lying, I didn't want Chris to see through a lie and blow me off there. I settled on a version of the truth.

Chris,

Your brother is worried about you. You don't know me, but I'm helping him find you. He's safe but worried. Reply to this message or to my cell, 410-555-7274.

Now I could only wait. I had to hope Chris would see the message, not be freaked out, and get back to me. My cell number gave him an easy way to figure out who I was. It would have to be enough. I wanted to look into his posting history on these forums, but it grew late, and I was tired.

I went upstairs. Gloria woke up when I entered the bedroom. She propped herself on one elbow. Her chestnut hair flowed down her shoulders and touched the white sheet of my bed. The lingerie she wore fit like someone made it just for her, and knowing Gloria, it was a possibility. I found myself staring. Gloria grinned.

Well, I wasn't *too* tired.

* * *

IN THE MORNING, I left the sleeping Gloria upstairs as I went down into the kitchen. One of these months, I would need to get my grocery shopping done. I made a cup of coffee and pondered my limited options. Some cracked wheat sourdough still looked good enough to combine with turkey sausage and a few eggs. A pretty basic menu, but it would do. I got two skillets going with a little olive oil and put the eggs and sausage on. The aromas of the food must have woken Gloria. She came into the kitchen and beelined for the Keurig.

"No kiss for the chef?" I said.

Gloria waited until her coffee brewed. She added sugar and creamer, took a long drink of it, and then kissed me. It tasted like spearmint and dark roast. "Priorities," she said, taking a seat at the table.

"I understand." I flipped the eggs and sausage patties and maxed out the toaster at four pieces. A few minutes later, I carried to the table two plates, each with two fried eggs, three sausage patties, and two pieces of sourdough toast. I sat opposite Gloria and buttered my toast.

"You always seem to know just what to make for breakfast," Gloria said after a few bites of her eggs and sausage.

"Years of morning-after practice," I said with a wink.

Gloria smiled and shook her head. "I might believe you."

"I might be telling the truth."

"Did you get any work done last night?" she said.

"You mean between bouts of being ravaged by a beautiful woman?"

"Yes," Gloria said, color rushing to her cheeks.

"I did some research, the kind you suggested. I found a few places Chris visited recently."

"Did you reach out to anyone who knew him?"

"Not yet," I said. "I didn't have much time. I found he logged in three days ago on one site, though, so I sent him a message."

"Any response?"

I shook my head. "I'll check after breakfast."

"You think it'll work?"

I buttered and added apricot preserves to my second piece of toast. My first cup of coffee was getting low. "No idea. If he hasn't responded by tonight, I'll try to find some people who knew him on those sites."

By the time I needed a second cup of coffee, Gloria did, too. I carried both back to the table. We finished, and I nearly fainted when Gloria volunteered to put the dishes in the sink. If she washed them, I would have dropped where I stood. While I went down the hall to work, Gloria climbed the stairs to get a shower. She didn't try to coax me into joining her; I must have looked serious about getting on task. I would have joined her had she asked.

* * *

WHILE GLORIA SHOWERED, I looked into Chris Sellers' activity on Coding Chat. He made over three hundred replies but only started three of his own threads. The pattern pegged him as a solid contributor. If I needed to track him down via other people, there should be no shortage of fellow coders he helped along the way. I focused first on the threads Chris replied to most often.

They all concerned malware reverse engineering. I studied it in college and worked at it on occasion since. Chris Sellers was probably more proficient than I at the moment, much as it pained me to admit. He offered a few pieces of general advice to the original poster. Then the person posted the code in question, and Chris provided a bunch of comments. I wanted to see how insightful they were.

I downloaded the code onto a flash drive. The exact functions of this malware had yet to be established. I would find out on a VM. I got out my laptop, fired it up, and logged into a fresh virtual machine. I copied over the malware code, compiled it, and ran it. I didn't notice a visible effect. My desktop looked the same. I searched for open processes and found nothing unusual. Maybe this malware didn't allow itself to be evaluated on a VM. On a lark, I opened a terminal window and examined the file list.

Then I saw it.

It took me a minute. I could have easily missed it. It was, after all, easy to overlook. It was exactly the point. Chris Sellers had been helping someone with a rootkit, a piece of malware able to hide from the user and subvert the operating system to mask itself. An extra file in the expanded listing I preferred provided the only indication, and I doubted most people would have seen it. Users and admins get accustomed to certain things, so much so they expect it. This rootkit took advantage of their tendencies.

I tried to find it in other ways and got stymied at every turn. This one dug its hooks into a lot of processes. I checked Chris' comments. He advised the original poster how this was a powerful and insidious tool and should not be trifled with. I couldn't read the original poster's intent. Chris must not have been able to, either, because he stopped replying after giving a long explanation and suggesting the poster leave well enough alone. This rootkit could do some serious damage in the wild. I wondered if anyone ever used it, and if an enterprising admin ever discovered it.

I heard Gloria come down. While I destroyed my infected VM and created another, I scoured the forums anew. Chris' replies centered on reverse engineering and esoteric coding challenges. From what I saw in his replies, he was a damned good programmer. In a moment of weakness, I would admit he had a small edge on me due to the recency of his research. No wonder Bobbi Lane held him in such high regard.

Instead of continuing with Chris' replies, I dug into the threads he started. One dealt with reverse engineering and how to handle a rootkit responsibly. Another solicited opinions on the finer points of Unix shell coding. The third intrigued me: it dealt with research into ransomware. I wondered again if Alberto Esposito found interest in Chris Sellers for the same reason. After some back and forth and solid suggestions, Chris posted his code. I downloaded it to a different flash drive.

My new VM finished building. The code allowed me to manage and deploy the ransomware, so I built another VM to play the victim. Ransomware tends to lock users out of their files. I created a few text files on the second VM so the software could encrypt and hold them for ransom. After verifying any communication medium on the laptop was disabled, I compiled and ran the ransomware.

The management console opened. This was software anyone could use. It gave a choice of how to encrypt the files, how much money to demand to release them, and ways to collect the funds. The hacker could choose what image to display on a victim's desktop. This was one-stop shopping for criminals. All they would have to do is point and click through a few choices, wait for their malware to infect some unwitting folks, and start making money. I had never seen such customization before. If this got into the wild—especially in the hands of someone like Alberto Esposito—it could cause a metric ton of damage. Not to mention, raise a lot of ill-gotten gains.

"Interesting stuff?" Gloria said from the doorway, making me jump in my seat. She padded into the room. "You were so wrapped up in your work."

"This is really interesting," I said.

"Did you find the guy?"

"No, but I discovered he's really good at writing malware."

"Is that a good thing?" Gloria said.

I leaned back. "It's a matter of perspective," I said. "The coding skills are good to have, though I'd like to see them put to better use. This program could cause a lot of damage."

"What does it do?" I explained the basics of how ransomware worked. "That's really shady," Gloria said.

"It is," I said. "So far, people who pay have gotten their files back. But there's no guarantee it'll keep happening."

"So people could have to pay over and over?"

"Potentially."

"What if this targeted specific people?"

"Good grief," I said, letting out a slow breath. "It would be like spear phishing on steroids."

"That actually made some sense," Gloria said.

WAS this malware the source of Alberto Esposito's interest in Chris Sellers? I still needed to know how Esposito got onto Sellers in the first place. Now seemed like as good a time as any to pay Danny Esposito a visit. I looked at my phone; it just turned one o'clock. I had been sitting with this malware for about four hours. Doing anything else sounded better.

I changed into more respectable clothes and drove to Hopkins. Several years went by since I was last on campus. During my senior year of high school, they recruited me hard, both for my academics and for the lacrosse team. I preferred computer science to engineering, opted for Loyola, and ended up not good enough to play varsity lacrosse. Despite the passage of time, I remembered where the admissions office was. I parked in an available spot and walked into the building.

A few students dressed like they didn't care if they got into Hopkins or not waited in the office. I asked the receptionist if I could speak to Danny Esposito. She eyed me and frowned. I didn't dress like a college student. She said Esposito was busy. Was there anyone else I could see? No, thank you. Was I OK to wait several minutes? I was. I took a seat next to a fellow who wore a sweatsuit and smelled like he recently sweated in it. I hoped Esposito wouldn't be long. Showing my ID could have reduced the wait, but I didn't want to put anyone in the office on edge right away.

A few minutes passed—and then a few more. I pondered the fact the receptionist and I favored divergent definitions of "several." She looked at me from her desk on occasion. Her short blonde hair framed a cute face, but she kept frowning at me as if I were suspicious. Perhaps I should hold her character evaluation in high regard. While I thought about it, Danny Esposito came out of his office. The receptionist pointed him to me.

Danny was shorter than his brother, probably about five-eight. He possessed a classic Italian complexion along with dark hair and dark brown eyes. He was built like a fire hydrant. When he walked, I could tell he was solid and strong. His gait showed an easy confidence. He could probably take care of himself in a fight, and if he couldn't, his brother the gangster would be a phone call away.

We went to Esposito's office. I closed the door behind me, causing my host to frown, but he sat behind his desk without comment. The desktop held stacks of folders and papers atop it, and the bookshelf featured more of the same. "Must be the busy season," I said after I sat in the uncomfortable guest chair.

"We're always busy at Hopkins," Danny Esposito said,

sounding like he worked in a pizza shop in the Bronx. I couldn't tell if his accent was real, or he affected it because he thought he should. "You got an application in?"

"Not exactly." I took out my ID and showed it to him. He looked it over and peered back with narrowed eyes. "I'm looking for Chris Sellers."

"I don't know who he is," he said.

"Sure you do. You were his graduate admissions officer."

"I got a heavy caseload."

The plethora of folders and papers confirmed it. "He wasn't just another case," I said. "This guy is smart, even on the Hopkins scale. In fact, he's so smart you told your brother about him."

"My brother?"

"Your brother."

"You've met my brother?" Danny said.

"I have."

"Then you know what he does."

"If you're trying to intimidate me, Danny, you'll need a lot more than an implied threat. I don't care what your brother does. He doesn't scare me and neither do you. I'm here about Chris Sellers."

Danny Esposito stared at me. I didn't say anything. He gave up after a few seconds. "I have work to do," he said. "You need to go."

"After we talk, sure."

"Maybe you didn't hear me." Now he scowled again. As glares went, it wasn't bad. It didn't make me quiver in my Clarks, but I could see it getting a freshman to bolt for the door. "Time for you to go."

"Danny, this is how it is: we're going to talk about Chris Sellers. You can't throw me out of here, and I'll prove it to you if you try. Let's make it easy and talk about Chris. When we're done, I'll leave."

Danny shook his head. He got up and walked unhurriedly around his desk, staring at me the whole way. I watched him. He was squat and strong, but I couldn't presume that also made him slow. I shifted in the chair, ready for him to throw a punch or try to grab me. He stood about a foot away and glowered down at me. I didn't flinch. He didn't stop glowering. We would hit an impasse soon.

After a few seconds, he said, "You hungry?"

I hadn't expected anything of the sort. "Uh, yeah," I said. "I haven't eaten lunch yet."

"We can talk about your boy over lunch, then. You're buying."

I stood, still alert for shenanigans from Danny Esposito. "Where are we going?" I said.

"The cafeteria. It's close."

"How's the food?"

"Shitty," he said.

* * *

An advantage to lunching after one-thirty is the dearth of people doing it at the same time. Barely a quarter of the seats in the cafeteria held occupants, and the lines were short. We got in one. Esposito didn't need to look at the menu boards, but I did. The fare and the smell of grease evoked memories of high school. I didn't trust anything like chicken salad, so I opted for a burger and curly fries. Both surprised me by still being warm. I risked a chocolate pudding not appearing to be concrete in a cup.

Danny Esposito had already selected a table. Like a good gangster's brother, he managed to find one without anyone sitting nearby. He chose a chicken salad sandwich and non-curly fries, and he started eating by the time I sat with him. "You must be brave," I said.

He looked at his food and gave a knowing nod. "The first time I got it, I was," he said. "It ain't bad. Good sub shops do it better, but for three-fifty at a college cafeteria, it's pretty good."

I took a bite of the burger. It had been cooked to medium. I did burgers at least to medium well. The flavor was good, though, and the toppings were fresh. "Why are you doing this?" I said.

"What, having lunch?"

"Talking to me."

Danny Esposito took a large bite of his sandwich. A little mayonnaise gathered at the corner of his mouth. He left it there. "You mean, why am I going against my brother?" he said.

"Yeah."

"My brother's an asshole."

"Good reason," I said. I tried the curly fries. They were adequate.

"Thing is . . . I'm an asshole, too."

"How do you mean?"

"You look like an athletic guy," Danny said. He ate a few of his non-curly fries and talked again before he'd finished chewing. "My guess is you can take care of yourself in a scrape."

"I do all right."

"You always done all right?"

"My parents made me take martial arts classes after some kid punched me a few times in sixth grade."

"You stick with it?" I nodded. Danny continued. "My brother wasn't much of a fighter. Didn't stop him from getting into his share of scrapes, of course. I was younger and not much help."

I shrugged. "Younger brothers shouldn't fight battles for older ones."

"Sure." Danny drank some soda and got a faraway look in his eyes. A minute later, he spoke again. "We got older. Alberto . . . got involved with some interesting people."

"I already knew about it. Doesn't make you an asshole."

"No. But whenever I'd get in trouble, I'd drop his name. 'Don't mess with me, fucker. My brother will kill you.' That kind of shit." He let out a dry chuckle. "Made me a coward, I guess. So yeah, my brother's an asshole for doing the things he did. I'm an asshole for riding his coattails."

I gave Danny a couple minutes there. The faraway look returned to his eyes. I took the time to finish my burger. It would earn a five out of ten. Were I in college, I might have given it a six, but I made better burgers on a skillet in our dorm room. When Danny appeared ready to talk again, I got back to it. "How long have you been here?"

"Five years," said Danny.

"How long have you been feeding names to your brother?"

The corner of Danny's mouth turned up. "I told you I was an asshole."

"I'm not judging. I'm trying to find a guy who's gone missing."

"You think my brother was involved?"

"I know he was."

Danny regarded me for a few seconds, then drank some more of his soda. "My brother has ideas," he said. "He wants to modernize things, bring the operation out of the stone age. He knows where I work and figured I'd be a good resource."

"The admissions office has to have access to student records. You know who the good ones are." He nodded. "And not long ago, you put your brother onto Chris Sellers."

"He's a sharp guy. I knew he could help."

"What if he didn't want to?" I said.

Danny shrugged. "My brother is persuasive. He usually gets what he wants."

"You mean by threats."

"Hey, I told you he was an asshole."

"How much of one?"

"Why?" Danny said with a frown. "What happened?"

"Chris is missing," I said. "I don't know if he's alive or dead."

"My brother's not a. . . ." he trailed off.

"Not a killer?"

Danny didn't say anything.

"Maybe calling him a killer is a little much," I said. "But he's killed before."

"That's probably fair," Danny said.

I leaned in. "What I want to know is this: if Chris told your brother to piss off, would your brother have killed him?"

"I don't think so," Danny said after a few seconds. He shook his head to emphasize the point. "He'd've been pissed, sure. But he wouldn't jump right to killing someone."

"You're sure?"

"I know my brother."

"I hope you're right," I said.

CHAPTER 7

When I got home, Gloria had left. She dropped by more and more but still spent most of her nights in her house. I understood; her house was far larger and fancier than mine. I enjoyed the great Federal Hill location; she enjoyed everything else. She didn't keep any clothes or random supplies at my house —a good thing as her bathroom supplies would have consumed much of my second floor. It would have been a step too far for both of us.

The last couple of times Gloria left, I missed her. I would have thought such a thing impossible a month ago. Our relationship of fun and convenience inched toward something more serious. For now, neither of us expressed any interest in wanting to formalize anything. I didn't expect the situation to change. I knew I wouldn't be the one to bring it up. If Gloria did. . . .

I tabled those thoughts and got back to work in the office. Chris Sellers' ransomware merited another look. Having skimmed it before, now I took the time to study it. I complied it onto a VM and really poked at it. Chris did a fantastic job writing it. I already infected a test VM. After reviewing the code until my eyes begged for relief, I saved the VM as it was. You never know when something like cutting-edge ransomware will prove useful.

With work done for the day, I went into the kitchen to make dinner. I again lamented the state of my refrigerator and pantry, but I found enough for what I wanted to do. I sautéed red peppers, green peppers, and onions in a skillet. While they cooked, I set the oven to low and put two wheat sub rolls in to get warm. In a smaller skillet, I fried two large Italian sausages. Once they cooked, I lowered the heat and added marinara sauce.

I took the rolls out of the oven, split them down the center, and added onions and peppers to each. Then I poured in a little sauce, added the sausage, and then topped it with more sauce. These would be messy but good. I ate in the living room in front of the TV while catching up on Netflix.

After dinner, I pondered going into Federal Hill but stayed home. In my younger days, I would have ventured out. Now I was happy to stay home with a full stomach and a good movie. I wasn't even thirty yet, and I was already morphing into a home-body. By forty, I might be a hermit with a beard down to my waist.

After the movie, I got back online and checked to see if Chris Sellers got back to me. He hadn't. Making dinner became the most productive thing I did since Gloria left. With those successes in the rearview, I called it a night.

* * *

AFTER WAKING THE NEXT MORNING, I made coffee in a travel cup and drove to the grocery store. My cart got heavier, my wallet got lighter, and at the end, I purchased enough to make a bunch of meals. I put it all away and made a simple breakfast of a bagel and bacon. An hour of shopping made me hungry.

I unwound and digested while watching SportsCenter,

then ran about four miles in the pleasant morning air. After a shower and another cup of coffee, I sat down in front of my computer, ready to work. It occurred to me I was all-in on trying to reach Chris Sellers. If he went dark and never responded, I didn't have a plan B. At the moment, I couldn't come up with one. If I failed to reach Chris Sellers and couldn't find a usable trace of him online, I would need an alternative.

I logged in on Coding Chat. The envelope icon at the top of the screen showed a red "1" atop it: I had a new message. It could have been the generic welcome-to-our-community crap, or it could have been a response from Chris Sellers. I opened the message.

Chris had gotten back to me.

You're right. I don't know you. I know that phone number belongs to a local private investigator I've read good things about. I hope it's you. Tell my brother I'm OK. He doesn't need to worry.

It was something, at least. Chris Sellers was alive. Or someone pretended to be him. I hoped for the former. He had sent his message an hour ago. Maybe I could catch him online. I fired off a reply.

Chris,

It's good to hear from you. I'll tell your brother you're OK. I need more, though. More importantly, he needs more. We have to know this is really you. I need to meet you. You can pick the time and place. Let me confirm you're alive and OK, and if you're in trouble, maybe I can help you. Reply or text.

After I sent the reply, I puttered around on the coding site for a while. A few people asked easy questions. I thought about answering them but decided my account was best used talking to Chris. In college, I offered to help someone with his code. It turned into helping multiple people for longer than I intended. I didn't need to go down that rabbit hole again.

As I looked at a couple of competent programs, Chris got back to me.

It's really me. I know I've put some people out. Unfortunately, I had to. I'll be at the Starbucks in Abindgon this afternoon at 1. Don't bring my brother with you.

This afternoon at one gave me plenty of time to get there, and I could even go to Z Burger for lunch afterwards. I could tell Brian I found his brother. Where he went and when he might come back would be for them to work out. It counted as a win for me.

Why couldn't all my cases be this easy?

Years ago, I heard it's acceptable to be up to fifteen minutes late to a social function. I have applied this maxim to everything over the years, taking great liberties with the intended meaning. Today, however, I sat at a table, iced vanilla latte before me, at five minutes to one. I knew what Chris Sellers looked like, so I would see him when he walked in. This Starbucks had two doors, one on the north wall and the other on the east. My table afforded a good view of both.

A pair of girls in University of Maryland tank tops and tiny shorts walked in. I found their clothes quite appropriate for the weather. About a minute past one, Chris Sellers walked in via the rear entrance. He wore a nondescript T-shirt and shorts and an Orioles cap pulled low over his face. The patchy beard growth gave me a moment of pause in identifying him. As he scanned the room, I raised my drink toward him. He started toward my table.

The other door opened. Alberto Esposito and a goon entered. Esposito saw me; his goon had eyes only for Chris. How the hell did they know he would be here? Once Chris saw them, he bolted back out the rear door. Esposito's man went after him, dodging around tables and patrons. I got up and ran after him.

The Abingdon Starbucks is in a small strip mall on a street dominated by fast-food restaurants and big-box retailers. There's also a Lowe's a quick sprint away. Chris took off in the direction of the retail stores. By the time I got outside, I was chasing the goon down Tollgate Road. Chris enjoyed a comfortable lead on the goon, who gained no ground as the pursuit wore on. Chris cut a hard left at the Chick Fil-A. His pursuer slowed. I dashed ahead of him and looked around for Chris Sellers.

He had disappeared.

I didn't see him in a parking lot or even in a car in a parking lot. No one I could see inside the Chick Fil-A looked like him. He could have gone in, run out another door, and taken off in another direction. If so, good for him—he would avoid Esposito's man, who wasn't built for a protracted chase. I eased my pace, then stopped and turned. The goon jogged toward me, then slowed to a walk.

Like most in his profession, this fellow was big, about six-five and built like a defensive lineman. The barbed wire tattoos around his biceps told everyone he had nary an original thought in his head. I knew he could bench-press me about thirty times but also knew I wouldn't give him the chance. He stopped about ten feet from me, sucking wind and glowering. Any fear factor the glare may have held got undone by the gasping. "If you're going to try and intimidate people," I said, "you might want to mix in some cardio."

"Go to hell," he said, the last syllable trailing off. He looked around.

"You're not going to find him," I said.

"I might."

"If you saw him, I'd get there before you."

He took a couple steps forward and glowered again despite

its lack of success the first time. "What if I just beat your ass right now?" he said.

"Brilliant," I said. "Look around, you moron. It's the middle of the day on a major road. I'm pretty sure it's the kind of attention your boss doesn't want."

He stood and pondered my words. "Fine," he said after a moment. "But I'm sure we'll see each other again." His breathing returned to normal.

"I'm counting on it," I said. I walked past him and back toward Starbucks. How the hell did Esposito learn Chris was going to be here today? Esposito had been in my office but neither he nor his driver touched anything. Their mobile jammer would have prevented any kind of wireless attack. I received no suspicious emails or texts. They couldn't have found out with my unwitting help. The alternative meant they had electronic eyes or ears on Chris Sellers. They didn't know where he was, but they knew where he would be thanks to the message he sent me.

I needed to discover how Esposito pulled it off. Chris Sellers struck me as too savvy to be a common malware victim. Esposito wasn't a code writer—why else would he be looking for one? I wondered if he kept someone like Chris on retainer, a cyber person who could go after fellow coders and hackers. I made a mental note to check all my systems and their security logs when I got home.

When I walked back into the Starbucks, Esposito sat at my table, sipping an iced coffee. I took a seat, and he smiled at me. I didn't return it. His man came in behind me. He joined us at the table.

"Matty, why don't you wait in the car?" Esposito said.

"Boss, I don't think—"

"You're right; you don't. I don't pay you to fucking think. Now go wait in the car. I need to have a conversation."

Matty looked at his boss, then glared at me. I winked at him.

He tried to add menace to the glare, then got up and stormed out. "Hard to get good help these days?" I said.

"You have no idea," said Esposito.

I drank my latte. It grew watery during my sprint down Tollgate Road. I didn't say anything. Esposito was a hotshot who returned to town with designs on running the show. He had to be impressed with himself. I knew he would talk if I gave him the chance. It didn't take long for him to prove me right.

"You must be wondering why I'm here," he said.

"I figure it's more than just the coffee," I said.

Esposito smirked. "I'd forgotten how funny you think you are." He paused and looked at me. "I'm a man of many parts."

"You're trying to be."

"And I'll get there. Without your help, it seems, and I'll remember your slight."

"It's good to be remembered," I said.

"Not this time."

"None of this tells me how you ended up here today."

Esposito took another drink of his coffee and lapsed into silence. He was enjoying himself. I wanted to know something only he could tell me. A prick like Esposito needs to drag these things out and savor them. I had done it a few times, too. Being on the receiving end of it wasn't fun.

"You're gonna have to keep wondering," he said.

"How anticlimactic," I said.

"Get used to being disappointed."

"I never have. I'll figure it out sooner or later."

"You think so?"

I gave Esposito a patronizing smile. "I do."

"What makes you so sure?"

"Because I'm smarter than you."

Esposito chuckled and sipped his drink. "You're smarter than me?"

"If you were a savant, Tony wouldn't have sent you to Cleveland."

"Is that a fact?" Esposito looked at me over the top of his plastic cup. "Maybe I'm smarter than you're giving me credit for."

"Maybe," I said, "but I'm still smarter than you."

His face twisted for a moment. Good. If I made Esposito angry, he might tell me something he otherwise wouldn't. Even if he didn't, he was a prick, and I liked pissing him off. "I have an interest in Chris," he said.

"I figured as much."

"Right, because you're so smart."

"Didn't need to be for something so simple."

"I came to you for ransomware. You weren't the first to turn me down."

"Why the obsession with Chris, then?" I said. "He writes good code, but this area is lousy with people who write good code."

"My interest in him goes beyond just code."

It meant money. I could ask to confirm, but I knew Esposito wouldn't divulge it. I probably pushed him as far as I could, and farther than I should have. "Fine," I said, finishing my watery latte, "but I'm going to keep looking for him."

"Because of his poor brother?"

"Yes."

"Be a shame if something happened to the kid."

I narrowed my eyes. "Don't."

Esposito held my gaze for a moment and laughed. "Relax," he said. "I ain't interested in the kid. Just Chris." The humor faded from his face. "I don't think you should keep getting in my way."

"It'll take more than Matty to discourage me."

"I have more," Esposito said with a thin, mirthless smile.

Why did all my cases have to be this complicated?

CHAPTER 8

I stopped at home long enough to change into workout clothes and pack a duffel bag. At the gym, I attacked the treadmill, pushing it harder than normal. After a half-hour there, I drank some water and recovered my wind before going to the heavy bag, the real reason I came. There are times everyone needs to hit something. This afternoon had been one of those for me. I put on my MMA gloves and went at it hard.

Matty's face filled my head, superimposed on the bag as I wailed away with fists and elbows. Esposito took a few good shots to the noggin, too. I went back and forth between them as I pummeled the leather. Fifteen minutes later, my arms felt like jelly and my gym gear was covered in sweat. I took a shower, put on the clean clothes in my bag, and got a smoothie from the juice bar.

Back at home, I finished the smoothie and sent Brian Sellers a text, telling him to call or stop by when he had a chance. Then I got online, went back to the coding forum, and sent Chris Sellers another message.

Chris, I don't know what happened today. I don't know how he knew. It wasn't from me. I can help you with him, and I can help your brother, but you'll need to trust me. Before you get back to me, make sure you're not infected with anything.

I decided to take my own advice on the last point. With all the malware sampling I did, my systems incurred a chance of infection. I destroyed all of the VMs I made in the last couple days, took the rest of my systems offline, and fired up the malware scanners. My phone could have been an attack vector, too, but I didn't want to take it down in case Brian called. It would have to wait.

I watched some of the malware scans run. It wasn't like there was anything better to do. Chris Sellers was in the breeze, Alberto Esposito plotted against him (and likely me, by this point), and I didn't accomplish much besides stirring the pot. So far, this would not go down in the annals of superior sleuthing performances.

The malware scans churned. I made a big pot of sweet tea to refrigerate. While it cooled, someone knocked on the door. After the impromptu meeting with Esposito and Matty earlier, I walked to the door with a 9MM behind me. Brian Sellers stood on my doorstep. I tucked the gun into the back of my jeans and let him in.

In my office, Brian saw me reholster the gun and frowned. "You can never be too careful in this city," I said.

We each sat on our respective sides of my desk. "Is that all it is?" he said.

"Let me worry about it. I saw your brother today."

My news got him to sit at attention. "You did? Where? How is he?"

"He's fine," I said. "I saw him in Abingdon. I reached out to him online at a coding site he posted on."

"So where is he now?"

"No idea. Unfortunately, someone else showed up, too, and your brother took off. I don't know where he is now."

Brian slumped in the chair. "Who was the other guy?"

I didn't like the look in his eyes. I would have worn the same one at his age, so I wanted better for him. "I can see you're angry," I said. "I would be, too. The other guy is a . . . gangster, I guess is the best way to describe him."

"You mean like a mob guy?"

"More or less."

"What's Chris doing with a mob guy?"

"I don't know. The mob guy wouldn't tell me."

Now my news made Brian frown. The anger hadn't left his eyes yet. "Wait, you know this guy?"

"I wouldn't say I know him," I said. "We met a few times several years ago."

"Is he dangerous? What does he want with my brother?"

"Yes, he's dangerous. It's why you need to get the wild look out of your eyes and let me deal with him." I waited while Brian took a couple of deep breaths. The anger on his face faded. Now he looked like a stressed-out high school kid, which counted as a small improvement. "I don't know for certain what he wants with your brother, but I can make a good guess."

"My brother's not a criminal," Brian said.

"I know. With his job, he couldn't be."

"You investigated him?"

"I had to. He was missing. I needed to know everything I could about him."

Brian nodded. "OK, so what's your guess?"

"Do you know what your brother did for a living?" I said.

"Sure, he was a programmer."

"It's what he told you?"

"My brother isn't a liar." I saw the anger bleed back onto Brian's face.

"You want a water or anything?" I said.

"Uh . . . sure," he said.

I went to the kitchen, got Brian a bottle of Harris Teeter's finest water and filled my own reusable bottle. I set his on the desk in the office. He picked it up, twisted the lid off, and drank about half in one gulp. "It's true your brother is a programmer," I said. "But do you know what kind of code he writes?"

"I never asked him," Brian said with a shrug. "He never told me."

"Do you know what ransomware is?" He shook his head. I explained it.

"My brother writes that?" he said.

"Yes. And I've looked at his code. He wrote really good ransomware."

Brian started to say something, stopped, and frowned in thought. I could visualize the gears turning inside his head. "So this gangster wanted my brother to write some for him?"

"It's my guess," I said. "He also asked me to."

"You?"

"Yeah. I turned him down. Based on the timing of everything, I think he went to your brother first. I might feel a little insulted by the order of things, but at least we both said no."

"You're sure my brother said no?" Brian said.

"You could answer better than I can, but I'm pretty sure he said no."

"Writing ransomware is why the gangster guy is looking for him?"

Would just being rejected cause Esposito to take such a keen interest in Chris Sellers? I turned him down, too, and he wasn't stalking me. I wondered if there was something else in play here, a factor I hadn't learned yet or a variable I needed to solve for. "As far as I know," I said.

"Can you handle the gangster?"

"I think so. It would be easier if I knew where your brother went. It's hard to help someone when you have no idea where they are or what they're doing."

"What do you need from me?" Brian said. He downed half of the remaining water in another big gulp.

"Nothing," I said. "I just wanted you to know what was going on."

Brian managed a tiny smile. "At least you found him, if just for a couple minutes."

"Now I need to find him again."

"You think the gangster is going to keep looking for him?"

"I do. And I don't know how he knew your brother would be at that coffee shop."

"He knew?" Brian said.

"I'm certain," I said. "There's no way he just happened to be there right when your brother and I were supposed to meet."

"You said this gangster is into software?"

"I'm already there. I'm running full malware scans of all my PCs, and I'll do my phone once you leave. I'm sure my stuff is good, but I have to know."

"I'm worried," Brian said after a moment of silence.

"I would be, too," I said. "I'm sure it's not reassuring, but it's true."

"Thanks."

"I'll let you know what turns up."

Brian nodded. "OK." He stood. "Be careful. This gangster sounds dangerous."

I offered my best inspiring smile. "I can handle him."

I hoped I could.

* * *

ALL MY COMPUTERS, including my phone, checked out clean. However Alberto Esposito learned of the meeting between Chris

Sellers and me, it wasn't with my unwitting e-help. I pondered dinner options when Gloria texted and wondered what I was doing for food and a nightcap. I invited her. She said she would be here soon.

A few minutes later, I heard a knock. The short time seemed fast for Gloria, but considering the rocketlike shape of her car, it could have been doable. My rumbling stomach made me glad she arrived quickly. I opened the door.

I had no time to react to the meaty fist walloping me in the face.

I staggered backward and went down, somehow avoiding slamming my head on the hardwood. Two legbreakers walked in. My cheek and jaw felt like someone hit me with a hammer. The lead goon walked up to me and raised his boot. I slithered out of the way before he could stomp a hole in my hardwood floors through my torso. In the end, I was still on the floor, unarmed, with two large men on their feet meaning to do me harm.

Not good.

I rose into a crouch. The goon who failed to stomp me now tried a punch. I blocked it and gave him a hard right cross in the balls. He doubled over. I shifted so he screened me from his partner and scrambled to my feet. I stood just in time to take a short left in the ribs. Breathing hurt. I deflected the next punch, then the next. He tried to grab me as his friend remained doubled over. I backed up and avoided his lunge.

He came at me again. I blocked his haymaker and hit him with two short punches in the gut. He backed off and lowered his hands to protect his midsection, so I clocked him in the jaw with an elbow. It staggered him but didn't put him down. I punched him in the stomach again, then kicked him hard in the face when he bent over. The combination put him down.

The first goon recovered enough to get back to his feet. He cursed at me and charged. I grabbed his arm and flipped him onto his back. From there, I kicked him in the face and put him in an armbar. He screamed as I wrenched in the hold. "This is the part where you tell me who sent you," I said.

He responded by reaching into his belt. I didn't see a weapon but didn't believe in taking chances. A hard kick to the face bounced his head off the hardwood, and he went limp. They were both knocked out in my living room. I heard footsteps coming up the front walkway onto the porch and stop. Gloria frowned at the spectacle. "Is everything all right?" she said.

"Get inside," I said. She did, and I locked the door behind her. "I don't know if these two assholes brought a third."

Gloria took the hint and went into the office. I fetched a couple zip ties and bound the wrists of the pair of jackasses who lay prone on my floor. Both had the size and build expected of their line of work. They looked to be around my age. Guys like these were used to ending fights with one punch, if they even needed to fight at all. When the opening blow didn't put me down, these two were in over their heads.

I took out my phone and called Joey. "Give me an hour," I said, "then come over. We have an errand to run."

"Something dangerous?" Joey said.

"Yes, and I can't think of anyone who'd make a better human shield."

"You're hilarious," he said.

"See you in an hour," I said and hung up.

After I called Joey, I called the police and reported what happened. They would send a car and an ambulance. Before they arrived, I took the cufflinks from my uninvited guests' shirts. Gloria sat in the office, hands clenched. "We might need to get delivery tonight," I said.

"C.T., what's going on?" she said. "Why are these men here?"

"I'll tell you all about it later. The police are coming to take them away. Then I need to run an errand." I smiled. "Sorry this isn't the night you had in mind."

A slow grin came onto Gloria's face. "Just come back in one piece," she said, "and I think we can salvage something."

"I'll do my best," I said.

* * *

Despite my vanity, I've never gotten a vanity plate on my car. They're too easily remembered by everyone. A random string of letters and numbers is one thing; MISTER E is quite another. While I waited for Joey, I ran Esposito's plate. He lived in the county. Interesting for someone who wanted to take over organized crime in the city.

I put the cufflinks in a small Amazon box. "Where are you taking those?" Gloria said.

"Back to the man who sent the goons," I said. Flashing lights made their way through the window. I opened the door. Two police officers approached, followed by paramedics. I talked to one of the cops while the second took the paramedics and dealt with the unconscious assailants. Another pair of cops showed up a minute later in a large police van. One went inside, and the other joined in talking to me.

I now gave my statement to both. When they asked what happened, I explained I had been expecting Gloria but instead got the goon party. "Sounds disappointing," the first cop said.

"On an epic scale," I said.

They knew I was a PI, and they checked out my license for a minute, finding everything in order. The paramedics offered to look at my face, but I declined. My teeth were intact. I'd weathered punches before. My face would swell and bruise but always healed just fine on its own. Three cops and two paramedics walked the now-handcuffed legbreakers out. Neither would look at me. Both got herded into the ambulance with a cop riding along. The police van pulled away, and the ambulance and other police car left a minute later.

Not long after, Joey showed up. I kissed Gloria goodbye, gave her some good delivery options, and left.

* * *

Esposito's address put him in a community called The Oaks. It was so named because it had streets like Black Oak and Rock Oak. I didn't have the slightest idea what a rock oak was, but Esposito lived there. Joey drove his BMW. He owned a 5 Series with a smooth ride and powerful engine. Maybe I would need to revisit the BMW dealer if my Lexus proved too costly to fix.

"Those assholes just showed up?" Joey said, picking up a conversation thread from a couple minutes before.

"Yep."

"You don't know why?"

"Esposito probably sent them," I said. "I pissed him off earlier."

"And now you're going to piss him off again."

"Yep."

"You ever think this move may not be the smartest idea?"

"I'd rather he worry about me than my kid client's missing brother," I said.

"Here's the thing," Joey said, "he ain't worrying about you. He's sending guys to take care of it. They fail . . . he sends a couple other guys. When they fail, he might send a guy with a gun."

"I have a gun, too."

Joey shook his head. "It's different. and you know it."

"OK," I said with a nod. "Should I just drop the whole thing?"

"You wouldn't be you if you did. Just be careful, is all."

"I will be."

"If something happens to you, though . . . dibs on Gloria."

I laughed. "It's good to know how far your concern goes," I said.

"I'm all about honesty," said Joey.

* * *

THE OAKS IS IN PARKVILLE, which sits between Carney and Towson. It's a short jaunt from the Baltimore Beltway. We slowed to cruising speed on Rock Oak. The houses here were brick duplexes with most featuring tacky metal awnings which went out of style around the time they started rusting over. Cars of varying vintages and quality lined the street. A few more peeked out from alleys. After a few blocks, we neared the address.

Vehicles packed both sides of the street all around the house. If Esposito were the type to jam cell phones, he was also the type to have some lackeys on the lookout. I couldn't simply walk up the steps to the walkway, leave the box on the porch, and walk away. Someone would stop me, probably before I put it down. I added a handwritten note to the box just to tweak Esposito a little more. Joey was right; I had to be careful here. Esposito was an asshole, though, and I wanted him to get his knickers in a twist.

Joey put a gun on his lap. He nodded at me. I got out of the Beamer and walked to a house in the next duplex. All the lights were off. As I went up the stairs and walkway, I looked over at Esposito's house. I couldn't see anyone keeping watch, but I knew they spied on me from somewhere. When I got to the porch of the decoy house, I stopped and crouched as low as I could. I waited. Nothing.

I padded across the grass to Esposito's house. Most of the

first-floor lights were on. No one sat on the porch. I couldn't see anyone in the windows. Then I saw a small camera above the door. Why have a goon keep watch when the electronic eye sees and records all? The camera was probably tied into the Wi-Fi. With some time, I could take it down, but the longer I stayed out here, the greater the odds someone would see me. I'd just have to smile for the video.

I crouched at the side of the house. No one came out. The only camera I could see was above the door. I stayed low and approached the porch. When I got there, I slid the box up to the door and started away. When I reached the steps, I stood and ran. Joey opened the passenger door, and I got in just as someone came out to have a look. Joey stomped on the gas, and the Teutonic turbo propelled us down the street.

* * *

AFTER WE GOT onto the Beltway, my cell phone rang. I had a good idea who was calling. "Hello?"

"It ain't like Amazon to make late-night deliveries," Esposito said.

"What about the handwritten note?" I said. "Must be a Prime perk."

"It was a nice touch."

"Thanks."

"You got my attention, C.T."

"Figured I would."

"My attention may not be something you want to have," Esposito said.

"I'll take my chances," I said. "I'm going to keep looking for Chris Sellers."

"So am I."

"Then may the best man win," I said.

CHAPTER 9

JOEY DROPPED ME OFF AND ISSUED ANOTHER WARNING TO BE careful. "You're just collateral damage in his war," he said. I promised to heed the advice. We both knew I wouldn't. Joey drove away. I took my gun out and walked around the front of my house before unlocking the door. I thought I smelled hot cheese and tomato sauce. When I got to the dining room, the two white boxes on the table confirmed it. Gloria chowed down on a slice topped with vegetables.

"Pizza?" I stated the obvious.

"I haven't had it in months," she said after swallowing her bite.

"What will all this bread and cheese do to your hips in a tennis dress?"

"I don't have to wear a tennis dress for a while." Gloria smiled. "Until then, I'm sure we can find some good uses for my hips."

"Count on it," I said, pouring myself some iced tea and throwing a slice of cheese and a slice of veggie on a plate.

"I hate to get back to business," Gloria said, "but what the hell just happened?"

She knew the crux of my case already, so I filled her in on recent developments.

"How did he know to be at the Starbucks?" said Gloria.

"It's a puzzle I'm trying to solve," I said.

"This Esposito is trouble. Promise me you'll be careful."

"I always am."

"Is that what you call going to his house to taunt him?"

"You'd be proud of how carefully I sneaked around."

"I'm serious," Gloria said, frowning. "It was dangerous."

"My job is dangerous," I said.

Gloria shook her head. "That was you creating danger. You didn't need to do it."

"Sometimes, you need to poke the bear."

Gloria closed her eyes and took a deep breath. "During your last big case, you got shot at," she said. "Then there was the time I had to toss you a gun because four men were looking for you. I don't want to worry about you on every case. And I don't want to worry that I'm going to get shot right along with you."

I put my pizza down. "I understand your concern."

"You do?"

"Yes. I don't want to get shot, either. When I started doing this job, I thought it would be easy. I figured I could do most of it from my computer. It hasn't turned out to be so easy. I do a lot offline, and some of what I do puts me in danger."

"Then why do you still do it?" Gloria said. "Your parents would support something else, I'm sure."

"No doubt they would. But I'm good at this. I'm good at finding things out. I've gotten better at dealing with people, and when it comes down to it, I can take care of myself in a fight. On top of it all, I'm helping people . . . people who probably couldn't get help anywhere else."

"That's important to you."

I nodded. "I didn't expect it to be. I used to think my parents' philanthropy was bullshit they did to feel good about themselves, but I like making a difference. Danger and all, I wouldn't give up this job."

Gloria looked at me and nodded. "I believe you."

"I hope so," I said. "It's the truth."

She smiled. "You believe in what you're doing. That's great."

I picked up the uneaten slice of cheese and took a bite. "It took me a while," I said, "but I've come around." And I had, as much as I didn't care to admit it. Some of my parents' altruism rubbed off on me. I wondered if Gloria would meet a similar fate. She was the hedonist I wanted to be a while ago. Something deeper lay beneath the surface, though. I recently saw her take an interest in fundraising. Maybe my indirect altruism would rub off on her. We spent enough time together to make it possible. Part of me wanted to be a good influence on her, to whatever degree someone like me can. Another part of me wondered what this desire meant.

* * *

LATER, I was still hungry. Gloria lay in bed fiddling with her iPhone. I went downstairs and reheated two slices of pizza. Then I felt hungry enough to have another. My dinner plans had been scuttled by the trip to Esposito's, and I didn't eat much after I came home. I pondered the case while I ate the third slice. Esposito and his pet goon showing up still bothered me. If he hadn't compromised me, he must have compromised Chris Sellers.

I hoped Chris trusted me enough to reach out again. He did a good job of vanishing the first time. I was still clueless where he had gone. Other than his occasional presence on a coding board, he left no online footprint I could find. This was a man who planned to unplug from the grid and then executed a well-plotted plan. I couldn't imagine disconnecting in the same way, but on some level, I admired it.

I put the remaining pizza in the fridge, feeling full after three slices. Sometime tomorrow, I would need to work those off. I went back upstairs. Gloria still diddled with her phone, but she yawned and her eyelids looked heavy. I got into bed beside her. She smiled at me and turned back to her phone. I checked for any messages from Chris Sellers, found none, and went to sleep.

* * *

WHENEVER GLORIA STAYED THE NIGHT—WHICH happened with increasing regularity—I woke up before she did. How she got up early for tennis lessons and tournaments, I couldn't fathom. I suffered no delusions about being an early riser, and she always slept later than I did. I walked downstairs, turned on the Keurig, and put a pod in it. While the coffee brewed, my cell phone rang. I didn't recognize the number. "Hello?" I said.

"What the hell did you get into now?" Gonzalez said.

"I didn't do it."

"What?"

"My usual response to the police," I said.

"So you didn't pay Alberto Esposito a visit last night?" Gonzalez said.

"Would denying it help?"

"Not really."

"What do you want, Gonzalez?"

"I think we should talk."

"We're already talking."

"In person, I mean," he said.

"Let me guess," I said. "This isn't the kind of invitation I should decline."

"You got it."

"Then I'd love to," I said, with as much sincerity as I could summon.

"You know where the Denny's in Perry Hall is?"

I frowned. Denny's? "Unfortunately, yes."

"See you in forty-five minutes."

Before I could answer, Gonzalez hung up.

"I'd be delighted," I said to the empty line.

* * *

FORTY-EIGHT MINUTES LATER, I squeezed the Caprice into one of the few remaining parking spots in the Denny's lot. The popularity of Denny's always mystified me. I understood its appeal at two AM after a night of drinking beer, but its allure stopped there. When I walked into the restaurant, Gonzalez nodded at me from the first booth on the left. It was a bit past the claw machine and a few booths from the restrooms.

Elegance.

Gonzalez possessed a tan Hispanic skin tone and dark hair worn short. A couple dots of gray in his beard yet none in his hair made his age tough to guess, but looking at his face, I went with late thirties. Gonzalez stood a shade under six feet and kept himself in shape, making his choice of restaurant all the more confusing. No sooner did I slide into the booth than a waitress appeared. All things considered, I would have rather sat across from her. I ordered coffee and skimmed the menu as I waited for Gonzalez to talk.

He didn't seem to be in a hurry. I noticed this restraint before with criminals. We worked together twice previously but enjoyed only limited interactions in person. Another few minutes would eclipse all the time spent with Gonzalez before. He sipped his coffee and alternated between looking at me and glancing around the restaurant. The waitress returned with my coffee. Gonzalez ordered the traditional Grand Slam breakfast. I ordered a western omelet with an English muffin and hoped the dish wasn't too difficult for a place like this. Maybe I should have opted for a plate of bacon and home fries. "I asked around about you," Gonzalez said.

"Good for you," I said. "I'm not surprised."

"Talked to a Captain Sharpe. He said you're a pain in the ass and you don't care about doing things the right way."

"I prefer to think of it as cutting down on paperwork," I said. "Save the trees."

"He also said you do good work and you get results."

"At least he got something right."

Gonzalez smirked. "They might cut corners in the city, but we try to do things the right way out here."

"Is breakfast at Denny's in your field manual?"

"I'm a humble public servant," said Gonzalez.

Before I could fire off a witty retort, the waitress returned with our food. She also freshened our coffees before walking away. My omelet was a nice shade of yellow, with some small scorch marks at the edges, just like I liked it. The muffin could have used another minute in the toaster but overall, I couldn't complain. I put butter and jelly on the muffin and cut my omelet as Gonzalez tore into his bacon.

"I take it you have people watching Esposito?" I kept my voice low.

"What makes you think that?" he said.

"The alternative is you have someone watching me. If you do, I can only hope she's hot."

My comment got Gonzalez to smile. "Yeah, we have people on Esposito. We know who he used to work for."

"You watch everyone who used to work for a gangster?"

"What if we do?"

I let his question linger as I ate some of my omelet and drank some coffee. The coffee was predictably mediocre, but the omelet tasted as good as it looked. I doubted I would do a lot of dining at Denny's, but it was good to know they had improved.

"He used to work for Tony Rizzo," Gonzalez said.

"I'm aware," I said.

"Then you also know he left town for a few years and recently came back."

"I do."

"Any theories?"

"I don't need to theorize," I said. "Esposito told me what he wanted."

Gonzalez frowned and put his fork down. "He did?"

"Yes."

"Why would he come to you?"

"Because I've known Tony Rizzo most of my life. He remembered me."

Gonzalez fell silent and sipped his coffee. His forehead showed deep frown lines. I never noticed before. Definitely late thirties.

"What did he tell you he was after?"

"He wants Tony's job," I said.

"He wants to run the Baltimore mob?"

"He might want the restaurant, too. It's a nice place."

"Did he say anything about the county?" Gonzalez said.

"Not really," I said. "But considering you don't really have anyone in charge out here, he might have an eye on consolidation. Or he might make a power grab in the county first, so he can bring more to bear against Tony."

"How did you factor into all of this?"

I told Gonzalez about Esposito visiting me to ask about writing ransomware. To his credit, and to my surprise, he knew what it was. He also didn't ask me if I agreed to do it, which I liked.

After a couple moments of eating, Gonzalez said, "You've told me all you know?"

"It's more than you knew," I pointed out.

"We're watching his house."

"But not listening."

"We didn't get a warrant for his phones."

"Sergeant, I'm disappointed. You can get directional microphones in a number of places, including Amazon."

"I told you. We try to do things right in the county."

"To the point you need people like me who do things the wrong way to fill in the gaps for you," I said. "Doesn't seem like a good method."

The waitress came back and asked if we needed anything else. We did not. She dropped off the check and walked away again. I could hear the bustle of people in the lobby waiting for a table.

"We'll get him," Gonzalez said, "and we'll do it the right way."

"Nice to hear," I said. "I'm looking at him, too, and I'm going to try and bring him down. If it's in the county, I'll give you a call."

"So I can arrest him."

"Exactly. For arresting someone like Esposito, you'll probably get a commendation. I wonder if your principles about doing things the right way would allow you to accept it." Gonzalez reminded me a lot of Rich. Wherever I went, I encountered a cop who loved to quote the rulebook.

"Sharpe was right," Gonzalez said. "You *are* a pain in the ass."

"I probably am," I said. "Just remember to thank me in your acceptance speech."

Gonzalez shook his head. He looked at the check. "You got it?"

"Is this also part of doing things the right way?"

"It's part of being a humble public servant."

"I'm not sure which part is worse," I said.

WHEN I GOT HOME, Gloria was finishing a breakfast she made herself. I acknowledged the rarity of the event, while being thankful my house wasn't reduced to ash. Judging by the smells in the kitchen and the crumbs on her plate, she made turkey bacon and toast. I would need to check the toaster and microwave for damage later.

I went to my office and got back to work while Gloria headed upstairs. A few minutes later, she came down. I looked for any message from Chris Sellers and again found none. "Already hard at work," Gloria said from the doorway. She wore capris and a Polo hoodie. Her overnight bag was slung over her shoulder.

"Heading home?" I said.

"You look like you need to work," she said, "and I have some things I need to do." Gloria came to my desk and planted a lingering kiss on me. "I'm sure we'll talk later."

"I'm sure we will."

A minute later, jet fuel ignited near my house and Gloria's rocket roared to life. I heard her drive away and pondered my next move in this case. My cell phone rang. It was Rich.

"I was deep in thought," I said.

"Then my interruption is no loss," he said.

"You wound me, dear cousin."

"We need to talk," said Rich.

"This is the second time I've heard those words from a cop today."

"Maybe something will stick this time."

"Don't count on it," I said.

"I'm serious."

"The last guy who said we needed to talk took me to breakfast. I'm holding out for lunch from you."

"Fine," said Rich, "how about The Abbey at one o'clock?"

"How can I say no to The Abbey?"

"See you at one," Rich said, and then he hung up.

I went back to work, such as it was. When I checked to see if anyone changed or downloaded Chris Sellers' code, I found it removed. I spent a few minutes searching other popular coding sites and repositories but couldn't find a trace of it anywhere. Chris had minimized his already tiny online footprint. If it got any smaller, it wouldn't even leave a dent in the sand.

Before Chris went all the way underground, I needed to find him. He removed himself from the coding community. Social media was a non-starter. Anna Blair showed no recent online activity. At this point, I needed to find a straw I could grasp. Then I remembered Bobbi Lane. Besides her pretty face and toned runner's physique, I recalled she and Chris worked for the same company. Maybe she could reach out to him on my behalf. I called her to run my idea past her.

"I still haven't heard from Chris," she said after we exchanged pleasantries.

"I'm not surprised," I said. I told her about contacting Chris online and the disastrous meeting at Starbucks.

"Can I help you find him?" Bobbi said.

"I hope so," I said. "Is his company email address still active?"

"Maybe. You want me to email him and ask him to meet you?"

"No. Not yet, at least. I only want you to contact him because you're concerned. If he answers, we go from there."

"All right," she said. "I'll email him right now."

"Good. Thanks. Let me know if you hear anything."

"I will." She paused for a second. Before I could bid her adieu, Bobbi said, "Do you want to go running tomorrow?"

I couldn't turn down an invitation like this. "Sure," I said. "Text me later, and we'll work out the details."

She said she would, and we both hung up. I used a lifeline. Now I hoped it paid off.

* * *

I GOT to The Abbey a little after one. The smell of burgers and beer welcomed me as I walked through the door. Several people sat at the bar, and about half the tables were full. Even with the more recent Fells Point location, the original Abbey in Federal Hill remained popular. The TV showed some sports-talk show on ESPN. I spied Rich in back near the bathrooms. He wasn't alone; Detective Paul King sat across from him and turned as I approached. An iced tea sweated in a tall glass in front of Rich, and King nursed a bottle of imported beer.

"Drinking on the job?" I said as I pulled out a chair beside Rich. It wouldn't feel as much like an interrogation if I didn't sit across from him.

"It's my day off," King said.

"And Rich dragged you out here anyway?" Rich rolled his eyes.

"It's The Abbey," said King. "Not much dragging required."

A waiter came to take our orders. I got a Santa Fe burger with fries and an Ommegang Abbey Ale. Rich and King both ordered boring basic burgers without even looking at the custom menu and its random exotic meats. One day, I would try the camel burger. The waiter left and returned after a minute with my beer. I took a sip. It was flavorful and a little hoppy. "OK, I've sipped some beer," I said. "Let the lecture begin."

"No lecture," Rich said, "just words of caution."

"Which you can't deliver without help?"

"You know about the task force I was on," King said. I nodded. "I did some asking around about Esposito."

"And?"

"He's a son of a bitch."

"I'm glad you brought him," I said to Rich. "This kind of piercing insight is hard to come by."

"Make your fucking jokes," King said. "It'll be real funny when you run into Esposito again."

"So what do you know besides the son of a bitch part?"

"He likes to take people."

"You mean kidnap them," I said.

"In a way," King said. "No ransom or anything. He just takes people who piss him off."

"And then what?"

"Then they usually die."

"Does he torture them?" Rich said.

"Don't know," said King, "but I doubt he's giving them a spa treatment." He looked at me. "You refused him. I'm glad you did, but it tweaked him a little. Then you beat up his goons and went to his house to piss him off. You're on his radar now. You might want to be careful."

I thought about the warning. I had already been taken once, in Hong Kong, and spent nineteen days as a guest of the Chinese penal system. It was an experience I didn't want to repeat or relive, and tightness spread across my chest at the memory of it. "OK," I said, "I'll watch my back."

"And stop trying to piss him off," King said.

The waiter brought our burgers and fries. He returned with

fresh beers for King and me and another iced tea for Rich. The Santa Fe burger was its usual delicious, spicy self. King's revelation about Esposito dampened the mood, however. Esposito was a prick, and I enjoyed tweaking him, but I would need to take him seriously. It sounded like he was prone to a viciousness Tony lacked. Maybe it was why Tony sent him away. Regardless, I would need to be vigilant.

CHAPTER 10

I GOT HOME AND PONDERED HOW I COULD FIND CHRIS Sellers or Anna Blair. Then I pondered some more. All my pondering didn't get me anywhere. They were in hiding. Chris already proved to be good at disappearing, which made me wonder about Anna. As long as Chris was with her, he could keep her hidden, too. But if they were apart, she would be left to her own devices. Maybe she was just as adept at vanishing as Chris but maybe not.

A quick MVA search got me her license plate. I didn't know if she would still have her own car. After all, if I could find it, Esposito and his cronies could find it, too. For now, it was the straw I decided to grasp. I didn't have many to choose from, after all. The next part of this plan would take more time and be a lot harder. Luckily, I knew a way to smooth it out.

I used the VM the BPD's network would treat as one of its own to access traffic cameras in the city and to tie into the county's feed. Once done, I wrote a script to convert license plate data to regular expressions and compare the output with Anna Blair's tag. It sounded like it would work.

I watched it run for a few minutes. The cameras observed tags and fed them through optical character recognition into a proprietary format (conveniently created by the makers of the camera system). My script took the output and turned it into a regular expression for comparison. It worked on every tag I watched. None were Anna Blair's, but at least I knew my system worked.

I let the script run. It would send me a text if it found a match. I had some downtime. Esposito knew where I lived, which bothered me. He already sent a couple of goons to my house. Next time, he might send more or send them armed. I packed two bags and headed out. First, I stopped at the gym and beat the hell out of a couple of heavy bags before finishing with a nice run on the treadmill. After a shower, I went to a nearby shooting range and killed a bunch of paper targets who definitely had it coming.

When I started doing this job, I didn't expect to spend many days hitting the heavy bags and shooting targets. Things always sound easier before you try them. I cleaned my gun at the range and packed it back into the bag along with the remaining ammo. This job proved to be more than I expected, and this case served as the latest example. Still, I liked what I was doing. Esposito was an unprincipled prick. The BPD could form another task force, but the first one didn't accomplish anything. I liked my odds better than theirs.

* * *

AFTER THE RANGE, I went home and made dinner. I wasn't feeling fancy, which turned out to be a good thing when I looked in the fridge. I bought a good stock of the basics but not much beyond. Basic it would be. I sautéed green peppers, mushrooms, and onions, added sausage, and served the whole thing with marinara sauce over rice. Anthony Bourdain wouldn't come around to try and learn my secrets, but it tasted good and filled me up.

Once I finished dinner, I checked my scripts. No hits on

Anna Blair's license plate. I hadn't expected any the first day. Hell, I didn't know if she would be driving her own car. When it came down to it, I didn't know if she was still alive. Such is the nature of grasping at straws. I washed the dishes and put them away before my phone chirped to indicate a text. It was from Bobbi Lane.

She wanted to run in the heat of midday, right at noon, and then get some lunch. I preferred the morning, but running under the sun's zenith with someone who looked like Bobbi Lane was much better than going out early alone. We decided she would come to Baltimore, and we would run laps around Federal Hill Park. We left lunch in the air. I checked back on my script, saw the expected zero results, and unwound with some Netflix before going to bed.

BOBBI LANE ARRIVED PROMPTLY at noon. Her small running shorts showcased her toned and shapely legs. She wore a tank top I could see the outline of a sports bra through, and her hair was pulled back into a tight ponytail. I sported my Under Armour shorts, shirt, and running shoes because I'm all about supporting the local companies. I showed Bobbi around the first floor of my house for a minute. Then we headed to the park.

The blocks we spent walking served as a warmup. Bobbi ran as soon as we got there. I already felt loosened up, so I fell in stride beside her. I would occasionally let her get a couple steps ahead so I could admire her running form. She set a good pace, and her breath came easily. Bobbi was a woman used to running. This pace was a little faster than my normal one. but I could adapt.

"I emailed Chris like we discussed," Bobbi said after we

finished our first lap. She talked as if she were strolling along. The run wasn't taxing her at all.

"Anything yet?"

"No response, but I know he read it. Our internal emails attach read receipts automatically."

"So the address still works," I said.

"And he still checks it," she said.

"I might need you to email him when we're finished. If he replies, I'll see if I can trace it."

"What if he doesn't?"

"Then you might need to hang out for a while," I said with a grin.

Bobbi smiled. "I can think of worse ways to pass the time."

I could think of better ones, but I kept my ideas to myself. Bobbi took off on a sprint. I matched her stride for stride for a quarter-lap. We fell back into a good rhythm. She lagged a couple steps behind before pulling even again. The sly upturn to her lips told me she had checked me out like I did her.

We did a few more circuits, about four miles in all, before breaking off at a walk back to my house. "Good run," Bobbi said. "We should do this more often."

"Anytime," I said. "It's good having someone to go with."

We got back to my place and pondered lunch. Our need for showers before going anywhere left it up in the air. "You have more than one shower?" Bobbi said.

"I do," I said, "but I have an old hot water heater. We'll have to go in shifts."

"You go ahead, then," she said, looking at her phone. "I'll keep searching for lunch places."

I went upstairs, put all my sweaty clothes in the hamper, and got into the shower. The hot water felt good. Bobbi put us on a pace faster than my normal one, plus two sprints. I adjusted the shower head. The hot water hitting my muscles loosened them up. Then a wider arc of light washed over the bathroom. The glass had already steamed over, so I couldn't see out. I wondered if Esposito's men came back. If they did, I only had hot water and a showerhead to fight them off.

Someone grabbed the door. I gripped the hose and metal head like a weapon. Bobbi Lane stood there, smiling. She, too, doffed her running clothes. The rest of her looked as toned and fit as her legs, with softness in exactly the right places. She stepped into the shower and pulled the door shut. "Hi."

"Hello," I said.

The conversation died there as Bobbi kissed me. She wrapped her arms around my neck. Water ran over her body. We kissed again. Before long, the hot water cooled to warm. I opened the door, grabbed Bobbi and a couple towels, and we left the bathroom for the bedroom.

* * *

LATER, when we were both dressed, Bobbi and I walked to Byblos and took the food back to my house. Federal Hill was awash in food options, and we decided on Mediterranean. Bobbi ordered a falafel pita with a side of baba ganoush and more pita. I got chicken shawarma with string beans and rice pilaf. We ate at my coffee table, sitting beside each other on the sofa, while she sent a follow-up email to Chris Sellers. I kept a laptop handy in case he replied.

"What in the world did Chris get himself into?" Bobbi said.

"Someone took an interest in his talents," I said.

"How? How does a gangster even know about Chris?"

"The gangster's brother works at Hopkins."

Bobbi shook her head. "He could get a pipeline of talent from a place like that."

I hadn't considered it, and the thought gave me a chill. How many other people did Danny Esposito pass onto his brother, and what were they doing now? Was Danny how Esposito knew where Chris and I were meeting? "He could," I said, trying to pretend the thought didn't disturb me.

"Have you talked to the brother?"

"Yes," I said. "He didn't sound eager to help his darker sibling again, but it could have been a ruse. I think I need to pay him another visit."

Bobbi took a delicate bite of her falafel. At her current rate, it would take her a hundred bites to eat something I would devour in twenty. "Does it ever make you nervous?" she said.

"What?"

"The job. Talking to gangster's brothers. Running into the gangsters themselves. It sounds dangerous."

"It can be," I said. "I'm not too proud to admit to some nerves here and there."

"Why do you do it? You said my company would love to hire you."

"They would."

"So why not do something safer?" she said. "Write code. Your biggest danger there is a faulty keyboard."

"I would say it's shitty documentation," I said, making Bobbi chuckle. She knew. "I'm good at this. I get to do things like write code for more interesting purposes."

"And the gangsters?"

"Part of the job. I thought I could do so much of this online at first, which hasn't turned out to be the case."

"You still do it," Bobbi said.

"It's growing on me." She didn't need to know about my arrangement with my parents. Maybe some of their persistent brand of philanthropy rubbed off on me after all.

"Try not to get hurt," she said with a grin. "I'd hate to have to find another running partner so soon."

"I'll be fine."

"You're already fine."

"Then I'll do my best to stay that way," I said.

* * *

After Bobbi left, I checked in on my scripts. Still nothing. Expanding my search area was a possibility, but I needed to be scientific about it. Simply adding counties at random would provide a lot more potential noise. I'd be looking for the same needle in a much bigger and more slapdash haystack. I required more information first.

I checked into Chris Sellers as much as I could for now. Anna Blair remained. I could only presume they went into hiding together. I started a thorough search into her life. Anna rented an apartment in White Marsh. Esposito would have gone there, and even if he were dumb enough to overlook it, my traffic camera script would have picked her up. I ruled it out.

With nothing significant from Anna herself, I moved onto her parents. They owned a house in Glen Burnie. Esposito would have gone there, too. If Anna went to either place, he would have found her and probably grabbed her based on what King told me about him. If Anna had been grabbed, Chris would come out of hiding. I hoped. If I couldn't find anything better, I'd need to follow up on the parents, but for now, I kept looking.

Anna still possessed one living grandparent on each side of the family. Her maternal grandfather had retired to Florida. The fact was worth noting. I wouldn't put a trip to Florida past Esposito, but he'd exhaust all the local options first. I came back to Chris emerging from hiding if Esposito's goons managed the snatch-and-grab with Anna. Her paternal grandmother lived in an assisted-living facility in Timonium, another place my traffic camera script should have found her.

I sifted through more family members and ruled them out for various reasons. Anna and Chris must be hiding outside the radius of my traffic camera script. I could have expanded it to all counties in Maryland and at least eliminate anywhere in the state. It would also provide a ton of input to churn through. In the meantime, I pulled her credit report and checked all her cards for recent activity. She withdrew $300 from a few different ATMs five days ago. Nothing since then. I kept watching her cards while I amended my scripts.

A hit came up.

Anna Blair used a credit card in Ocean City.

It was always possible someone stole her identity—or at least her credit card—and used it. This represented the first real lead I uncovered since I got Chris Sellers to answer me on the code forum. I quickly changed my script to look for Worcester County traffic camera activity, grabbed my phone, and got in the Caprice.

A drive to Ocean City loomed ahead of me.

* * *

AFTER CROSSING THE BAY BRIDGE, I pulled over and used my phone to open a secure tunnel into my desktop. Anna Blair's car triggered a number of traffic cameras. I could trace her path from the ATM and narrowed her location to about a one square block area. Once I got there, I could reduce the scope the rest of the way. I drove to the block, which had a smallish hotel on each corner.

Anna Blair drove a silver Subaru sedan. I saw just such a car at the third hotel, and it matched her tag number. I parked the Caprice in an available space, called up a picture of Anna from social media, and headed into the lobby of the Ocean Getaway Inn. The fellow behind the desk looked young enough to be bumming his way around after high school. His polo was untucked, and his nametag, which read "Vince," sat crooked below the collar. "Need a room?" he said.

"I need to find someone." I showed him my ID. He looked at it like I offered a look at my pet lizard.

"I don't know if I should be talking to you."

"Got something to hide?"

"What?"

"Let me guess," I said. "Your guests pay for discretion."

"Yeah," he said, nodding. I hoped he convinced himself. "That's it."

"Not at the rates you charge, they don't. Now you can help me, or I can talk to your boss."

Vince resigned himself to his fate. "OK, OK. Who are you looking for?"

"A woman named Anna Blair."

After a little typing and head-shaking, Vince said, "No one here under that name."

"How about Chris Sellers?" I said.

He checked and got the same result.

"How about this woman here?" I showed Vince the picture of Anna Blair on my phone. "She should have come back a couple hours ago."

"Yeah, I remember her. Miss Curie."

"Curie?"

"Yeah," Vince said, "Marie Curie."

I rolled my eyes. "Do you know who Madam Curie was?"

"Was? What do you mean? She's in 312."

"Google her," I said as I headed for the stairs. I took them two at a time, got off at the third floor, and found room 312 quickly. While I knocked on the door, I pondered what I would say. Nothing like having a plan.

"Who is it?" a nervous voice said from the other side of the door.

I held my ID up to the peephole. "Take a look at my ID," I said. "I'm trying to help you and Chris."

"He's not here."

"Then I guess I'll focus on helping you for now," I said.

I waited. Anna didn't say anything else. She was on the third floor so there was no other way out of the room not involving a thirty-foot drop. Maybe she scrutinized my ID. Maybe she wondered how such handsomeness could be conveyed in such a small photo. Or she could be holding a gun. I moved to the side as much as I could while still holding my credentials to the peephole.

The chain unlatched. The deadbolt turned. The door opened. Anna Blair looked exactly like the picture I found on Facebook. She was pretty, though I would have put Gloria and Bobbi Lane above her. I chided myself for the thought. Anna's brown hair looked newly-washed. She wore a plain black T-shirt, pink gym shorts, and no shoes. "Who says I need help?" she said.

"You opened the door," I said.

"Why do you think I need help?"

"Brian came to me. He's worried about his brother and by extension, you."

A small smile played on Anna's lips. "He's a good kid."

"Yes, he is," I said. I looked around to make sure no one took an interest in our conversation. "I'd rather not talk right here. Is Chris somewhere nearby?"

"Somewhere, yes. We're not staying together. He called it a single point of failure, I think."

I liked the term, even though Chris was the one Esposito and his men were after. From what I heard about Esposito, I felt he could get Anna to give up Chris' location. "Probably a good idea," I said, working on my diplomacy.

"Look, I'll talk to you," Anna said. "But I'm not telling you where Chris is." I watched her face for a tell, even a glance in one direction. Nothing.

"All right," I said. "I have just the place in mind."

* * *

Ten minutes later, we sat in a booth at Tequila Mockingbird. I've always loved the name and liked the food, and this combo is enough to get me to go back every time I visit Ocean City. Those visits became less frequent after I left my teen years behind. Ocean City is great until you travel to some spectacular beaches throughout the world. It still held local appeal to me, though, in part because of places like Tequila Mockingbird. It was decorated like a thousand other Tex-Mex restaurants, and chips and salsa appeared on the table as soon as we took seats.

Anna Blair sipped a margarita. I nursed a very non-Tex-Mex IPA while we waited for our food. "Tell me what happened," I said.

She frowned. "You know Chris is really good at writing code." I nodded. "Like, really good." I nodded some more. She seemed to want the acknowledgment. "Anyway, this guy wanted him to write some bad program for him."

"Alberto Esposito," I said, keeping my voice down. "And he wanted ransomware."

"That sounds right. Anyway, Chris agreed to help him at first. Then . . . I guess it dawned on him who he was working for; I don't know. He stopped and told the guy he was done."

"And he wouldn't return the money he'd been paid."

"He worked for the money."

"Esposito sees it differently," I said.

"Whose side are you on?" Anna said, frowning.

"Yours," I said, "but once Chris knew who he made a deal with, keeping the money wasn't smart."

"Whatever." She shook her head. "Anyway, he told me we needed to get out of town, so here we are."

"Here you are."

"What do you mean?"

"I found you without a lot of effort," I said. "I've been looking for a day or so."

"Sure, but you're a detective."

Fajitas sizzled from about twenty feet away. The sound grew closer. Our waitress dropped off our food. Unlike Anna's fajitas, my fish tacos did not sizzle, but steam rose off them, and they smelled terrific. "My point," I said, "is it didn't take a lot for me to find you, and I'm probably not the most motivated guy looking."

Anna assembled a fajita. She ordered chicken, and it came with the usual array of colorful vegetables, sour cream, guacamole, and tortillas. She skipped the guac entirely, committing a serious fajita *faux pas*. I let it pass. "How did you find me, anyway?" she said after a couple bites.

"You used a credit card."

"Shit." She shook her head. "I just got that card. Thought it was safe to use."

I tried my tacos. The fish had a tasty seasoning to it, and the slaw, pico, and guac complemented it nicely. "The place you used it is far enough from here so no one would find you right away," I said. "I used something else, too. But you need to be careful. Chris does, too."

"We will."

We ate our dinners in silence for a few minutes. I broke it with a question. "How long do you guys plan to stay on the run?"

"What do you mean?" she said.

"I mean, you can't just chill here for a couple weeks and go back like nothing happened."

"Huh." Anna pursed her lips. "I guess I never thought about it like that."

"You're on the run for a while. You need to be ready."

"I am," she said, adding a quick and forceful nod. Too quick and forceful. I wasn't convinced.

"Here's my card," I said, sliding one across the table to her. "I'll stick around here for a day or two and see if we have any unexpected company. In the meantime, you and Chris need to come up with a plan. Living on the lam doesn't suit you."

"I'll talk to him."

"Any chance you'll take me to see him?"

Anna shook her head. "No."

"All right. At least tell him we talked. I reached out to him earlier and was going to meet him until Esposito rolled in."

"He mentioned that to me," she said.

"I still don't know how Esposito knew."

Anna fell silent. She wasn't going to be any more help. When the waitress returned, I paid the check—in cash, so as not to contribute to the credit card trail—and took Anna back to her hotel. From there, I checked into the Sea Spray Inn across the street. I felt Anna didn't know what she got herself into, and the feeling made me more worried for her and for Chris than before.

CHAPTER 11

THE NEXT MORNING, I PULLED A T-SHIRT AND GYM SHORTS out of my overnight bag and went for a run along Coastal Highway. It wasn't Federal Hill Park, but it gave me about a half-hour of exercise. Later in the year, with more coeds walking to the beach, the scenery would be improved. I got back to my room, showered, dressed, and declared myself ready to stop all forms of malfeasance.

First, though, I wanted breakfast. Stopping malfeasance is harder when you're hungry. I went to the General's Kitchen, glad for the light offseason crowd, and ordered an omelet with wheat toast and home fries. The coffee was good enough to merit a second cup. On the drive back to my hotel, I took a lap through the Ocean Getaway Inn's parking lot. Anna Blair's Subaru was gone. I didn't think much of it. She said she and Chris weren't staying together.

Back at my hotel room, I renewed my efforts to find Chris Sellers online. If Anna went to see him, he could be online now. I checked all the haunts I knew for him and came up empty. Bobbi Lane said his company email address still worked, but he hadn't answered her. I sent her a text wondering if anything changed. She replied a few minutes later and said it hadn't. She also wondered when we could go running again. I suggested tomorrow. She asked where I was, and I told her.

After coming up empty on finding Chris, I checked my traffic camera script to see if I could get a clue where Anna was. I didn't get any hits for her car. It definitely left the parking lot. Even if someone stole it, the traffic cameras up and down Coastal Highway would have seen the car. Yesterday, I told Anna I found her via her credit card. Now I wondered if she and Chris were paranoid enough to wonder about traffic cameras. If she didn't want to be tracked, she could have swapped her license plate or simply taken a bunch of back roads.

Maybe she didn't want to be found again.

* * *

A couple hours later, I walked across the street and checked the parking lot. The Subaru was still missing. I went inside. Instead of Vince, a cute redheaded girl of college age worked the front desk. She grinned dimples at me as I approached. "Can I help you, sir?"

"I hope so," I said. "I was supposed to meet my friend here yesterday, but I got delayed. I hope she hasn't checked out."

"Have you tried calling her?" she said, frowning in confusion as if I hadn't considered the obvious. Did I look so much older and more technophobic to a college-aged girl?

"Well, part of my delay left me without a phone, or I would have. Can you tell me if she's still registered?"

Vicki, according to her nametag, pondered my problem for a moment before offering a cheerful nod. "I can check for you. What's the name?"

"Curie," I said.

"I'm sorry. She's already checked out," Vicki said after a quick search.

"Unfortunate. Do you know when?"

"Seven o'clock this morning."

"Wow," I said. "She got an early start. OK, I'll have to get a phone and reach her, then. Thanks."

Vicki gestured to a phone at the end of the desk. "You could use ours." She lowered her voice. "We're not supposed to let people use it, but it sounds like you need it."

Social engineering works. Never believe otherwise. "Thanks," I said, "but I don't want to land you in hot water." And I didn't. I knew what I needed to know. Vicki gave me another smile as I walked out. Anna Blair had been gone for hours, and she knew to evade traffic cameras, so I couldn't keep track of her. She also knew not to use her credit card. I really needed to stop telling people things.

I got back to my hotel room. Anna and Chris were in the wind again. I could only presume she told Chris how I found her, so now they'd both be careful going forward. It still concerned me if I could find them, Esposito could find them. They were careful before. If I didn't know where they went, I couldn't help them.

I checked out and drove up and down Coastal Highway for about an hour, hoping to luck into spying Anna Blair's Subaru somewhere. I came up empty. Without anything else to pursue, I headed back home.

* * *

AFTER I GOT to my house, I checked my traffic camera script. No hits. I looked for Anna Blair's credit cards. Nothing. On a lark, I tried Chris Sellers' cards. Nothing. They vanished from the grid again. I hoped they were better at hiding this time. While I wanted to find them, I wanted to make sure Esposito and his cronies couldn't.

I logged onto codingchat.com and sent Chris a message.

Chris,

I found Anna. It looks like you two have gone off the grid again. I can help you, but you need to let me. If I found you before, I'm worried Esposito will find you now. You should be worried, too. Reply to me here or at my cell: 410-555-7274.

I didn't have an idea of how to keep looking for them. They were ahead of me from the jump, and could have gone myriad places in the hours before I realized they were in the wind. The elapsed time since opened up more possible places. I didn't even have a way of narrowing them down at the moment. They could have driven north from Ocean City, up through Delaware, and could be eating lobster in Maine right now for all I knew.

My phone rang. Of course, it was Brian Sellers. When life hands you lemons, sometimes it follows up by pelting you with more of them. He'd keep calling.

"Hi, C.T., it's Brian."

I was used to old people telling me who was calling. People Brian's age grew up with caller ID. Then again, maybe he lumped me in with Luddites like Vicki at the hotel did. "Hi, Brian," I said, summoning my diplomacy.

"Have you found Chris?"

"I would have told you if I had."

"Oh." I could almost hear him deflate over the phone.

"I found Anna, though," I said.

"Oh!" Life came back into his voice. "That's a good thing, right?"

"Maybe. If I can find her, the people she and Chris are hiding from might be able to also."

"You said you found her." He paused. "What happened?"

"Yesterday's news," I said. "She and Chris left early this morning. I don't know where they are right now."

"Can you find them again?" Brian said.

"I'm working on it."

"Can I do anything?"

"Keep trying to reach him. You never know; it might make a difference one of these times."

"I can do that."

"I'm going to keep trying, too," I said. "If I found them once, I should be able to again."

"Good luck," he said.

I declined to say I would need it, even though I would.

*   *   *

GLORIA CALLED as I sat down to eat dinner. I made steak kabobs with rice pilaf. At least they would reheat well. "How's your case going?" she said.

I liked her taking a greater interest in my cases, but I wasn't sold on talking shop with her yet. It felt a little odd. I wanted some separation between my professional and personal lives. The fact of Gloria consuming more and more of my personal life was something we would need to hammer out one day. I liked her, but I wondered if our relationship of fun and convenience was morphing into something more. "Well," I said, "and not so well."

"What do you mean?"

I told her about finding Anna, what I learned, and then Anna's early departure. "You'll find them again," Gloria said.

"I hope so," I said. "My concern is I found them before, and I'm still not the only one looking. What if I'm not first to find them the next time?"

"You found her before, you can find her again."

"I'll try. I need to before the other guys do."

"Do you know where you're going to look next?" she said.

"Not really," I said. "They could be anywhere along the east coast by now . . . or well past the Mississippi River if they made a turn."

"Are they both from around here?"

"I think so." I would have to check about Anna.

"Then I doubt they packed up and drove to Kansas," Gloria said.

I nodded. "They don't really see themselves as on the run. Anna made it clear enough, and I don't think I changed her mind. They think they're just holing up until all this blows over."

"See? You should listen to me more often," Gloria said. I could hear the smile in her voice. Her smile was terrific, and it forced me to reciprocate.

"It all depends on what you say," I said.

"I could whisper some suggestions into your near next time I see you."

"I'll definitely listen to you more, then," I said.

LATER, I came back downstairs. There had to be better ways of trying to find Chris Sellers than the ancient messaging feature of a coding forum. Brian gave me the email address he checked most often (he said he didn't have one for Anna). I sent an email, saying pretty much the same thing I'd been saying all along. If I needed to type it again, I could add *this is a recording* to the end of it.

I didn't expect a response while I kept working and wasn't disappointed. Chris didn't have much reason to trust me, even if his brother did. I doubted my little tete-a-tete with Anna won me many favors, especially considering what I told her. Maybe he'd catch another glimpse of Esposito or one of his goons somewhere and realize I was the better alternative.

Until then, I didn't have any brilliant ideas on how to find him. Nor did I have any bad ideas, short of driving around and scrutinizing silver Subarus. I wasn't desperate enough to try it yet. On a lark, I checked the results of my traffic camera script again. No hits. I didn't expect there to be any. Low expectations make disappointment impossible. This case kept reinforcing the idea.

I didn't want to let Brian Sellers down. His brother made a stupid decision, but the kid didn't need to pay the price for it. I didn't have any ideas for the night, however, and after not being disappointed at my lack of results for anything again, I went back upstairs.

CHAPTER 12

THE NEXT DAY, I CHANGED INTO A RUNNING OUTFIT AND drove to Bobbi Lane's apartment in White Marsh. She told me she had a nice five-mile course planned for us. As I pulled the Caprice into her complex, I remembered I needed to resume my new-car searching. My Lexus was still MIA. The Caprice had its uses, but everyday driving was not among them. I went into Bobbi's building and rang her doorbell. She answered in a tank top and a pair of running shorts accentuating her legs. To my surprise, she kissed me at the door. "Ready to go?" she said.

"After you," I said. I followed her down the stairs and onto a nearby trail, watching with interest as she transitioned from walk to run. I settled in beside her at a good pace. Bobbi fell behind at some point. and I imagined she watched me with the same interest I watched her. The trail moved from paved to grassy a few times, winding into the woods. It was mostly level with a few hills not providing much of a challenge. We ran out to a checkpoint, paused for some water, and turned around.

With the end of the trail in view, Bobbi decided to turn the last leg of our run into a sprint. Despite the fact I played lacrosse from sixth grade through my senior year of college, I've always been more of a distance runner than a sprinter. Bobbi bolted from a normal run into a dead sprint. I took off right behind but couldn't catch her. She hit the end of the trail two steps ahead of me, stopped, and doubled over, catching her breath.

"Not much of a sprinter?" she said, straightening.

I drained the rest of my handheld water bottle. "I'm built for distance," I said.

Bobbi smirked at me. "Yeah, your stamina's not bad."

We went inside and drank more water. Bobbi's apartment was small, smaller than the one I leased in Fells Point after first returning from overseas. Her living room featured a new LED TV with a loveseat and two recliners. The dark brown furniture went nicely with the beige apartment-grade carpeting. The kitchen featured stainless steel appliances but not much counter space. The living area was open concept, with the cooking area flowing into a dinette with a round table sized just right for its two chairs.

"I only have one shower," Bobbi said after we had downed a tall glass of water each.

"And probably a dinky water heater, too," I said.

She peeled her tank top off, revealing a sports bra beneath. I barely set my empty glass on the counter before Bobbi grabbed me and planted a kiss on my mouth. She pulled my sweaty shirt off and tossed it aside. "Yeah, it's pretty small," she said, steering me down the hall into her bathroom. I lifted her to sit atop the sink as we kissed some more.

"I wonder how long the hot water lasts," I said as I lifted Bobbi's sports bra over her head.

"Let's find out," she said.

* * *

IT LASTED ABOUT TWENTY MINUTES. We cranked it up pretty high to massage our muscles after the run. Once the water dropped to warm and then to tepid, we retired to Bobbi's bed. Later, we lay side-by-side, tired again but refreshed at the same time. Bobbi propped her head up on her arm and looked at me. "I could get used to these runs," she said.

The sun coming in the window danced on Bobbi's light mocha skin. She never looked prettier. I couldn't help comparing her to Gloria but stopped as quickly as I started. Gloria and I enjoyed a relationship based on fun and convenience. So far, Bobbi and I had the same thing going. Comparing one to the other wouldn't end well for anyone, especially me. I felt like I would need to choose between them at some point. You're not in college anymore, C.T.

"I could, too," I said. And I could.

"Any luck finding Chris?" Bobbi said.

I shook my head. "The trail seems to have gone cold." I gave her a brief rundown of finding Anna Blair and her subsequent vanishing act. "I'm not sure what else I can try at this point."

"You want me to try emailing him again?"

"It can't hurt."

"We miss Chris at work," Bobbi said. "He's really good. Covering his slack has really been tough."

"Are you picking it up?"

"Some of it. I'm sort of divvying it with someone else."

"Anyone at work have any insight into where Chris might have gone?" I said.

"I wish," Bobbi said. "We've talked about it enough. He never really told us much about his private life, you know? Some people are just like that."

"Then you have those who Instagram their every meal and tweet the details of how it came out."

Bobbi chuckled. She showed dimples when she smiled or chuckled. It was absurdly cute. "I hope you find him."

"Me, too," I said.

"If you do, does that mean we can't . . . run together anymore?" Bobbi said.

"I don't see why it would."

"Good." Bobbi lifted herself up and lay atop me. "I think we were talking about your stamina earlier," she said, kissing my neck.

"You categorized it as merely 'not bad,'" I said.

"You suppose I need to upgrade that?"

"I'll prove it to you."

My boast made Bobbi smile.

AFTER LUNCH AND ANOTHER SHOWER—THIS one alone—I finally put on my change of clothes and left Bobbi's apartment. I drove home, checked my traffic camera scripts and email, and found nothing of promise or interest. I left my house and walked to a local coffee shop. When I left and walked home, I noticed a certain large gentleman following me. Rich always tells me how unobservant I am about things like this, and he has a point. For me to notice a tail, this fellow had to be bad at tailing.

I settled in at a normal walking pace, using store and car windows to confirm he was still behind me. He didn't seem to notice, not as though I expected him to. I was no expert at this. and he was even worse. I slowed, and he gained on me before adjusting his own pace. This guy most likely worked for Esposito. If Gonzalez put a tail on me, it wouldn't be someone so inept. I took out my phone and queued up a Bluetooth exploit, slowing even more as I pretended to text. Captain Obvious wasn't in range yet, but if I could get him about ten feet closer, he would be. I kept at the slower pace, and he matched it. As I neared my house, I stopped and faked a conversation, all the time keeping an eye on my special app.

When the goon came within ten meters, a red line on the app went green. I touched the *Exploit* button, and it did its Bluetooth magic, compromising one of the most wide-open and vulnerable protocols in the world. Writing this program was easy, and even with the supposed advances in Bluetooth security, it had yet to fail me. It didn't fail me this time, either; the program successfully cloned the goon's phone. Now I would know his texts and calls as he got them. I remembered how Esposito distrusted electronics.

It made me smile.

When I got home, I dumped the goon's phone information onto an extra SIM card and inserted it into a spare phone I kept for situations like this. I keep three extra phones in case there's more Bluetooth hackery to be done. The spare came online with the SIM card and provided me a perfect clone. Any text or call he made or received, I would be privy to. I hoped he would contact Esposito and one of them would know where Chris and Anna were hiding. Then again, I hoped no one in Esposito's crew knew anything about where Chris and Anna were hiding.

I glanced at, then ignored some rather lascivious texts between my incompetent shadow and a girl. His texting game was weak, but she seemed amenable to his limited charms. A short while later, I overheard a call with nothing to do with the case. Being a PI isn't all glitz and glamour. We're allowed to beat people up, and we usually get the girl in the end, but along the way, things like this happen.

At about six, the dearth of useful activity on the cell phone made me hungry. I bought some fresh pita bread at the market, so I made a dinner getting me in touch with my nonexistent Greek roots. I sautéed onions and green peppers in olive oil, removed them, and cooked sliced steak in butter and spices. When the steak was mostly done, I added the onions and peppers back in and whipped up homemade tzatziki. While the steak cooled, I chopped lettuce and tomato and made myself a couple of stuffed steak pitas.

I had eaten all of the first pita and about a third of the second one when the stolen phone rang again. This time, I heard Esposito's voice on the other end of the conversation.

"Jerry, where are you?" he said.

"At home, boss," Jerry said. "What's up?"

"I finally got a line on that fucking guy and his girl."

"The one who skipped with your money?"

"Of course the one who skipped with my money."

"Where are they?" I hoped Jerry would ask.

"The Dewey Inn in Dewey Beach," Esposito said. "Get over to my house now. We're going to get them and bring them back."

"I'm on my way." Jerry hung up.

I put my pita down and grabbed my car keys. The Caprice had a powerful V8. It could get there quickly. I counted on it to beat Esposito and his goon squad.

Dewey Beach. I knew approximately where it was but never been. My parents favored Ocean City in Maryland, no doubt because they shared a luxurious condo with a couple of other families. My GPS told me the shortest route would start the same way as the trips to Ocean City: Route 50 over the Bay Bridge. I weaved in and out of traffic, keeping the Caprice above 80 and above 90 when I could. I also kept a sharp eye out for police; getting pulled over would give Esposito and his men a chance to overtake me.

The Bay Bridge slowed me. One lane was closed due to the offseason for beach traffic, and there were enough cars in the two remaining lanes to force me to plod along at about 60. After the bridge, I gained speed and made up some time. I got onto Route 404, then Route 16, which would take me into Delaware. The narrower state routes required driving slower. I maintained about 15 over the speed limit but needed to be more vigilant for Johnny Law, who enjoyed more places to hide off the highway.

A little while later, I turned onto Coastal Highway. About eight miles remained to the Dewey Inn. I considered trying to reach Chris or Anna in advance but didn't want to spook them. They had fled (though not very far) before, and I didn't want to panic them again. The Caprice devoured the last few miles, and I turned with screeching tires into the parking lot at the Dewey Inn. It was a three-story hotel finished in stone the color of sand. I didn't see any silver Subarus in the parking lot, but I also didn't see any car like Esposito's. Yet.

I parked in the registration lane and went in. It was a few minutes after eight-thirty, and no one was checking in, so I walked straight to the sixtyish man behind the desk. I showed him my ID and pictures of Chris and Anna on my phone. "I know they're staying here," I said, "and I need to find them before someone else does."

"Someone else?" He gave me a wary look.

"Someone whose associates will toss you around and smash this place looking for them," I said. "So unless you want those things to happen, I need a key to their room now."

A minute later, I sprinted up the stairs to the second floor, armed with a keycard to room 215. I found it about halfway down the hall on the left. The card opened the lock, and I pushed the door into the room. Anna Blair stood up from the sofa and looked at me with wide eyes. Chris Sellers glanced around in panic, looking between the door and the balcony for a means of escape.

"What are you doing here?" Anna said.

"I heard Esposito knows where you are," I said. "He and some of his men are on their way. We need to move."

"Who the hell are you?" Chris said.

Anna answered for me. "He's the detective I told you about."

"Great, we all know each other," I said. "Let's chat later. Time to go."

I walked past Chris and looked out the window. Their room offered a spectacular view of the parking lot and Coastal Highway. I saw two cars pull into the parking lot. The lead car, a large black sedan, showed the damned MISTER E license plate. "Shit," I muttered.

"What?" Chris said, standing beside me at the window.

"They're here," I said. Two of Esposito's goons got out of the other car and started for the front door. "We're going to need to take the back way out. Let's go." Anna gaped at us as we moved, so Chris herded her along. I led them to the stairs, looked at the handy fire evacuation diagram, and found the rear exit past the basement pool and fitness center. We went down, coming out in a hallway. The fitness center and pool were on opposite sides. Ahead was a glass door to the outside.

"Let me go first," I said. I took my gun out and heard Anna gasp. I walked to the door, looked through it in both directions, and slowly pushed it open. I didn't see anyone. "Let's go," I said. Chris and Anna followed. We hugged the building as we made our way around the side toward the front. I unfortunately left the Caprice directly in front, right where Esposito could see it, and where he'd probably have a crony waiting for us.

Sure enough, he did. I peeked around the corner of the building and saw one of his goons standing between the Caprice and Esposito's car. He hadn't seen me yet. I turned back to Chris and Anna. "Where's your car?" I said.

"Out front," Anna said, casting her eyes down when Chris glared at her. "It was the only spot I could find."

"Argue later," I said. "For now, wait here and stay down."

"What are you going to do?" Chris said.

"Deal with the welcoming committee."

I put my gun away and walked around to the front of the building. The goon noticed and turned to give me the once-over. I hadn't seen him before. Hopefully, he wouldn't recognize me, either. He didn't make any aggressive move as I walked closer to him.

"Damn wife never remembers where she leaves the car," I said, shaking my head.

The complaint drew a sympathetic smirk and nod from the goon. I patted the pocket of my windbreaker. "You got a smoke?" I said.

"Sure," he said as I approached When he reached into his jacket, I gave him a hard kick in the balls, then two elbows to the head. He dropped. I found a gun in his jacket, so I tossed it onto the roof. I crouched and moved to the Caprice, looking into the lobby. Esposito and one of his goons got into an elevator. The other one pummeled the poor man behind the desk.

I waved Chris and Anna to me. They kept low and scurried to the Caprice as I unlocked the doors. "Get in and stay down," I said.

"Where are you going now?" Anna said.

"To stop the guy in there before he beats the clerk to death." I closed and locked the doors behind them, then walked into the lobby. Esposito's henchman held the clerk against the wall. Even from ten yards away, I could see the clerk was already unconscious, his face beaten into a bloody mess. The lackey stared at me as I approached. He let the clerk go, and the poor fellow sagged to the floor, somehow not hitting his head in the process.

"I know you," he said.

"How nice for you," I said. "Want to try your shit on someone who can fight back?"

He flashed a sinister smile and came at me. I blocked one punch, then another, and answered with a short jab into his solar plexus. The goon backed off, breathing hard. I pressed the advantage, launching two kicks he blocked and a third he didn't. The kick to his midsection staggered him. I moved forward and took a glancing blow to the face before blocking a couple other punches. He threw another, and I grabbed his arm, locking it in a hold threatening to snap his elbow. He grunted in pain.

Esposito and his other crony would have been up to the second floor and room 215 by now. To end this, I gave the goon a quick kick to the back of his leg, which dropped him to one knee. Then I let go of the arm lock long enough to slam his head into the counter. A smear of blood remained as his head bounced off, and he slumped backwards, unconscious. I picked up the front desk phone and called 9-1-1. "There's been an assault at the Dewey Inn," I said. "Send police and an ambulance or two." I hung up before the operator could finish her follow-up question, sprinted outside, and got into the Caprice.

"What happened back there?" Anna said as I fired up the engine.

The wheels shrieked as I stomped on the gas and we left the Dewey Inn's parking lot. "I convinced the guy he needed to treat the hotel staff more courteously," I said. Two figures emerged from the hotel in my rearview mirror. I also heard sirens in the distance.

"What the hell have I gotten into?" Chris said as we drove away. I watched for any cars following us and didn't see any.

"We'll have about two hours to discuss it," I said.

* * *

We rode in silence until we crossed the Bay Bridge. Anna sat beside me up front, and Chris Sellers rode in back. I saw no signs of Esposito or any other forms of pursuit. In the recesses of my mind, I realized I should have taken the five seconds to wipe my fingerprints off the hotel phone. The Dewey Beach police would dust the scene and discover I was there. My prints were confined to the phone and a couple of doors, and they could get lost in the mass of prints all over the doors. I could probably explain things to the police's satisfaction, but I didn't want to have to go back to Delaware and do it.

A minute later, I said, "Chris, I think we need to call your brother. He's the one who asked me to find you."

Chris frowned. "Not yet," he said.

"The kid is worried sick about you."

"Don't you think I know?"

"I'm not sure," I said. "You take money from a gangster, disappear with your girlfriend, and then go even further off the grid when I manage to track you down. So you'll forgive me for not knowing how much you prioritize your brother and how he feels about this whole fucking mess you created."

Chris stared at me in the rearview mirror. "I guess I deserved that," he said, his expression softening.

"And now I think I deserve an explanation," I said.

"You do?"

I jerked the wheel and pulled onto the shoulder, ignoring the horns of protest from a couple nearby cars. The Caprice shuddered to a stop beside the highway. "What are you doing?" Anna said.

"It's a long walk back," I said, unbuckling my seat belt and half-turning to face Chris. "But I'm sure Esposito won't be too far behind. You can probably hitch a ride with him."

"Come on," Chris said. "We need to keep going." He looked between me and the rear window as if his head were on a swivel.

"Then start talking."

"Chris, listen to him," Anna said. I could hear desperation in her voice.

"Or what?" Chris said, ignoring his girlfriend.

"Or you can practice your hitchhiking," I said.

Chris shot me a defiant look. "You think you can get me out of the car?"

I laughed at him. "You stupid asshole. I just took out two of Esposito's goons in about fifteen seconds. So yeah, I'm pretty sure I can toss you out of my car."

The defiant look fled Chris' face. He was a smart guy. I could almost see him doing the math in his head. He relented with a nod. "OK, fine, I'll tell you what happened. Just get us out of here."

I buckled up again, stomped on the gas, and merged back onto Route 50. Esposito was slippery. He might have gotten away from the hotel before the police arrived. I made sure to keep the Caprice above 80 and checked the rearview mirror often, both for police and jackass gangsters.

"There's someone I want to talk to when we get back," I said. "You can unburden your soul then."

CHAPTER 13

WHEN WE GOT CLOSER TO BALTIMORE, I CALLED JOEY. "IT'S almost eleven," he said.

"Sorry," I said. "I know how badly you need your beauty sleep."

"You're hilarious. What's up?"

I gave him the brief version of what happened with Chris and Anna. "They don't do a very good job of running and hiding," I said. "They might need the help of a professional."

"Let me guess," said Joey. "They're in your car right now."

"How did you know?"

"It seems I'm working late tonight. How far away are you?"

"About twenty minutes."

"Bring snacks," Joey said and hung up.

"Who's that?" Anna said.

"Someone who might be the answer to all your problems," I said. "If I can keep him well fed."

I found a 24-hour Super Walmart nearby featuring a bakery. The breads had been picked over, but the sweets were still in good supply. I grabbed a blueberry pie, a box of donuts, and a package of store-baked chocolate chip cookies. We got back in the car and drove the rest of the way to Joey's. I took the back roads to minimize the chances of encountering Esposito.

Think of the devil, and he shall call. My phone rang. "Keep quiet," I told Anna and Chris as I answered on speaker.

"You're a very meddlesome man," Esposito said.

"I don't know what you mean," I said.

"You expect me to believe you weren't at the Dewey Inn recently?"

"I don't really care what you believe. But yes, I was there."

"So you have Chris and his girlfriend?"

"No," I said. "They were gone by the time I got there."

"I'm not sure I believe you," he said.

"What you believe is your business." In the passenger's seat, Anna looked at me with wide eyes. Chris, to his credit, sat in the backseat and sulked in silence. "But I asked the guy at the front desk, and he said they recently left. Their room looked like it."

"He let you into their room?"

"You can get a lot more out of people when you talk to them rather than have one of your goons beat them half to death."

"He'll live," Esposito said.

"So will both of the assholes I dealt with."

"Ralph has a bad concussion."

"Ralph should learn how to talk to people."

"You might do well to learn that yourself," Esposito said and hung up.

"He has a point," Chris said. "You might want to watch how you talk to him."

"Tell you what," I said. "You return the money you stole, and maybe he'll pay for me to go to charm school."

Chris shook his head. "He's dangerous."

"And you stole his money," Anna said, pounding on the console. "If you know he's dangerous, why did you steal his money? Especially after. . . ."

"After what?" I said when she trailed off.

"Nothing."

"Don't worry about it," Chris added quickly.

"Why do I have the feeling I'll definitely need to worry about it?" I said.

* * *

A HALF-HOUR LATER, we sat around Joey's kitchen table. Chris and I each ate a cookie. Anna declined any of the treats. Joey already put away two cookies and was halfway through a piece of blueberry pie covering most of the plate he put it on. Anna frowned at Joey's eating. Chris, for his part, looked like he wanted to be anywhere else. He probably did. I didn't care.

"The first thing you need to do is call your brother," I said to him. He shrugged. "He's worried about you."

"Brian shouldn't worry about me," Chris said.

"He does. He hired me to find you. If you don't call him, I will."

Chris looked at me and pursed his lips. He didn't answer and didn't make a move for his phone.

"Jesus Christ, Chris, call your brother," Anna said. "For the first time in a while, don't be such an asshole."

He glared at Anna like she hit him. Anna stared back. This went on for a few seconds until Chris relented and pulled out his phone. "You're right," he said. He made the call, saying, "Hi, Brian" as he walked into the next room.

Anna shook her head as he left. "Ever since this mess began," she said, "it's like he's been a different person."

"Stealing a gangster's money will do it to you," I said.

"Why not give it back?" said Joey.

"It's complicated," Anna said.

I knew she wouldn't simplify it here, not with Chris around. On a different tack, I said, "Why not simply leave?"

"I love Chris. When he told me what he did, I was mad, but . . . I love him. I never thought it would end up like this."

Joey finished his pie as Chris walked back into the room. "I want to hear it from the top," I said.

Chris sat heavily in a chair and nodded. "All right. About a month ago, a guy approached me and told me his brother had a proposition for me."

"Danny Esposito," I said.

"Yeah," Chris said. "His face was familiar, but I couldn't place him."

"You'd seen him at Hopkins?" Chris nodded. "But he wasn't your graduate admissions officer?"

"No."

I wondered how Danny Esposito knew about Chris, then. Did the graduate admissions department share records of all their prospective applicants? "Anyone want coffee?" Joey said, interrupting my thought process, such as it was.

No one did, so Joey made a cup for himself on his Keurig. If Chris and Anna were going to need his services, he'd probably be up for a while. "OK, Danny Esposito comes to you with an offer," I said. "Then what?"

"I recognized him, so I figured I'd hear him out," Chris said. "Otherwise, I would've blown him off. He arranged a sit-down with his brother."

"Where?" I said.

"Why's that matter?"

I took a deep breath. Helping Chris was trying my patience, which wasn't a boundless resource. "Because it's a place he might go back to," I said. "Where was it?"

"I don't know . . . some Chinese buffet in Towson."

"Towson or Parkville?"

Chris pondered the question. "Parkville, I guess. Off Loch Raven."

I thought I knew the place he referred to. "OK, so you met Danny's brother. Did Danny come along?"

"He was there at the beginning," Chris said. "He left before we got down to business, though. It was like he . . . didn't want to be involved."

It seemed consistent with my prior conversation with Danny Esposito. "Tell us about your dinner conversation," I said.

"He introduced himself," said Chris. "He didn't tell me he was a mobster or anything, but I got a feeling it was something like that." I saw Anna shake her head in my peripheral vision. I knew the question she wanted to ask and sympathized. "He said a business associate did things the old way and didn't believe in technology. But if I wrote some ransomware—he didn't call it that in a restaurant, but I knew what he meant—then the whole operation would be modern. He asked me if I would do it and offered to pay me fifty thousand."

"You said your feeling was he might be a mob guy?" I said.

Chris nodded. "Yeah."

"And not in so many words, he asked you to write ransomware for him?"

"Yeah."

"And—"

"Why the hell did you say yes?" Anna broke in. She pounded Joey's kitchen table so hard I thought she might dislodge a tile. "Why, Chris? You're such a smart guy. Why the hell would you write that kind of software for a gangster?" Tears rimmed her eyes as she fell silent.

"I wanted to give you a nice wedding," Chris said in a small voice. He looked at Anna. "I know the kind you want." He looked at me now. "I do OK for salary, but I have a lot of student loans for undergrad and grad school. We could get married, but it would be a small wedding." He shrugged. "I wanted to give her the kind she deserved."

Tears slid down Anna's cheeks. "I don't need a big ceremony," she said. "I just want a wedding with you in it." Her head bobbed as she cried. Chris stood and walked to her. Anna jumped up, and they embraced, holding each other in silence for at least a minute.

"This is all really touching," Joey said, "but if I want to watch teary lovefests, I have cable."

After a few more seconds, Anna and Chris returned to their chairs. "Where were we?" Chris said.

"In the middle of your deal with the devil," I said.

He nodded. "He hinted at what he wanted and why. I knew I could write it, so I said yes."

"You never thought about him using the ransomware?"

"I guess not," Chris said.

I shook my head. "So you agreed to do it. Then what?"

"I went to work on it. I already wrote something similar . . . a little more primitive. All I needed to do was update it a little."

"I looked at your code," I said. "It's impressive."

"You're a developer?"

"Among other things," I said, "but we can compare our bona fides later. What happened next?"

Chris sighed and stared at the ceiling. If Joey's kitchen chairs would have allowed him to lean back, he would have. "At some point . . . I guess I realized what I was doing. Or who I was doing it for. Or both. He gave me a number to reach him, so I called. Told him I wanted out."

"Let me guess," I said. "He told you a deal's a deal."

"Pretty much, yeah. He said he paid me and I would finish the job if I knew what was good for me."

"So you went into hiding?"

"Soon after," Chris said with a nod. "I wrote a little more code, decided I couldn't finish it for him, and stopped."

"And skipped town with his money?" Joey said.

"Yeah."

"You took Anna with you," I said. "What about Brian?"

"I didn't want him to have to go with us," Chris said. "He should finish school."

"I mean, you took Anna with you where she would presumably be safe. But you left Brian to fend for himself."

Chris started to say something, then stopped. His jaw clicked shut, and he frowned. "I didn't think of it like that," he said after a few seconds of thought.

"You didn't think the mobster you just ripped off would discover you had a brother?" I said.

"I guess not."

"You're lucky nothing happened to Brian."

"I think you should take him with you," Joey said.

"What do you mean by take him with me?" Chris said.

"Let me tell you what I do," Joey said. He leaned forward in his chair, and his size allowed him to cut an imposing figure. "I help people disappear . . . start over. I turn a bad beat story into a new life somewhere else. You get a new identity, a job history, everything."

Anna stared at Joey and frowned. "How do you do all of that?"

"I have my methods."

"How much does all of this cost?" Chris said.

"For the three of you?" Joey said. "Considering C.T. referred you, I could do you all for thirty-five."

"Hundred?"

Joey laughed. "Thousand. This takes time. It's art *and* science."

"I'm not paying thirty-five thousand for a fake ID," Chris said.

"You get a lot more than a fucking fake ID." Joey's eyes narrowed. I couldn't recall the last time I saw him offended. "But have it your way."

"At least think about it," I said. "Esposito is going to find you sooner or later. He might even find your brother and try to use him to draw you out."

"Fine," Chris said, "I'll think about it. Is there anywhere we can all stay for a night or two?"

"I have a place," Joey said.

"We'll need to get Brian," Anna said.

Joey tossed me a key. "You know the place?"

"Unless you've gotten a new one, yes," I said.

"Good." He looked at Chris. "Keep the place neat. It ain't your hotel room. This is part of my business."

"We will," Chris said.

"And I'll let you know what they decide," I said. "Thanks, Joey."

We left Joey's house. I went first, made sure no one untoward lurked outside, and waved Chris and Anna out. From Joey's house, we left to pick up Brian.

* * *

CHRIS CALLED Brian from the Caprice. He was waiting for us. Brian and Chris hugged. Then they both got in the car before I could tell them we needed to keep going. Maybe Chris was learning. I got back on I-95 and headed toward Columbia. "Where's this safehouse?" Chris said from the rear seat.

"Columbia," I said.

"That's convenient to a lot of things," Anna said.

"It's most convenient to staying indoors and not being seen," I said. "The place is part of Joey's business. It gets professionally cleaned three times a month . . . more often if necessary. He also has someone keep the pantry stocked. I'll buy you some perishables once you're there."

"Is there an alarm?" Brian said. I was glad someone asked the question but wished it came from one of the adults.

"Yes."

"You know the code?"

"No, but I know how to find it. It changes every time he puts someone up in the house."

"Your friend takes security seriously," Chris said.

"He has to," I said, finding Chris' eyes in the rearview mirror. "I wish everyone took it so seriously."

Chris frowned. "I guess we deserved that."

"You did."

We made the rest of the drive in silence. I turned onto Puppy Breath Court—which is the most Columbia street name in the city—and drove slowly. The houses here were all large Victorians, many with unnecessary pillars surrounding their front doors, and two-car garages. I doubted any of them could be purchased for less than $600,000. Joey put his clients up in style. Signs on the street advertised a neighborhood watch, and most houses posted alarm system signs in their manicured front yards.

I pulled the Caprice into the driveway of Joey's house, sitting right before the end of the cul-de-sac. "Stay here for a minute," I said as I got out. I didn't see anyone paying extra attention to us. No one followed. Still, I walked around the exterior once, checking the doors and windows and finding nothing unusual. I waved at Chris, Anna, and Brian, and they got out of the car. Joey texted me on the drive, and I looked at his message now.

Sir Laurence Olivier really hated Picasso.

His text meant the alarm code would be 387657. It also meant Sir Laurence's myriad talents included a keen eye for weird art. I used the key Joey gave me and unlocked the door. The alarm emitted a quiet but shrill whistle as we walked in. I entered the code; the screen flashed *ALARM DISABLED*, and the whistle fell silent. I tossed the keys to Chris. "Don't make copies," I said. "There are only two. One of you won't have a key. Too bad."

"I understand," Chris said.

"You'd better," I said. "Joey is helping you here, and you haven't even paid him yet."

"I don't know that I want a fake ID."

I bit down my initial and very uncharitable reply. "It's a new life," I said in a measured tone. "You get all new papers, Social Security numbers, job history, everything. And it stands up to scrutiny."

"How does your friend do it?" Anna said.

"You'll have to ask him," I said. "I know a little, but he's a savant at this stuff."

"Where would we go?" Brian said.

"Your destination is between you and Joey," I told him. "He recommends places you don't have family or anyone else who might call you out."

They all thought about it. "I'm going to get you a few perishables," I said. "I shouldn't be long. When I come back, I'll knock on the door six times. Don't open it for anyone but me."

"Why not take a key?" Anna said.

"What if the goon squad finds me?" She frowned. "It's unlikely, but it could happen. If they get the drop on me and take my keys, you're compromised. Get comfortable. I won't be long." She nodded.

As I left, I jerked my head for Brian Sellers to follow me. We walked into the living room. Despite being the youngest of the trio, he was definitely the adult in the situation. I held out a prepaid cell phone. "You're giving me a phone?" he said.

"A burner," I said. "It has my cell programmed in as a pizza shop, along with a few decoy numbers."

"What's it for?"

"Keep it with you all the time," I said. "Your brother and Anna . . . well, I wouldn't trust them to think their way out of a wet paper bag."

"My brother's pretty smart," Brian said, a little defensive.

"Recent events don't concur," I said. "Anyway, keep this with you. If you're in trouble, shove it down the front of your pants."

He frowned at me. "Why?"

"Because no macho goon will search your junk. Take it." He took the phone and charger.

"I hope I don't need it," he said.

"I hope so, too," I said. "But considering what's happened so far, I think you should have it. Don't tell your brother and Anna about it."

"All right." Brian nodded. "Thanks for finding them." He moved in for the hug, paused, thought better of it—perhaps cued by my grimace—and settled for a handshake.

"Thank me when this whole mess is behind us," I said.

I left the house and got groceries from a nearby Safeway. With the perishables delivered, I headed back home. No one followed me. At least something was right with the world.

CHAPTER 14

I WENT TO BED A FEW MINUTES AFTER GETTING HOME. THIS case wore me out. I trusted luck for no crises in the night. When I woke up the next morning just after nine, it felt like the best sleep I'd gotten since Brian Sellers wandered into my life. I pushed my good fortune on the no-interruptions front and went for a run around Federal Hill Park. My luck continued.

A half-hour later, I went back home, showered, and pondered breakfast. I took the easy way out, putting sausage into a skillet and making toast. Cooking only for oneself is hard to beat. I sat at my table with coffee and orange juice and enjoyed my breakfast. Chris Sellers hadn't done anything stupid yet, but I reminded myself it was barely ten o'clock. He had plenty of time to wreck his day and mine. No more Esposito goons came to visit me. Joey didn't tell me his house burned down. This could turn out to be a good day.

After breakfast, I checked to see if my infection of my inept tail's phone was still paying dividends. It wasn't. All I got was a "No connection" message. Either he discovered my intrusion or got a new phone. Discovery was less likely. Esposito ran a pretty tight ship with respect to technology and phones were cheap. If I didn't dislike him so much, I would respect his operation.

I still wanted to keep tabs on Esposito and his cronies. Getting close to his house again wouldn't be easy. The whole crew knew the Caprice, I left in Joey's car last time, and Gloria's red Mercedes rocket was way too distinctive. Walking by on the sidewalk or the alley behind the house would give me away and lead to me being quickly outnumbered. So I did the only reasonable thing I could do in the situation.

I rented a car.

* * *

MY GRAY HONDA ACCORD looked like about a third of the cars on the road. I parked it on the opposite side of the street from Esposito's house and about a hundred feet away. I wore sunglasses, a hoodie, and a hat, counting on the trifecta to prevent me from being discovered. Armed with a tablet and a high-strength antenna, I went to work.

Finding Esposito's wireless network was easy. Unless a neighbor named his or her network "ESPO," I found the right one. For a guy who swapped out his employees' cell phones on a recurring basis, he didn't practice good security when it came to picking his SSID. He did use the recommended WPA2 encryption, at least. People used WPA2 because it was hard to compromise. Previous wireless security like WEP and WPA folded to hackers too easily. WPA2 was more robust.

Robust but not impenetrable. The past couple years saw great advances in cracking WPA2 encryption. It took a determined adversary (check) with lots of time on his hands (check) but it could be done. My tablet ran Kali Linux, the preferred operating system of people whose ideas about computer security mirrored my own. Metasploit, a framework meant for penetration testing but used by hackers the world over, boasted of the latest and greatest WPA2 cracking techniques. I streamlined them a bit with a custom script. First, I tried the well-publicized KRACK vulnerability, but it didn't work. I then chose my script-enhanced module, entered a few inputs, and launched the exploit. Now I needed to wait.

About twenty minutes into my vigil, a goon strolled out of Esposito's house. He spent a few seconds looking around, then walked off the porch and down the steps toward the sidewalk. I was parked across the street to his left. He headed in my direction. I sank a little lower in the seat. If he saw me, he didn't give any indication. He walked up to a black Dodge Charger on the other side of the street and got in. I guessed the distance at about twenty-five feet away.

It left his phone in range for a Bluetooth attack. I fired it off as his Charger rumbled to life. He backed up a bit and pulled away. I looked down at my phone. He got out of range before the Bluetooth hack finished. Alas. I still had the Wi-fi hack in progress. With the right tools in place, Esposito may have known someone assaulted his network. I didn't figure him for having such defenses, however. Changing phones and using jammers were simple mitigations. Active monitoring of a network took time, tools, and manpower. Plenty of businesses didn't do it. I didn't think Esposito would divert resources away from his desired takeover of Tony Rizzo's enterprise to find some techie to watch Wireshark looking at network traffic.

The module kept running. The more traffic Esposito's network generated, the faster it would work. Still, its speed was relative. A patched router running WPA2 would not succumb quickly, even on a busy network. I budgeted two hours of time for this. Based on the rate my progress bar inched across the screen, the guess appeared to be accurate. The time itself wasn't a concern; I felt exposed sitting here on the street. Spotting me from the house wouldn't be easy, but it could be done. I considered moving the car, but it might draw unwanted attention, and a shift out of range would force me to start over. All told, sitting it out proved the more acceptable risk.

And so I sat. And waited. And waited some more. About forty-five minutes later, another employee of the Esposito enterprise walked out of the house. He headed in the other direction, up the block, and down an alley. When a car didn't emerge a minute or so later, I grew concerned. This guard may have gone out on a patrol, and his radius could include my inconspicuous Honda. It would be more conspicuous with me in the driver's seat and a tablet on the passenger's seat.

The Oaks had alleys all over the place. Like in downtown Baltimore, they ran behind many of the houses, offering more parking and other means of getting around. I needed to be prepared if Esposito's lackey popped out behind me. I pulled my hat down lower and made sure the sunglasses hid my eyes. The tablet would be a problem. I closed the Kali window, shrugged out of my jacket, and used it as a cover. Sure enough, the guy walked out of an alley about a hundred yards behind my car and across the street. To make my job as hard as possible, he crossed the street.

I reclined the seat and shifted to lie facing the passenger's seat. All I could do was pretend to be asleep and hope he passed by. If he challenged me, I planned to be ready to act. I heard his footsteps on the sidewalk as he approached. He slowed as he passed the Accord. Then he stopped. I could feel him looking at me. If he already knew me and looked long enough, he could recognize me.

He stood there.

A moment later, I heard his footsteps move on.

I remained lying down and faking sleep. The last thing I needed was to pop up and have this goon see me and come back to investigate. After a couple minutes. I figured I was in the clear. I opened my eyes and poked my head up. I didn't see him, which could be a good or a bad thing. He could have finished his patrol and gone back inside. Or he could have run into the house and summoned reinforcements, who were now arming themselves to come and shoot holes in yours truly. I took my gun out of the glove compartment and kept it handy.

And I waited.

No one came running from the house. I kept watching it. Five minutes passed. It didn't take a bunch of trigger-happy men so long to grab their guns. I couldn't see the back of the house, and it occurred to me they might run out the back and use the alleys to get behind me. It seemed unlikely, but I kept an eye out. While I did, I checked my progress on the tablet. About sixty percent.

I split my time watching the house, the alleys I could see, and the laptop. No one came gunning for me. My WPA2 attack continued its slow, steady progress. About a half-hour later, it finished. I gained access to Esposito's network. The first thing I wanted to do was enable some kind of persistence, so I could keep tabs on his traffic and find out if he knew anything about the Sellers brothers and Anna Blair.

There are many ways to establish a persistent presence. The most common is to leave some code behind, usually a rootkit to compromise targeted systems and allow you easy access. I've done it plenty of times. I didn't think it was the right call this time, though. Esposito struck me as too paranoid about technology. He would run frequent malware scans. He would reinstall his operating system. He would buy a new laptop. I couldn't count on a rootkit to get me there.

Instead, I went after his router. He changed the default password, so I set about cracking the one he used. The job took another forty minutes, during which time I kept an eye out for any more patrols. With access to Esposito's router, I added a rule to send all its traffic to a server not attributable to me instead of its normal gateway to the outside world. It would slow his network a little, and he might notice the speed reduction, but I counted on the fact he wouldn't replace the router as a mitigation. Most people don't.

Before I could hunt around for information about my clients, however, another of Esposito's men walked out of the house and did the alley patrol. I started copying files from the usual places people store documents. Complicating this effort was the fact I wanted to be gone when the lackey made his rounds. I started the car and drove away. My laptop antenna delivered a lot of range, but it would lose its connection soon. I wanted some good data before it happened.

As I drove to the end of the street, I saw the goon emerge from an alley in my rearview mirror.

* * *

When I got home, I took my laptop to the office to inspect my ill-gotten gains. First, I checked the files I snagged from Esposito's computer. He didn't run any kind of encryption, which I found surprising (and even a little insulting). Based on what I got, it didn't look like Esposito knew much about the Sellers brothers and Anna Blair. If he did, he either didn't keep it on his computer or he kept it in a folder I didn't have time to grab before the flunky patrol made its rounds.

The files came from a Windows computer so I kept them on a Windows computer. I preferred Linux for most of my work, but I didn't want to run into the problem of the operating system throwing up its hands at trying to parse a Microsoft Office file. Windows, thanks to the *findstr* command, at least offered me some ability to comb through the information quickly. I didn't find anything on Chris, Brian, or Anna. I also looked for "Rizzo" and came up empty.

After a few more minutes, I wrote off the data from Esposito's PC as a loss. If I had more time, I might have found something. I pondered going back. Parking a silver Honda on the street again would not be an option. The plan would mean another rental car parked somewhere else, and then I still would have to deal with his lackeys going out on patrol. An idea came to me about how I might pull it off better next time if I needed to. If I could avoid doing such a risky task again, I would.

I logged into my server. Thanks to the routing rule I added to Esposito's router, it used my server as its gateway. Years ago in my high school and college days (and even into my time in Hong Kong), encryption wasn't so ubiquitous. People still read and sent email over unencrypted web connections. They would transfer files with FTP and their chat programs were in plaintext, so someone like me on the wire got to see both sides of the conversation.

Encryption changed—and ruined—it all. Every self-respecting webmail client now ran over HTTPS, the encrypted web protocol. FTP died an overdue death. IRC added security for chats and conversations, and then there were the encrypted options like Skype and WhatsApp. In short, eavesdropping on people's online conversations became a lot harder. As someone who doesn't want the government reading mine, I liked it. As someone with a case to solve, I hated it.

The good thing is smart hackers found ways around it. The server I sent Esposito's traffic to ran a program to downgrade encrypted HTTPS connections to unencrypted HTTP. A savvy user could sometimes spot the difference in their address bar— your browser won't come out and lie to you, after all—but most people didn't notice it or ignored it. I knew Esposito was smarter than the average bear when it came to large-scale security, but would he notice anything? I counted on the probability he didn't, at least not for a while.

With the SSL part of the HTTPS connections stripped off, I could see where Esposito went online. I could read his emails. I could see his passwords after he entered them (and I made notes). Nothing he did at the moment concerned Chris, Brian, or Anna, however. The problem with hijacking a person's traffic like this is most people are boring and will do boring things. Esposito, as much as he may have fancied himself some high-tech gangster, was as humdrum as anyone else.

I couldn't watch the uninteresting traffic any longer. To flag items about the Sellers brothers, Anna Blair, or Tony Rizzo, I wrote specific filters in my packet sniffing program. Then I realized how hungry I was. All this sitting, goon dodging, and felonious computer activity had given me quite an appetite. With my filters running, I walked out into Federal Hill to find some lunch.

* * *

I CAME BACK about a half-hour later with a bag of Greek deliciousness. There are few things in this world not improved by the eating of a chicken souvlaki pita. I paired it with fries despite knowing I should opt for rice or a salad. The fries were just too good, and I was too hungry and too eager for my computer chicanery to work. I ate at my kitchen table, dunking the fries in way too much tzatziki as I pondered what else I might do for the Sellers brothers.

A potential answer (or more problems) came when Joey called me. "I was just thinking about you," I said.

"Oh yeah?" said Joey. "What's the occasion?"

"I'm eating too much too fast. Who else could I think of?"

"You're hilarious."

"What's up?" I said.

"Have you heard from the asshole and his girlfriend yet?" Joey said.

I hadn't, and I didn't know if it should concern me. "No," I said. "Maybe they're doing a good job keeping their heads down."

"Yeah. Or maybe they're dead and bleeding all over the place."

"Do people usually check in with you?"

"Sometimes," Joey said. "I like to check on them every now and again."

"Driving by can't be good security," I said.

Joey chuckled. "I got cameras," he said. "They're well-hidden but there are a few around the house. I don't keep any in the bathrooms or bedrooms, though."

"I'll bet you've still seen some things you can't unsee."

I could hear the shudder in Joey's voice. "You have no idea."

"If you have CCTV in the house, what are you worried about?" I said.

"I haven't seen any of them on my monitors."

Unusual. I didn't know where Joey hid his cameras, but people tended to move around houses. A couple in hallways and the living room should spot people as they walked around, even if they weren't doing much. "I presume you have a continuous feed?" I said. "And you can rewind to look for anything unusual?"

"Of course," Joey said. "I paid a lot for the system. It does even more. But the thing is I don't see them anywhere, and I don't see anyone else. No intruders, nothing."

"And they haven't left?"

"Unless they jumped out the bedroom windows, I'd've seen it."

"You want me to check it out?"

"They *are* your clients," Joey said.

"They're actually paying you," I pointed out.

"You carry a gun." I laughed. "Fine, you're *licensed* to carry a gun," Joey said.

"All right, I'll check. Take my time off their tab."

"Unless you're buying me food, your time is worthless to me," said Joey. He hung up. I looked at the little of my lunch remaining. Could Chris and Anna have been stupid and managed to leave without being seen? I still liked Brian Sellers, but his brother and his brother's girlfriend were more trouble than they were worth.

I grabbed my keys and headed for Columbia.

* * *

I COULD HAVE CALLED any of them. The issue was talking to someone on the phone doesn't necessarily tell you if they're in trouble. Being told at gunpoint to stay calm and sound normal can be quite persuasive. I wanted to check this out in person. Chris and Anna acted dumb before. I didn't put it past them to do it again.

It occurred to me Esposito might have a lackey following me. I wanted to get to Columbia as fast as possible but also didn't want to lead the enemy right to the safehouse. Someone like Rich would spot a tail quickly. I didn't have his observational skills or experience. As far as I could tell, no one followed me, but someone who knew what he was doing could have lurked back there.

As a precaution, I took a more circuitous route than normal to Columbia. Getting there from Baltimore was a straight shot down I-95, and then either Routes 175 or 32, depending on where in Columbia you wanted to go. I took an unusual route through the city to get to the highway, then got off at Route 100. I looped around a roundabout an extra time, and got back on. Then I took Route 100 until it terminated at Route 29 and took it into Columbia. As far as I could tell, no one shadowed me.

When I got close to Joey's house, I made unnecessary turns

and doubled back on myself at least once. Again, no one popped up in the rearview, so far as I could tell. I turned onto Puppy Breath Court, scoffed at the name one more time, and parked four houses down from Joey's. No cars followed me onto the street. I got out of the Caprice, kept low, and dashed to the house. I didn't see anyone lurking around or watching me from the other houses.

I knocked on the door as quietly as I could while still making sure they could hear me inside. Footsteps moved toward the door a couple seconds later. I took my gun out and stood to the side in case an Esposito miscreant beat me here. The deadbolt slid back and the door opened. Anna Blair looked back at me. The worry of before no longer scrunched her face, and she looked prettier.

"C.T.?" she said. "What's going on?"

"Can I come in?"

"Sure." She moved aside and I walked in.

"Is anyone else here?" I said as Anna locked the door behind us.

"Just the three of us." She looked at my gun and frowned. "What's wrong?"

"Have you been here all day?"

"Yeah." Chris wandered into the living room. "We've basically stayed in the bedrooms all day," Anna said. "We all took some snacks up last night."

"We've been careful," Chris added, sounding a little defensive.

"All right," I said. "I'm only checking up on you, making sure everything is OK."

"You could've called," Chris said.

"And you could've been at gunpoint and said whatever you were being told to say."

"You and Joey are worried about us," Anna said.

I nodded. "Where's Brian?" I said.

"In his bedroom," Chris said. "Probably trying to do some schoolwork."

I didn't stay for much more conversation. They were OK was the important part. I gave Anna and Chris another safety reminder and then left. On the way home, I called Joey and told him everything was fine. While I drove, I kept an eye out for anyone tailing me, but I didn't see anyone.

* * *

After I got home, Gloria called and asked if I had any dinner plans. I did not, in fact, so she said she would join me soon. I liked our relationship of convenience. Gloria and I moved in the same social circles. If people still used the word, they would have called her a socialite. To borrow another term, we were friends with benefits. While I certainly enjoyed spending time with Gloria, I wondered if inviting herself over for dinner strained the bounds of our casual arrangement.

In about a half-hour, Gloria arrived and let herself in. She wore a tight pair of jeans looking as if tailored to accentuate her curves. She wore a dark green sweater with a neckline just low enough to be interesting. Her chestnut hair was tied into a ponytail, which for Gloria constituted a bad hair day. She only pulled it back if it didn't look good worn the usual way.

"Hey there," she said, sitting down next to me on the couch and kissing me.

"Hungry?" I said.

"Starving, actually."

"What are you in the mood for?"

Gloria contemplated that, and I noticed she was very pretty when she got pensive. "Pub food," she said after a moment.

Of all the types Gloria could have answered with, I would have put her choice near the bottom. She liked fancy restaurants where entrees cost forty dollars, waiters were clad in black tie, and someone valeted the car. I liked those places too, but I also entertained a strong affinity for things like burgers and pizza—which could be found for way less than forty dollars. "Seriously?" I said.

"I know, right?" Gloria said. "I never eat pub food. I just . . . want it for some reason."

"You're not going to start craving pickles and chocolate at midnight, are you?"

She gave me a light punch on the arm. "I'm not pregnant." The news was certainly a relief. "I just want pub food."

"Irish pub or sports bar?" I said.

"Sports bar might be pushing it."

"More's the pity," I said.

* * *

I took Gloria to the James Joyce Irish Pub on President Street. It was in an area I grew up calling Fells Point, but it rebranded itself as Harbor East. Like any area rebranded for hipness, it featured nearby housing, access to public transportation, pubs, and a Whole Foods. No hipster neighborhood can be complete without the addition of a Whole Foods.

We started with some homemade Irish brown bread and a Guinness each. For as buttoned-up and prim as Gloria could sometimes be, it was good to see her let her hair down and eat and drink like a normal person. Maybe I rubbed off on her in the culinary respect. For dinner, I ordered the beef and Guinness stew and Gloria surprised me by getting a shepherd's pie. "When in Rome," she said when she noticed my puzzled expression.

"Hear, hear," I said, and we clinked our glasses of Guinness.

"How's your case going?"

I sighed. "OK, I guess. I found the kid's brother and his girlfriend. They're probably the dumbest people who ever went on the run."

Gloria chuckled. "That bad?"

"It's like they don't want help," I said. "They don't seem to understand the fact if I found them without a lot of trouble, other people could, too. For smart people, they're pretty stupid."

"What's happening to them now?" Gloria said.

"I took them to see Joey," I said, lowering my voice. The restaurant grew more crowded; Gloria leaned in a little to hear me. "They should be on their way soon."

"If they're smart enough to get away."

I hadn't considered them wanting to hang around. As dumb and stubborn as Chris and Anna seemed to be, they might insist on staying local. They might eschew Joey's help altogether and count on Esposito forgetting about them. I hoped Brian would be the voice of reason, telling them they couldn't do it and why. But they showed no signs of being able to listen to reason so far. What cause did I have to be optimistic?

"You think they're not?" Gloria said.

"Maybe," I said. "And the thought might keep me awake tonight."

She shot me a lascivious wink. "I hope that's not the only thing keeping you awake tonight."

I smiled. "Here's to insomnia."

CHAPTER 15

GLORIA LEFT THE NEXT MORNING. SHE SCHEDULED AN early tennis lesson and would compete in a practice tournament in the afternoon. For the first time, she asked me if I would come. She chewed on the corner of her lip subtly after asking. I told her I would try if the case allowed me. She said she understood, gave me a lingering kiss goodbye, and set off for a day of tennis.

After she left, I made breakfast. Without Gloria to distract me, my thoughts drifted back to Chris Sellers and Anna Blair. Would they keep their heads down long enough for Joey to set them up someplace else? And what would happen after they got there? The old Simpsons episode with Homer wearing a *Witness Protection Program* hat leapt to mind. I wished they would stick it out for Brian. He needed to finish high school, and give college a try without worrying his brother would take two to the head.

I made a simple breakfast of wheat toast, two scrambled eggs, and turkey sausage. I carried it all plus a mug of coffee to my office to see what the day held in store. The SSL-stripping attack on Esposito's router continued to pay dividends. No significant traffic traversed it now, so I looked back on what I missed last night. Some web surfing and a few emails, none of which made a difference in anything I did. I knew he still wanted to find Chris

Sellers. Why was he so quiet about it, then? Was he eschewing going online in favor of issuing all his orders in person or on the phone?

After breakfast with nothing to do in the case, I acted like so many other members of my generation and did the Netflix and chill. I was content to keep getting my chill on when my phone rang. It was Bobbi Lane. "Hello?"

"Hi, C.T.," she said. "You up for a run?"

I had eaten a hearty breakfast. Running off the calories—and anything else we might choose to do—with Bobbi sounded like a good remedy. "Sure," I said. "Your place or mine?"

"Can we do mine? My car's not the best right now."

I said we could, and we agreed on an hour, giving me almost thirty minutes to kill, so I went back and checked on Esposito's traffic. It looked like he (or someone else in the house) spent an enthralling morning reading the news. I kept on the alert for a smoking gun, and I couldn't even find an empty cap pistol. Now I knew what network analysts felt like. I still didn't love my job, but I also didn't envy theirs.

Not much changed as I watched. Most people have boring Internet habits. Even visits to adult sites aren't interesting from a traffic perspective.

With nothing of note happening, I got in my car and left for Perry Hall.

* * *

LATER, after we got ran, showered, and spent some time in the bedroom, Bobbi pulled things out of the fridge. "Want turkey burgers?" she said.

"Sounds good," I said, sitting on her couch. This was our third time running, showering, and having sex until we tired ourselves out. I could get used to it, and I got the distinct feeling

Bobbi could, too. My thoughts drifted back to Gloria. We didn't owe each other anything, and she was popular and outgoing enough to have someone else to have fun with. Still, I wondered how long I could keep seeing both of them, however informal the arrangements were. In college, doing this didn't make me feel like a cad. Five years out of grad school, it did. Funny things, consciences.

"Can you give me a hand in the kitchen?" Bobbi said.

I went in to see what I could do. Bobbi cooked three turkey burgers on a George Foreman grill. I didn't hear much sizzle from the grill, but I could smell the ground turkey broiling. "What do you need?" I said.

"I still need to toast the buns and make a salad," Bobbi said. Her kitchen was small and the grill, the rolls, and the salad ingredients she spread out consumed nearly all the counter space. I got to work slicing and dicing vegetables and selecting the perfect avocado to accompany the turkey burgers. Bobbi busied herself seasoning the turkey as it cooked and toasting the buns. I added my sliced and diced veggies—including carrots and artichoke hearts—to a bowl of lettuce and spinach. It needed dressing, so I rummaged around in Bobbi's fridge and cabinets.

I mixed a simple vinaigrette, whisked it until my arm grew tired, poured it into the salad bowl, and tossed everything together. Bobbi took the turkey burgers off the grill, set each on a roll, and added lettuce, tomato, and avocado. I availed myself of a dash of barbecue sauce from her fridge. Bobbi carried her burger and two domestic light beers to her small dining room table; I carried the salad and my burger.

Bobbi and I were both hungry, so we wolfed down salad and half our burgers without talking. After another round of salad, I slowed down. "What's wrong with your car?" I said after another bite of my burger.

"It's getting old," Bobbi said. "I bought it in college, and it wasn't new then."

"You've got a good job now," I said.

Bobbi frowned. "It's OK. I mean, I like it. It just doesn't pay a lot. I was an intern before I got the job so they're not paying me much."

"Sounds like you should be looking for a job, too."

"I am," Bobbi said. "My résumé is on the coffee table. You mind looking it over while I clean up?"

Except for learning the basics of it in high school, I had never assembled a résumé. Still, how hard could it be? I sat on the couch and looked at Bobbi's CV. She led with her education. My teacher in high school, good old Mr. Williams, impressed on us to lead off with job history. Everybody went to school somewhere, he would tell us. Where you've worked is more important. However, Bobbi had a master's degree in a STEM field, which was worth shouting from the rooftops.

Her job history was sparse. She listed some good accomplishments at her current job. I saw she interned at Hopkins while going for her master's. *Developer and Website Designer, Graduate Admissions Office.*

Uh-oh.

Below the department address, I saw what I dreaded.

Supervisor: Daniel Esposito.

Shit.

There were a million ways the revelation could be bad for my current case, and I couldn't think of a single thing to counter it. Chris Sellers went to Hopkins for his advanced degrees. Bobbi likely could have accessed his information. She could have fed it to Danny Esposito, who in turn gave it to his brother. I now wondered if she even contacted Chris when I asked her to.

I was sleeping with the enemy—or at least the enemy's mole.

So much for getting used to running and sexing with Bobbi.

I thought about what to do. My hand almost crumpled Bobbi's résumé so I set it back down. I was mad enough to confront her here and now but was it my best move? Did she still provide any value to the Esposito brothers? Severing the connection could make them unpredictable. I didn't want to risk it with Brian, Chris, and Anna.

Bobbi washed dishes in the sink when I walked into the kitchen. She smiled when she saw me. Its warmth made her even more beautiful. I needed to know to what level she was involved in this whole mess, but pursuing it would have to wait. For now, I simply wanted to get away. "Hey, I need to go," I said. "A detective's life is never easy."

"So soon?" Bobbi said. She shot me an adorable pout. Dammit, why did she have to work for Danny Esposito?

"Yeah, I'm afraid so," I said. "But I'm sure I'll talk to you soon."

Bobbi wrapped me in a hug and gave me a lingering kiss. I wished her involvement could be chalked up to coincidence. She was a great girl. I didn't want her to be in league with the enemy.

I left her apartment expecting to be disappointed.

I POUNDED on the Caprice's steering wheel as I drove away. Part of me thought I should have seen this coming. Bobbi had been nice and helpful all along. She was pretending to help me, probably trying to get information out of me—and I told her some things about the case—all while feeding information to the Esposito brothers. Another part of me thought the only part of her involvement I knew for certain was feeding Chris' name to Danny Esposito. The rest was above her pay grade.

The more I thought about it, the more the second one made sense. Bobbi worked in the office. Her job gave her access to records, and her knowledge of the people would have been something Danny Esposito didn't have. She gave him Chris' name, and he then gave it to his brother. Afterward, though, Bobbi didn't have to be involved. She worked with Chris. When I said he was missing, I didn't recall a guilty reaction from her. A nice, caring person like Bobbi would have felt bad if she thought she had something to do with Chris' disappearance.

Of course, I wanted the second option to be true.

Wanting it didn't make it so, of course. I would need to be careful around my run and fun partner. Breaking all contact with her while working this case made the best solution. If I did talk to her, I needed to stop giving details of the case. I told her about Esposito, Chris and Anna going into hiding, and other things. If she were feeding information to Danny Esposito—and, by extension, his asshole brother—then I'd given her some choice intel.

While considering what to do about Bobbi dominated my thoughts, Joey called. "They left," he said when I answered.

"What?"

"They left the house."

"Seriously?" I said.

"Yeah," Joey said. "A half-hour ago. Cameras saw them leave and walk up the street."

"A half-hour ago?"

"I figured they might have gone out for a walk. Stupid . . . but no need to panic. However, a half-hour is a long walk."

"All three of them went?" I said.

"Yeah."

"Goddammit." How dumb could they be over and over? "I was headed home, but I'll go to Columbia instead. Maybe I'll catch them at the house."

"Let me know," Joey said and hung up. I could hear the frustration in his voice. His job required his clients to listen to him, thus maximizing their chances of survival. When they flouted his advice, especially after they had already displayed some bone-headed behavior, frustration was bound to set in.

I stayed on I-95, bypassing the Baltimore exits and continuing to Columbia.

* * *

I GOT to Joey's house and saw one light on inside. Joey hadn't called back or texted, so I knew they hadn't come back yet. If the three of them went for a walk, they were gone for fifty minutes now, and I hadn't seen them on my way into the neighborhood. This wasn't good. From the car, I called Chris and Anna, getting no answer from either. I didn't call the burner phone I gave Brian Sellers. If something bad happened, I didn't want to give away him having a secret cell phone.

There was no activity on the street. I got out of the car and made a loop of the house. Nothing looked out of the ordinary: no windows broken, the doors looked unmolested, and no corpses lay in the grass. What the hell would possess Chris, Brian, and Anna to leave? They enjoyed a good situation here. Esposito didn't know where they were, and Joey was going to relocate them. All they had to do was sit in the house for a few days and wait. And they couldn't even do something so simple to save their asses.

I called Joey. "You want me to break in?" I said when he answered.

"No sign of them?"

"None."

Joey sighed into the phone. "No," he said. "There's no point. The cameras haven't shown anything since they left."

"All right."

"Thanks for the courtesy call before breaking in."

"It's always good to try new things," I said.

* * *

Gloria called as I drove home. I ignored it and let it go to voicemail. She would want to do fun things which would distract me from working. On a normal night, I'd be all about Gloria's usual methods of distraction. Tonight, however, I needed to focus on the case at hand. Three people's lives could depend on me.

Joey lived closer to Columbia than I did, so I stopped at his house. He frowned when he answered the door and didn't change his expression as we sat and discussed what happened. "Did you see anything before they left the house?" I said.

"Like what?"

"Did one of them get a phone call? Did you see them go online and look something up?"

"No," Joey said, shaking his head. The frown remained in place. "They all went into the kitchen, looked in the fridge and the pantry, and then left."

"Did they talk?" I said.

"Sure, but my cameras don't get audio. I ain't trying to eavesdrop."

Joey brought up one of his extra computers. He was the only person I knew who could match me in terms of technology owned and used. I knew more about how to use it (and misuse it) but Joey owned at least as much of it as I did, and when it came to specialized things like printing, he was way ahead. From his PC, I opened an SSH connection to my server.

Esposito was still in the dark regarding the stripped SSL at his router. I combed through a bunch of captured web traffic and didn't find anything of interest. "What about text messages?" Joey said.

"From his computer?" I said.

"You're the one who says this guy hates technology," Joey said with a shrug. "What happened to his guy's phone you knocked over?"

"Didn't stay knocked over for long."

"So maybe this asshole doesn't trust phones," said Joey. "Maybe he thinks texting from his PC is more secure."

In absence of a better theory, I decided to work with it. It sounded plausible on some level. I added a traffic filter, further narrowing my results to anything using HTTPS and connecting to an SMS device for texting. The filter gave me a slew of results. There was a signal here the whole time, and my initial filter put too much noise in the way. How much time did I already lose?

Joey sat with me as I combed through the captured SMS messages. Swaths of them were unimportant, but then we hit a goldmine. Esposito and one of his cronies exchanged texts not even two hours ago.

Esposito: *I think we have a line on the girl.*

Crony: *How?*

Esposito: *Looks like she used a credit card again.*

Crony: *Seriously?*

I flashed on the same thought. After I found Anna and Chris the first time, I warned her about doing things like using her credit card again. These people would never learn, and now they endangered poor Brian, too. All he wanted to do was find his brother again. Maybe they were being held captive together.

I kept reading.

Esposito: *Different credit card. It was actually her mother's.*

Crony: *I guess the geek you got paid off for you.*

Esposito: *He did. I want you to get the asshole who took my money and anyone who's with him. If he doesn't have it or doesn't want to pay, let's see how long he sticks to his greed when other people are involved.*

Esposito hired his own hacker. For someone who hated technology, he embraced it in selective ways. It made sense, though.

Now I wondered how long my router hack would last. I couldn't count on it long-term.

"Her mother's credit card," Joey said. His frown remained and, if anything, only deepened. "Jesus Christ."

"Just because he picked them up in Columbia doesn't mean they're still in the area," I said. I combed through the rest of the conversation, but Esposito never gave his goon any instructions about where to take Chris, Brian, and Anna. It must have been understood.

"We don't know where they are," Joey said.

"No," I said. "Esposito was out of town for a few years. Now he's back. He'd have to set something up quickly to be able to hold people he's captured."

"One of Tony's old places?"

I shook my head. "No way Tony would go for it."

Joey and I both stared at the monitor, looking for some bolt of inspiration to emerge from the pixels and strike us. Joey relented first. "What now?" he said.

"Not much to do but wait," I said.

"For what?"

"Esposito is a braggart. He'll want to rub this in my face, especially after Delaware."

"So you think he's going to call and taunt you at some point?" Joey said.

"I know he will."

"Better hope he does it before he kills one of these three."

"I am," I said.

CHAPTER 16

I didn't do waiting well. It's something I've never had the patience for. I can stand by while computer processes take their time and do their things. Those are logical delays, and I know what the results will be. Those, I can handle. Other things, not so much. I have little patience for just waiting, especially when the result is a giant unknown. At this point, I didn't even know if Chris, Brian, and Anna were still alive.

After I left Joey's, I went back to his safehouse. Before, I snooped around the property. Now I needed to look inside. Joey would see me on the cameras and understand. I wouldn't scratch his precious locks. Based on what he described, I didn't expect to find anything, but I was willing to be surprised. I drove to the safehouse, parked across the street and a couple houses down, and surveyed the scene.

The street was as empty and boring as the last time I visited. I got out of the car and did another circuit around the house. As before, nothing. I walked up to the front porch, looked around for miscreants and curious neighbors, saw neither, and got to work. Joey chose good locks. It took me almost two minutes to get past the regular lock, and a little longer for the deadbolt. Every so often, I would knock on the door to keep up appearances for the neighbors. Almost five minutes after I started, I walked into the house.

The alarm was silent. I turned it off via the keypad. It flashed a SYSTEM DISABLED message before returning to its usual blank green screen. Checking houses after people vanished could not be counted among my many talents. Still, I saw it done on TV plenty of times. How hard could it be? The house had a basement, so I started there. Armed with pocket flashlight and gun, I went down the steps.

The stairs opened into a large rec room Joey never did anything with. He didn't need to; really; the house had two living rooms, and he didn't live here anyway. The room was at least twenty by ten and being devoid of all but carpet and air was easy to declare empty. I moved on to the extra bedroom. Nothing. Ditto the full bath and laundry room. All that remained was an unfinished storage room.

I stood outside the room and felt for the light switch. I flipped it on. Nothing. I moved to the other side of the doorway, gun at the ready. Leading with the flashlight, I took a tentative step into the room. The flashlight was small but powerful; its LEDs could disorient someone if shone right in their face. The beam lanced through the darkness and showed me the emptiness of the room. Even Joey's built-in shelves held nothing but a small box of cleaning supplies.

The first floor was equally vacant like the basement. Two living rooms, a dining room, a small study, and a half bath held not even a cricket. Joey said Chris, Brian, and Anna gathered in the kitchen before heading out of the house. I searched the kitchen table, all the cabinets and cupboards, the drawers, and the pantry. I peered under and behind appliances. All I found was nothing.

Brian was a sharp kid. He should have been aware of the stupidity of what Chris and Anna considered. Maybe he left a message somewhere. I went back through the first floor, looking under couch cushions, pulling out desk drawers, and stopping just short of ransacking the place. Still nothing. If I hadn't known three people occupied this house just a couple hours ago, only their dirty dishes in the sink would have betrayed them.

Expecting to find more of the same, I went upstairs to three bedrooms, two full baths, and a large linen closet. The master bedroom contained a walk-in closet with enough space to fit another bed, along with a sitting room, and a bathroom bigger than my bedroom. I looked inside, under, and behind everything I could and found nothing.

The second bedroom was smaller, about three-quarters the size, with a small walk-in closet. It was as empty of anything useful as the master. Ditto the smallish third bedroom, the second bathroom (I even looked inside the toilet tank), and the linen closet. I couldn't claim to be surprised by the lack of anything resembling a clue, but I still felt frustrated.

On my way out of the house, I offered a giant shrug to one of the first floor cameras. I turned the alarm back on, locked the bottom lock from the inside, re-locked the deadbolt with my burglar's tools, and left.

I HAD GIVEN Brian Sellers a burner phone. It wasn't the latest and greatest model of smartphone, but it could do a few things those phones do. Chief among them, at least for my current interests, was beacon its location. I presumed (or hoped) no one found and took the phone. I also trusted Esposito wasn't holding Brian somewhere with a cell phone jammer in place. This was my shot in the dark, and I needed it to work.

When I got home, I logged into my computer. I knew the SIM card ID for the phone I gave Brian. I could use software to track its location. The technology, at its best, would be accurate to about a hundred meters, so I wouldn't know exactly where Brian (and, I could presume, Chris and Anna) was being held, but I would have a general idea. The thought came to me how Brian needed to keep the battery charged. I expected he did. Joey kept a few of the most popular charger types in the safehouse.

If my software didn't provide a reliable location for Brian's phone, I would ask Joey to install and run it, too. A second point could make for a more accurate location estimate. I waited as the software ran, checking cell towers for communications. Towers in Baltimore lit up. Esposito hadn't taken them far. After a few seconds, I had an area: somewhere at the Port of Baltimore.

I sighed. The port was a big place with many warehouses, shipping containers, and vessels in which to hide someone, or three someones. And metal containers could inhibit cell signals. Adding another data point—or two for triangulation—may not get me a more searchable area. I needed to try, though, so I called Joey and told him what I wanted to do.

"You didn't find anything in the house?" he said.

"Nothing," I said. "My angle was Brian would have objected to what Chris and Anna wanted to do and left something I could use. No such luck."

"How do I get this software?"

"I put it on an SFTP server," I said. I gave Joey the address, confident he would know how to download and install it.

"Ok, I have it running," Joey said a couple minutes later. "What now?"

I told him the SIM card, how to run the search, and how to combine his results with mine and narrow the area. "It's working," Joey said after a few seconds. "Hitting a few towers . . . now focusing on one."

"I can see it on my screen," I said.

"But you're missing out on me narrating the action," said Joey.

"You're no Al Michaels," I said as the program finished. It showed me the same location as before.

"No luck?" Joey said.

"No. The port itself could be the problem. Lots of metal. We may not be able to get any better than this."

"Now what?"

"No idea," I said.

* * *

"Can you get a warrant?" Rich said. We sat in my living room drinking a couple of beers. An oatmeal stout for Rich and an IPA for me.

"Do they let you apply online?" I said.

Rich rolled his eyes. "This doesn't sound like a joke."

"It's not. And I don't have any proof, short of an app used to trace the location of a burner cell phone to the port."

"It's a big goddamn place," Rich said.

"Hence, why I wanted some help in looking around."

"It doesn't work on guesses."

"Because I don't have a warrant?" I said. "Because your system is great and wonderful?"

"It's not about the system," Rich said. "It's not even about getting around the system. The Port of Baltimore is secure. Companies there have their own security. They don't much like cops with warrants, but they can't do anything about it. You go down there with your usual unauthorized snooping, even if you have cops with you, and they're going to bounce you out. And there won't be anything you could do about it."

I downed the rest of my beer and looked at Rich. He shook his head. I got myself another IPA from the fridge, then plopped back into my recliner. "So what do I do?" I said. "I can't just sit here and do nothing."

Rich took a drink and thought about it. "You said the younger brother has the burner phone?" he said.

"Yeah. He's the only smart one in the trio."

"Then reach out to him. You have the signal. The phone is on."

"I don't want to risk it," I said. "It would give away he has the phone."

"They may already know," Rich said.

"I've thought the same thing."

"Then did you think the phone might be planted?"

"Meaning what?" I said.

"Meaning they found it and stashed it at the port, hoping you'd discover it's there. And then when you come and look for it, you find a welcoming committee to meet you."

I considered the possibility somewhere in the cynical recesses of my brain. My time in Hong Kong gave me plenty of practice with worst-case scenarios, and my experience has colored my worldview ever since. "I tossed the idea around," I said.

"And?" said Rich.

"And it's one of the reasons I'd rather wait for Brian to contact me."

"If he can."

"If he can," I said.

It could prove to be a big if.

* * *

Later, I settled into an uneasy sleep. Gloria called again after Rich left. I didn't answer, but I texted her and said it wasn't a good time with the case. While I liked Gloria, I didn't want her to come by. To my relief, she stayed away. I would have been bad company anyway. I went to sleep wishing I could do more, knowing I was better off to wait for something else to happen and dreading the eventuality.

I woke up around eight and lay in bed, staring at the ceiling and straining for a good idea. None came. After about fifteen fruitless minutes, I got up, changed into running clothes, and hit Federal Hill Park hard. I pushed myself for over four miles, working in even more sprints than Bobbi Lane and I did. When I finished, I drove to the dojo where I trained and wailed on a punching bag for a while. I drove my fists, elbows, knees, and feet into the bag as if abusing it would provide me an epiphany. All it did was tire me out.

I drove back home, showered, and ate a late (and large) breakfast. I whipped up an omelet, toast, turkey sausage, coffee, and a banana. I earned the calories . While I washed my plate in the sink, my phone rang. The number looked familiar and not in a good way. "Hello?"

"Well, well, well." Esposito. The fucker probably called to gloat. "I wasn't sure you'd pick up."

"Mystery solved," I said. "What do you want?"

"Seen Brian or Chris lately?" he said. I didn't answer. "What about Anna?"

"You have them." I didn't want to sound too certain and risk burning my compromise of Esposito's router. I doubted it could last forever, but I didn't need to lose it right now.

"You're damn right I do." Laughter threatened to spill into everything Esposito said. I never wanted to punch him more and wanting to punch him had been a constant condition since our first meeting. "What are you going to do about it?"

"I'm not begging for their lives," I said.

"No?"

"No."

"Why's that?" Esposito said.

"Because you're an asshole," I said. "Also, I don't beg for anything. But mostly because you're an asshole."

"You know I could have them killed, right?" he said.

"Come on. If you were going to resort to murder, you'd just do it. Me calling you a name wouldn't be a factor."

"You think you have this all figured out?" Esposito said. The lurking laughter vanished from his voice. Now I heard anger replace it. I imagined him getting red-faced, and the mental picture provided me a small measure of satisfaction. I would take little bits of satisfaction where I could get them at this point. "Tell me this: if you're so fucking smart, where do I have them? Huh?"

"I don't know," I said. I wasn't about to give away knowing anything about the Port of Baltimore.

"That's right," Esposito said. "You don't know. You did all you could to keep them from me, and I ended up with them anyway. Now I have them, and you don't know shit."

"Great. I don't know anything. I'm an ignoramus when it comes to where asshole mobsters hide people. Now what?"

Esposito took a deep breath. It hissed in my ear. I was getting under his skin. While I didn't think he would hurt or kill anyone based on how our conversation went, I didn't want to push him too far. He was about as stable as a see-saw.

"I wanted Chris," Esposito said after a few seconds of deep breathing. He sounded calmer, probably not red-faced anymore. Pity. "You know it. I don't really need his brother or his girlfriend."

"You're going to let them go?" I said.

"I'm going to let one of them go. The girlfriend. I'm keeping the brother to make sure Chris does the right thing."

"All right," I said. "What am I supposed to do about it?"

"You know these people," Esposito said. "They trust you, for whatever it got them. I'll release the broad to you later today."

"Her name is Anna."

"Whatever. You want to pick her up or not?"

"Of course I do," I said.

"Good," said Esposito. "I'll call you later and tell you when and where. Just you. No cops, no feds, no friends. Just you. We'll be watching. You want to make sure I know this broad's name, you probably want to keep her alive."

"Yes, I do."

"Good. Come alone, then, where and when I tell you." Esposito hung up.

Prick. At least he was releasing Anna. Maybe she could tell me something about where she, Chris, and Brian were being held. Presuming they were together. Even with Anna's pending return, a cloud of uncertainty still trailed this case around.

With luck, I might shed a bit of light on the mess.

GLORIA CALLED AGAIN after a couple hours. I had hoped it would be Esposito calling. For the first time in my life, I felt a twinge of disappointment that a beautiful woman was calling. "You're a hard man to reach."

I told her the recent developments in the case.

"Wow. He's going to let her go?"

"So he says," I said.

"You don't believe him?"

"For now, I have to take him at his word. Chris is the one he wants, and I guess a younger brother is more incentive to keep working than a girlfriend."

"You deal with some very shady people," Gloria said.

"Don't I know it?" I said.

Gloria wanted to have lunch, but I declined. "I don't know when he's going to call," I said. "And I don't know if he's going to do something like tie up Anna and throw her in a tub so I only have a certain amount of time to get there."

"You think he would do that?" Gloria said.

"He's an asshole, and he has a little flair for the dramatic. I wouldn't put it past him."

I told Gloria I would talk to her when I found more time. She said she understood. My thoughts drifted to Bobbi Lane, and I purged them as soon as they came. Bobbi wasn't the enemy, but I didn't want to see her right now. Thankfully, she hadn't called or texted since I left her apartment two days ago. It would be a complication I could live without.

While I waited for Esposito to call, I fired up my phone-tracking program. It still showed Brian's burner being somewhere at the Port of Baltimore. Would I have to go near there to get Anna? It would give me a chance to snoop around. The hell with Rich's warning: if I got a chance to poke around the port, I would take it. If Esposito didn't know about the burner, he didn't know about my ability to track it. Maybe this would be the leg up on him I'd needed ever since I plucked Chris and Anna from him in Delaware.

It was worth the hope.

* * *

A FEW MORE HOURS INTO the afternoon, the call came.

"Where is she?" I said.

"You get right down to it, don't you?" Esposito said.

"How do I know her life isn't in the balance?"

"It's not."

"I should just take you at your word?" I said.

"I'm not a liar," he said. "I think your buddy Tony is behind the times in a lot of ways, but he definitely taught me the value of being straight with people."

"All right," I said, "I'll take you at your word. Where is she?"

"How familiar are you with White Marsh?"

So much for stashing Anna at the Port with Brian. I should have realized Esposito would be too careful. Even if he didn't know about the burner phone and my ability to track it, keeping Anna near Brian constituted an unnecessary risk. "Familiar enough."

"Good," Esposito said. "She's in a house not far from the mall." He gave me the address on Necker Road. "It's right near where the road dead-ends. Should be easy to find."

"Good. I'll go and get her."

"You're welcome."

I was disappointed it came to this. Esposito was doing something nice. My proper upbringing compelled me to thank people who did nice things. Esposito was also an asshole who did a lot of terrible things. Because I resisted the urge of my upbringing, he now threw it in my face. "Thank you," I said through clenched teeth.

"I'm sure that was difficult," he said.

"Good talk. I'll be on my way now." I hung up.

I had a woman to rescue.

* * *

THE CAPRICE's V8 surged as I got onto I-95 and stomped on the gas. It would never be much to look at, but under its hood an eager engine could get down to business on the open road. One of these days, when this damned case was over, I needed to keep looking for another car. The Caprice would be useful in spots, so I would keep it. For everyday driving, presuming my Lexus wouldn't recover, I required something looking better and running smoother.

I went through the Fort McHenry Tunnel, got off at Route 43, picked up Belair Road, and made a right onto Necker. It was a narrow street with houses and parked cars on either side. Other roads connected off it with names like Silver Teal, suggesting they should be in a place like Columbia. I took Necker almost to the end, where it narrowed even more and saw a squat white house. It looked pretty plain with an aging roof, nondescript shutters, and a narrow, pitted driveway matching the street. I backed the Caprice in to park in case I needed to get Anna out of here quickly.

No other cars were in the driveway. This end of the street was isolated from the rest. There was a small cluster of townhomes at the very end of Necker. On the other sides, grass and trees surrounded the house. Esposito chose a good place to stash someone. Few people out here would see anyone coming and going. I looked at the house. No lights were lit. Dusk had settled. I would need my flashlight. I brought my .45 also. Esposito told me Anna would be here. He didn't say the rest of the house would be free of goons.

I expected the front door to be locked and would not be disappointed. The lock yielded to my picks in under a minute. Flashlight and .45 leading the way, I walked into the house. Picking the lock had not been a silent endeavor, and the area was quiet enough anyone inside would have heard the Caprice. I couldn't count on the element of surprise. "Anna?" I said.

No answer.

"Anna, are you here?"

Nothing. I looked around the living room, dining room, and kitchen. I didn't see Anna, nor did I see any evidence anyone had been in this house in the last week. The fridge was empty of perishables. There were no dishes in the sink, no mail or magazines on a table anywhere. I got a bad feeling. What if Esposito chose this house because its owner wasn't home?

"Anna?" I called again as I reached the bottom of the stairs leading up.

Still no answer. Not even a muffled cry or a whimper.

I took the carpeted stairs two at a time, stopping at the landing. The flashlight showed me four closed doors and a closet. No goons. No sign of activity. "Anna?" I said again. No response came. I flipped on a hall light. No one had stuffed Anna into the linen closet. The two small bedrooms at the far end of the hallway were vacant of all but cheap furniture. I checked the bathroom. Empty, including the tub.

I opened the last door. It was the master bedroom. "Anna, you in here?" I said as the door swung open.

Then I saw her on the bed.

She had been shot several times in the torso. Her white shirt turned red with blood as did the blanket she lay on. Anna's eyes were frozen open as if looking for a rescuer who wouldn't make it in time. I felt her neck for a pulse. Her skin was cool to the touch.

I found no pulse.

The son of a bitch killed her. King had told me Esposito was ruthless.

Outside, I heard cars screech to a stop. Red and blue flashing lights flooded the windows.

Great. Not only did Esposito murder her, but he called the cops when he knew I would be here.

I put my gun away. No point in making it appear I shot her. I looked at Anna. Five bullet holes punctured her chest. Any of them could have been fatal. All were small as if made by a .38 or nine millimeter. I wondered how long she had been here. Her body was cool. An hour? Two?

The door burst open downstairs. "County police," I heard a man shout.

"Up here," I said. "There's a dead woman."

Three cops came up the steps, their guns held before them. "Freeze!" one of them said to me.

"I found her like this," I said.

"Get on the floor!"

"Not happening."

The three cops approached. "That a gun at your side?" the one who told me to freeze said. His name tag identified him as Winters.

"Yes," I said. "You'll find the license in my right front pocket." I put my hands up. There was no point in resisting. I had no intention of getting onto the floor to be sat upon and cuffed, but I wouldn't resist a reasonable search.

"You shoot her?" Winters said.

"I told you, I found her like this."

"Uh-huh." He looked at my PI license and gun permit. "Private investigator?"

"Yes, I am."

"And you just happened to come here and find a dead woman."

I rolled my eyes. "Feel her neck," I said. "Then feel the hood of my car. I got here fifteen minutes ago. The hood should still be warm. It'll certainly be warmer than her body."

Winters half-turned. "Check out the hood," he said. One of the other cops went back down the stairs.

"Let's say you didn't kill her," he said. "Know who did?"

I felt confident Esposito hadn't killed Anna himself. Ordering it done made him as guilty as whoever pulled the trigger five times, but I had no idea who. "Not really," I said.

"Not really?"

"You know a Sergeant Gonzalez?" I said. "I'll be glad to talk to him."

Winters was about to say something when the cop who had gone outside sprinted up the stairs. "Hood's warm," he said.

"Warmer than her body," I said again.

The cop who went to the car moved into the room and put his fingers on Anna's neck. "He's right," he said.

"We're going to need you to come with us," Winters said.

"You have to know I didn't kill her," I said.

"I don't have to know anything," Winters said. "You will come with us. You can pick the easy way or the hard way."

I needed to talk to Gonzalez. Resisting here wouldn't help me, and more importantly, it wouldn't help Chris or Brian. If they were still alive.

I went with the easy way.

CHAPTER 17

I sat in the interrogation room. After Winters took my gun, phone, and wallet, the BCPD gave me a cup of water and made me wait forty-five minutes and counting. I did not consider this an even exchange. While I knew they must investigate Anna's murder, they couldn't have any reasonable suspicion I did it. What then was the point of having me sit here? I could help them. At the very least, I could talk to Gonzalez.

Instead, I sat. At least they hadn't taken my watch. I began a fascinating study of watching the second hand do its herky-jerky dance around the dial. Anna was dead. I couldn't find them, and she died. Had they been at the port? Should I have defied Rich and gone anyway? I would never know if any more positive action would have made a difference.

I recalled my conversation with Esposito. He said Anna's life wasn't in the balance in a phone call a few hours before I found her dead. I wondered if she had already been shot when Esposito called me the first time. He knew her life wasn't in the balance because he'd already had her killed. Or maybe he ordered her shot afterward. Either way, Anna was dead a couple hours by the time I arrived at the house on Necker Road.

The realization spurred another thought. I had only been there maybe fifteen minutes when the BCPD rolled up. It meant Esposito or someone in his operation watched the house. When they saw me go in and look around, they called the cops. And there I was, carrying a gun and alone in a house with a woman who died from multiple gunshot wounds. Even though it would be easy to prove my gun hadn't killed Anna, the police would have to be suspicious and take me in. Thus removing me from the case while I sat here and waited.

If I didn't hate Esposito so much, I would have admired his strategy.

What seemed like an eternity later, Officer Winters entered the room, and Gonzalez came in behind him. "Finally," I muttered.

"It was my day off," Gonzalez said, sitting in the chair opposite me. Winters stood against the wall behind him. "I barely know you. You're lucky I came in."

"It's obvious I didn't kill Anna Blair," I said. "You're lucky I've sat here and waited while you two stuck your thumbs up your asses."

Gonzalez glared at me but didn't take the bait. His patience was probably a good thing. My frustration got the better of me there. "I know you didn't kill her," he said.

"So I'm free to go?"

"Not so fast. I also know you've gotten tangled up with Alberto Esposito." He paused. I didn't fill the gap. "I'm going to presume this poor girl did, too."

"Yes," I said, fighting my natural inclination to stonewall. "She's the girlfriend of someone he's interested in."

"And he killed her."

"More likely he ordered it done," I said.

"Whatever," Gonzalez said, waving his hand. "Semantics. Do you know where Esposito is now?"

"Come on," I said. "We both know where he is. He's at home. He'll have an airtight alibi for whenever your ME says Anna died. The goons with him either won't know anything or will have the same alibi."

"You sound like you've done this before," Winters said.

I shrugged. "You know it's how it'll go down."

Gonzalez said, "OK, let's say you're right. What are you going to do next?"

"I'm going to find the other two people Esposito took captive," I said.

"Wrong," Gonzalez said. "You're done. A woman is dead. Now maybe you could've stopped it from happening and maybe not. But she's dead. You shouldn't risk anyone else's life."

I leaned forward in the uncomfortable chair. It was my turn to glare. "You think I could have stopped her murder and just sat on my ass and didn't do anything about it?"

"Not what I meant," he said.

"Whatever." I stood. "I'm done here. You two can piss off."

"Where are you going?" Gonzalez said.

"Am I under arrest?"

"No."

"Then I'm leaving," I said.

"You can't go," Winters said.

I turned and glowered at him. "Then come and stop me," I said.

He didn't.

I left.

* * *

I COLLECTED my stuff from the desk officer. From the police station, it was a short drive to Bobbi Lane's apartment complex. I pulled into her lot. Her car was there. I caught a break; I didn't want to call ahead, so I had to count on her being home. I parked in a guest spot, went into her building, and banged on her door. Soft footsteps moved inside and came toward the small foyer.

Bobbi opened the door halfway. Her dark hair was pulled back into a ponytail. She wore a tank top and a pair of yoga capris. Under better circumstances, I would have been glad to see her in such a getup. Bobbi saw it was me and smiled. Then her smile faded. If I looked as angry as I thought I did, I understood. "C.T., what's up?" she said.

"She's dead," I said.

"What? Who?"

"Anna."

Bobbi frowned in thought. "Anna?"

"Anna Blair," I said. I pushed the door open all the way and walked in. Bobbi's eyes went wide and then recognition crept across her face.

"Chris' girlfriend?" she said.

"Do you know another Anna Blair?"

"Why come here and tell me?" Bobbi said. "You can't think I had anything to do with someone dying."

"She didn't just die," I said. "She was shot five times in the chest. She bled out on a bed in a house she'd never been in before."

My description made Bobbi pale. "That's terrible," she said, "but I still don't know why you're barging in and telling me."

"Because you gave Chris' name to Danny Esposito."

"What?"

"Don't play dumb, Bobbi. You're too smart for it. You worked for Danny Esposito. He may have mentioned wanting someone good at writing code, and you gave him Chris' name."

She looked at me for a moment before giving a single nod. "OK, I did," she said. "Danny had access to student records but wanted a recommendation. I took a class with Chris and thought he was really good." She paused. "What does that have to do with Anna?"

"Because Danny wasn't asking for himself," I said. "His brother is a mobster. He wanted Chris to write malware for him. Chris agreed to do it. Then they had some kind of falling-out."

"Oh, my gosh," Bobbi said, her hand covering her mouth. "Oh, my gosh. So you're saying Danny's brother ordered Anna killed?"

"Yes."

"No," Bobbi said. She shook her head and when it obviously proved insufficient, she shook it again, harder. "No, no, no."

"Let me guess," I said. "You never thought this would happen."

"I didn't know anything about Danny's brother." Tears rimmed Bobbi's eyes. "C.T., you have to believe me. I didn't know."

I watched her while she wiped at her eyes and a tear escaped and slid down her cheek. "You know what, Bobbi?" I said. "I do believe you."

She smiled. "Great, I—"

"I just don't give a shit," I said. "You gave up Chris to Danny. Whether you knew anything or not, what you did started the series of events ending with Anna Blair bleeding out in a strange bed."

"But I didn't know!" Bobbi cried in earnest now. She reached out for me to comfort her, and I took a step back. Rejection made her cry more. "You believe me," she said. "You said you believe me. I didn't know anything like this would happen."

"And now you do. Actions have consequences, Bobbi. You have to live with what you did."

She sobbed as I walked past her. Part of me felt sorry for her.

Bobbi was a great, sweet girl, and I knew she didn't realize giving her boss Chris Sellers' name would lead to someone getting killed. But it had, and she needed to know her role in the tragedy and own it.

"Don't go," Bobbi said. Tears stained her mocha cheeks and spilled from her eyes. I fought the urge to hold her. "You can't just tell me something like this and leave."

"I can," I said, "and I am because I don't want to be around you right now."

I walked away. Bobbi stood in her foyer, crying with the door open. As I walked down the stairs, I heard it slam.

* * *

From Bobbi's apartment, I drove home. I still felt conflicted over laying the blame on her. Even if she didn't mean to land Chris right in the soup, though, she did, and Anna Blair paid for it with her life. I couldn't let it go. Any comparisons I once made between Bobbi and Gloria now landed on Gloria's side. If I survived this case, I would be twenty-nine in a few months. Maybe this was my wake-up call to put carrying on with two women behind me. I wasn't in college anymore.

I parked a few houses down from my own. As I started up the walkway to my front door, I heard footsteps approaching. I turned. Matty, Esposito's goon from the debacle in Abingdon, approached. "If you're here to dissuade me," I said, "there'd better be more of you."

"Just me," he said, stopping a couple paces short of me.

"Did you kill her?"

"I don't know what you're talking about," Matty said with a wolfish smile.

"You know damn well," I said.

"What I know is the cops hauled you off," he said. It meant

Esposito had eyes on the Necker Avenue house, and this dolt confirmed it for me. He continued as if he hadn't given me a piece of information. "Maybe you killed her."

"Your boss was right—thinking isn't something you're good at."

Matty glared at me. "Yeah?" he said. "I think we still have Chris and his brother. I think you have no fucking idea where. So I think you shouldn't run your mouth."

Now was my turn to smile. "Then make me shut it," I said.

He came at me. Matty was a big fellow, probably six-five and a good 260 pounds. A lot of it was muscle. He was quicker than I expected, so I used his momentum to shove him away and get time to set myself. He came again, leading with a couple of hard punches. I blocked them. The force made my arms sting. Not letting him hit me would be a superior strategy.

After another two punches, I countered with a short left to Matty's midsection. At the same time, he launched another hard left, and I didn't have a defense for it. My jab hit him, but his punch hit me a lot harder, blasting my breath away. He followed it with a right that caught me flush in the face and knocked me down.

So much for not getting hit.

My head throbbed, and I struggled for breath. Complicating those woes, Matty knelt atop me and put his hands around my neck. He squeezed. I couldn't breathe, and I didn't have a lot of breath to begin with. I used both my arms to box his ears. His winced but didn't let go. I did it again. He still didn't let go. Darkness crept into the edges of my vision, and I saw stars.

My thumb jabbed hard into Matty's left eye. He pulled one hand off to cover his eye. I did it to the other one. Now he released me and covered his face. I sucked in a deep breath, then shoved him to the side. He rubbed at his eyes while I lay on my walkway and tried to fill my lungs with oxygen. I wished it were a faster process.

Matty got up and stood over me again. When he knelt once more, I kicked him as hard as I could in the midsection. He doubled over, which allowed me to kick him in the face. The boot bent him back the other way and sent him to the ground. I kept breathing, my lungs thankful to drink in fresh air. I scrabbled to my feet before Matty did.

Over the years, I've learned a couple different fighting styles. Every lesson I took in a dojo stressed fighting with honor. Avoid a fight if you could, but if you couldn't, use what you've learned with honor and respect for your opponent. My opponent, however, recently tried to strangle me, and he also might have killed Anna Blair. Before Matty could get up, I planted my foot and kicked him hard in the gut. This second boot dropped him to the ground on his side. I kicked him again as he struggled to protect himself.

Matty covering his midsection left his face wide open. I drew my fist back and walloped him square in the nose, splaying it against his face with a satisfying crack. Now he covered his face, so I stomped on his stomach with as much force as I could muster. This prick may have killed Anna, and he tried to kill me. I stomped again and again on Matty's gut, snapping a couple ribs. Blood rimmed his lips even as it ran from his nose.

I fought down the urge to keep going. If I did, I knew it would be impossible to stop, and I didn't want to beat this asshole to death a few paces from my front porch. I took a step back out of his reach and crouched beside the fallen Matty. "Where are Chris and Brian?" I said.

"Piss off," he said.

Matty's hands covered his nose. I leaned closer and hammered my fist down onto them, crunching his broken nose again. He yelled in pain. I leaned back, out of his reach again. "Same question," I said.

He coughed a couple times and spit some blood at me. "Fuck off," he said.

"I'm trying to be nice here," I said. I noticed a set of car keys poking out of Matty's pants pocket. "But maybe I don't need to be." I grabbed the keys and pressed the lock button on the keyfob. A late-model BMW 3 series chirped its alert back at me.

"You're probably not smart enough to read a map," I said. "I'm going to guess you have a nav system." Matty frowned above the hands still covering his nose. "Which means I don't need you to tell me shit." I grabbed him by the hair and bounced his head off the pavement a couple times, knocking him out. If it cracked his skull at the same time, I didn't care.

With Matty down for the count, I took out my phone and looked up how to get location information from a newish 3 series. Then I got my laptop from the house.

* * *

WHILE I DOWNLOADED the information from Matty's navigation system, I called 911 for the police and an ambulance. The download finished a minute later. I locked Matty's car, activated the alarm, pocketed his keys, and stashed my laptop inside. Then I sat on my front porch and waited for the cops and the paramedics.

They arrived about three minutes later. One of the paramedics looked at Matty while the other checked me out. The two uniformed BPD officers looked all around for any evidence they could find. The paramedic told me one of my teeth had been knocked loose, and I would need to get it checked out. When he finished with me, he joined his partner, who fetched the gurney to put Matty into the ambulance.

The officers came to me after the paramedic left. They were Jennings, whom I knew a little and a younger officer named Turk. "Want to tell us what happened?" Jennings said. He looked to be about forty. Maybe he was training Turk, who looked like he started shaving all of two weeks ago. He was about as big as Matty, however, so the baby face only went so far.

I gave them the rundown, omitting the part about getting the navigation info from the BMW. "When he was knocked out, I called nine-one-one," I said in conclusion.

"This guy drive here?" Jennings said.

"No idea," I lied. "He was here before I was."

"We didn't find any keys on him," Turk said. His voice matched his body.

"There you go, then," I said.

Jennings said, "This guy local?"

How much should I tell them? I already held back the information about the car. Once Matty woke up, he wouldn't rat out Esposito. If the BPD knew about him, though, and if they worked with the BCPD, maybe Esposito would feel some pressure. "He works for a guy named Alberto Esposito," I said.

"That name supposed to mean anything?" Turk said.

"Minor-league gangster trying to make it to The Show," I said. "He's based out of the county, as far as I know."

Turk started to say something, but Jennings cut him off. "We'll talk to the county about him," he said.

"You might want to talk to Sergeant Gonzalez," I said.

"You been working with him?"

"To the extent I work with anyone, yes."

"Why do I think you know more?" Turk said.

"Because you have correctly deduced I'm a genius," I said. "Perhaps you'd like to talk philosophy? Programming?"

"Just be around if we have more questions," Jennings said,

shaking his head. He smirked, while Turk looked like he just sucked on four lemons in succession.

"I'm always available for the BPD," I said as they left.

Once the police and paramedics pulled away, I went back inside. I had information to comb through. My calculation was Matty drove to wherever Esposito kept Chris and Brian. Even if he didn't navigate there, his GPS would store the location. I logged into my laptop and got to work.

* * *

I HAD several locations to sift through. Eliminating some was easy: my house, for instance. I also eliminated Necker Avenue (the GPS gave me an address in the townhouses a block past the house where Anna died) because it would have been combed over by the police. The townhouse nearby was unlikely, but I needed to consider it a possibility.

Entries not corresponding to navigated directions were represented in coordinates. I used Google Maps, which happily took coordinates and matched them to real places I could work with. I filtered out things like gas stations and convenience stores. Other businesses remained possibilities until I could eliminate them. How did I know Esposito didn't know someone who would stash (or could be strong-armed into stashing) two captives at a furniture store?

All of this could be made easier if Brian Sellers would use the burner phone I gave him. At this point, I wondered if some Esposito lackey discovered the phone. Even if it went undiscovered, the battery could have run out by now. I pulled up the phone mapper. Nothing. The blips at the port no longer registered. I went back to the navigation data dump and made more notes.

At the end of another twenty minutes of converting coordinates into addresses, I owned a manageable list, most of the addresses being in Baltimore County. The list would be more manageable if I could split it with someone. The excitement of the evening made for a late night. Tomorrow, I would recruit Rich. In the meantime, I took a guest parking pass out to Matty's BMW, which had fortunately not been towed away yet. He had an orange 335i with an automatic transmission, a color and shifter I would not have chosen for myself. Still, it gave me another automotive option not on the blacklist of the entire Esposito organization. The tinted windows would allow me a certain measure of privacy as I snooped around possible hideouts.

It was late, but I wanted something to do. I could check out one or two addresses on my own. I set out to do a bit of light recon. The first was a sub shop I never heard of in Essex. I probably never heard of most sub shops in Essex, but the map did not show this one with a favorable location. It set a little ways off of North Point Boulevard, meaning road traffic might find easier parking lots.

Tino D's was more of a shack than a sub shop. There would be no room to eat inside; this was only a carry-out operation. The building looked like a long wooden shed. The roof begged for replacement, and its cries went unheeded for years. But unless the small building hid a sprawling basement, this was no place to stash two captives. They would have a bathroom at least, but unless they were going to sleep in the walk-in cooler, I needed to look elsewhere.

I checked out one more place. A game store in nearby Dundalk popped up on the navigation roll. It sat at one end of an aging strip mall. I didn't see any other cars in the lot. All the lights inside were off. Unlike Tino D's, this was bigger than a shack, and I could see inside. Posters for games I heard of (and even tried in college) stared back at me. Like Tino D's, however, this place would need a huge basement or warehouse area to house two captives. And even if it had those things, where were the goons who would need to keep an eye on things?

While I eliminated two possibilities, I didn't feel very accomplished as I drove home. Rich and I could run down the other choices tomorrow. As I neared my house, an incoming text made my phone vibrate. At a traffic light, I checked the text.

It was from Brian Sellers.

CHAPTER 18

It's Brian. We're OK. In some industrial place, idk where. Will text again when I can.

I read the message a couple times. A car behind me honked. I looked up, saw the green light, and started driving home again. Brian and Chris were OK. He had kept the phone hidden and charged, and finally found a chance to text. Brian was a smart kid. Now I just needed to be able to use his communication to narrow down his location.

Another, darker thought occurred to me. Esposito or one of his goons found the phone and sent the text. They wanted to bait me into their trap. Chris and Brian had joined Anna in the choir invisible, and now I, the last credible witness against the Esposito gang, needed to join them. I thought about what the message said. It didn't sound like bait. A baiting text would have given me a location counting on me to blunder into an ambush.

I had no intention of getting ambushed, and I did not blunder anywhere. When I got home, I would hope Brian left the phone on and try to track his location. Maybe he turned it off again to conserve the battery and avoid detection. If I texted back, I risked revealing the phone to his captors. I needed to wait for Brian. In the meantime, I would work on finding him.

* * *

At home, I fired up the phone-tracing program. Nothing. Brian's burner wasn't online. He had texted about twenty minutes ago. I checked the tower history of the phone. If I knew what towers it bounced off of, I could narrow its location.

Many things are great theories but don't work so well in practice. This turned out to be one of them. The phone showed a bunch of locations. It was like someone drove Brian around while he texted. Was he in the back of a truck? The trunk of a car? Were they being moved from one spot to another so no one would discover them? This case got stranger and stranger, even when I thought I experienced a minor breakthrough.

I kept watching the phone app. Considering the hour, I didn't expect it to come back online. If not staring at my screen with flagging hope, I would have been in bed. I considered making coffee and staying up to see what happened. As the clock struck one, however, I called it a night. Odds favored Brian being asleep wherever they were holding him, and if he left the phone off to maximize the battery, I wouldn't find him anyway.

I would have to try again tomorrow.

* * *

After breakfast and a fresh round of no results, Rich called. "Haven't heard from you in a few days," he said.

"Been busy trying to save the world," I said.

"How's your quest working out?"

"Not so well," I was forced to admit. I told him about finding Anna Blair dead in the house on Necker Road in the county.

"Jesus," he said. "I wonder why they killed her."

"They didn't need her. If they wanted Chris to sit down and crank out code, Brian's life is all the motivation they need to provide. He's the brother. Keeping Anna around becomes more trouble than it's worth."

"And you found her?" Rich said.

"Yeah."

"You OK? I know you don't have a lot of experience with dead bodies."

"I hope I never do," I said. "I'm OK. The cops questioned me, of course. Gonzalez knows I didn't do it."

Rich said, "You playing straight with him?"

"I think you and I define 'playing straight' differently. By my definition, yes."

"But probably not by mine," Rich said with a chuckle. "I guess it's time Gonzalez got used to your charms."

"If I crack this case and bring him in on the arrest, I'm sure he'll like the perks he gets," I said. "It works well for someone I know."

Rich changed the subject. "What are you doing now?"

"I gave the younger brother a burner phone. He's turning it on when he can. I'm trying to track it when he has it on. He texted last night, but I haven't found the phone yet."

"That the first time you've heard from him?"

"Yes," I said. "Until I can find the phone, I have to wait to hear from him again. Maybe he can give me some more info this time."

"What are you going to do when you locate him?" said Rich.

"What do you mean?"

"I mean I don't think you've thought this through. Esposito is careful. He might be moving the kid and his brother around so they're never in one place too long. Means he's resourceful, too. You can't just walk in there, take those two with you, and walk out."

"I'm not expecting to," I said.

"So what's your plan?" Rich said.

"I figured I would call some reinforcements. And maybe some strategy help. You've done this a lot more than I have."

"At least you're thinking about it."

"See?" I said. "I'm learning."

"We might make a real detective out of you yet," Rich said.

"Don't wish such a fate on me," I said.

* * *

LATER, I still worked on trying to find Brian and Chris. The phone didn't come back online. I still had Matty's list from his navigation system. Based on how Brian's phone moved around while it was online, I presumed Esposito kept Brian and Chris in multiple places. Maybe a regular (or irregular) rotation. If the phone didn't come back online soon, I would have to go back out and survey the places Matty visited.

My planning, such as it was, got interrupted by a knock at the door. I wasn't expecting any visitors. Maybe Gloria got tired of me not answering and not talking to her much. If she came by to distract me, I could live with it. I walked to the front door and looked through the peephole. A woman stood with her back to me. All I could see was dark hair. I opened the door.

The woman turned around and showed me a tentative grin. I gasped.

"Gabriella?" I said.

Gabriella Rizzo was Tony Rizzo's daughter. We were the same age (technically, she was a week older) and grew close after we first met at age ten. As we got older and moved through high school, it became obvious she liked me. And I liked her. She wanted me to take her to both our proms senior year. While I wanted to, I couldn't. At the time, I showed no interest in a long-term relationship—a view I still held—and didn't want to break Gabriella's heart, and then have her mob boss father order my death. A vengeful, murderous father is always a factor.

"Hi, C.T.," she said with a smile giving my knees a twinge of weakness. Gabriella had always been tall, standing about five-eight. In heels, she pushed six feet. She possessed a tan Italian complexion, coal black hair, and eyes as green as grass. Her shirt and jeans went well with her complexion and figure. I'd not seen Gabriella since before I left for Hong Kong. In the intervening four years, she managed to get even prettier. I reminded myself her father still ran organized crime in Baltimore.

"It's been a while," I said.

"Too long," she said, wrapping me in a tight hug. I smiled as we embraced. She held the hug longer than I expected. I didn't mind. Holding her close felt good.

"What brings you by?" I said. "How do you even know where I live?"

"Your parents told me," she said. "And I came by because I think we need to talk."

"Uh-oh, I'm getting 'we need to talk.' Don't we need to be dating or something first?"

Gabriella smiled again. It had the same effect. If she stood in my doorway much longer, I might marry her. "We need to talk about Alberto Esposito," she said.

"You know about him."

She nodded. "Can we get some lunch?"

"Your father's place?" I said.

"No," Gabriella said. "I don't want to have this conversation with him around." She paused in thought. "Or in public at all. Can we get some carry-in or delivery?"

"I'm sure we can find a good spot. Come on in."

Gabriella entered my house. I wondered, not for the first time with this case, what the hell I was getting myself into.

* * *

WE WALKED a few blocks to Maria D's on Light Street. A while passed since I indulged in sub shop food, and Maria D's always proved itself worth the indulgence. Gabriella spent her formative years in an Italian restaurant, so I knew she wouldn't object. She opted for a turkey burger. I took the plunge and got a pizza steak sub. We each ordered fries, and based on being in for a penny and in for several pounds, I got us a fried mushroom appetizer to share.

About ten minutes later, we walked back to my house. Thus far, Gabriella hadn't said anything about Esposito or why she decided to visit. She was her father's daughter in several respects. Tony preferred not to talk business in public. He demonstrated an uncanny ability to lower his voice so you could hear him across the table, but no one nearby could.

"Didn't you go to China?" Gabriella said when we were back inside. She sat next to me on the couch, and I spread the food out on the coffee table.

"For about three and a half years," I said.

"Why?" Gabriella put a few fried mushrooms and a spoonful of ranch on her plate. "Why would you go all the way over there?"

"I wanted to see the world," I said. I munched on a mushroom. "I was in Europe for six months seeing some things, collecting passport stamps."

"Did you stop in Italy?"

"For a few nights. I think I have a picture where it looks like I'm holding up the Leaning Tower."

Gabriella chuckled and gave me a light shove on the shoulder. "Oh, my god, you're such a tourist," she said. "Everyone takes that picture."

"So you did, too?" I said.

"Sure . . . when I was like, six."

"OK, so I was older than six. But I saw a lot of Europe."

"And then you went to China?"

I nodded. "You know I've always been into computers?"

"Sure," said Gabriella.

"I knew some people who lived in Hong Kong."

"Hackers."

"Hackers," I said. I ate another mushroom. So did Gabriella. "I learned some things in classes but taught myself most of it. A book here and there but a lot of trial and error. They were doing some real cutting-edge stuff, and they were doing it against the Chinese government."

Gabriella said, "So they were . . . what's the word . . . hacktivists?"

"More or less. They did some good things, but they tended to have an angle of personal gain. Doing good things for maybe some not-so-good reasons."

"I can see how you would fit right in," Gabriella said with a grin.

I grinned, too. "Yes, well . . . guilty as charged, I suppose. I got there and started working with them. They showed me a lot of things, things I'd never done or learned. In return, I paid for a bunch of upgraded equipment."

"You financed their operation?"

"Basically. I also worked on helping Americans who were being targeted by the government and a few dissidents."

"Did they help you with that?" Gabriella said. She ate her last mushroom. There were a few more in the container, but she eschewed them for her sub. She put half the burger and a handful of fries onto a different plate.

"Here and there," I said. "They were mostly into embarrassing the government. If helping me would make it happen, they were in." I grabbed the last few mushrooms. Added to at least half the sub and a bunch of fries, I would need to run an extra lap or two tomorrow. My mind flashed to running with Bobbi, and I banished those thoughts. I would do my laps alone.

"What happened, then?" Gabriella said. "My dad said something about your parents getting you out of China."

I told Gabriella about the Chinese government discovering us, the police arresting us, my nineteen days in the Chinese prison, and my eventual release. "They said they didn't want to see me again, and I assured them the feeling was mutual."

"Wow," Gabriella said. She rubbed my forearm a few times, then picked up her sub. I took the chance to start eating mine, too. Both barbecue sauce and ketchup were on the table for the fries. Gabriella disappointed me by selecting ketchup. I, of course, opted for the superior barbecue sauce.

After a few minutes of eating in silence, Gabriella said, "Alberto Esposito."

"The bane of my recent existence," I said around a mouthful of fries.

"You know he wants to take over from my father."

I nodded. Gabriella frowned. She must have thought I didn't know. "He came out and told me," I said. "He wants to modernize the operation."

"He told you," she said. "Wow."

"He did." Now I frowned. Gabriella's surprise struck me as more than normal. "Gabriella . . . you're not working with Esposito, are you?"

"Of course not," she said. "I just happen to agree with him."

"Really?"

"I don't want him to push my father aside. But Dad is stuck in the old ways. He's still messing with things like protection and construction. This isn't the 'eighties and 'nineties anymore. Everyone is online. Everything is online. People's refrigerators can tell them when they need eggs, for Christ's sake. And Dad doesn't want any part of that. It's . . . I don't know. It's weird."

"Because he should want a piece?" I said.

"Yes," said Gabriella. "There's a lot of money to be made online. People like my dad all over the world are using ransomware to make money. Why not him?"

Her words forced a smile. Gabriella was her father's daughter in many ways, and may have even surpassed him in business acumen. "Why doesn't he have you running the show?"

"Ugh." Gabriella shook her head. "This is no business for a broad," she said, mocking her father's voice. She did a creditable impression. "He doesn't want to turn his operation over to me. My dad's great disappointment is that he never had a son."

"He's crazy," I said. "He has to know you'd do a good job."

"I think he does. He sent me to college. Got my MBA. I know money. I know how to make money. My dad . . . doesn't think I'd be good at the parts of the job that don't involve money."

"He doesn't think you'd want to kill people." I picked up a couple fries. They grew tepid while we talked.

Gabriella leaned back on the couch and nodded. "That's the part he doesn't think is right for 'a broad.'"

"Could you do it?" I said.

She shrugged. "I don't know. I've thought about it. Hell, I was raised around it. I knew what my dad did years before he told me."

"You've always been smarter than he gave you credit for."

"Thanks," Gabriella said with a wan smile. "But the other side of the business . . . I don't know. I don't think I could do it myself."

"You wouldn't have to," I said.

"I know."

We lapsed into silence. Gabriella finished her turkey burger and, having eaten half my sub already, I started on the second half. We both ignored our fries at this point.

"Esposito found someone to write the malware for him," Gabriella said after a few minutes.

"I know," I said. "It's who I'm trying to find." I caught her up on Chris and Brian Sellers and the late Anna Blair.

"Esposito's brother runs his mouth," Gabriella said. I thought it was a rough segue until she clarified. "I talked to Chris. Asked him what Esposito wanted and how much he paid, so I gave him a little more to leave it alone and work for me someday."

I felt my mouth fall open. Whatever I thought to say died in my throat. Gabriella filled the gap. "I told him he had to return Esposito's money," she said. "I didn't want him double-dipping." She sighed. "I guess he decided to keep it after all."

"Yeah," I said. "I guess he did." What the hell? This got weirder and weirder all the time. Here came Gabriella, back from getting her MBA and whatever else she was doing, injecting herself into the case. Did her father know she did any of this? Would he be OK with modernizing if his daughter were the one leading the effort?

"I know I've dropped a lot on you," she said. "I'm sorry. None of this was ever supposed to happen. If Chris had just returned the money, none of it would have."

"Would it really be so simple?" I said. "Chris tells Esposito he changed his mind, hands him the money back, and Esposito is going to be fine with it?" Gabriella looked at me. "Would your father be OK with it?"

"He wouldn't be happy," Gabriella admitted. "But with the money returned, I think he'd be all right." I wasn't convinced, and Gabriella picked up on it. "Look, people like my dad aren't used to being refused, but they're definitely not used to people stealing from them. That's a lot, lot worse."

She made sense. Being refused was a matter of life. People

changed their minds. Someone stealing from you was disrespect. I could see men like Tony Rizzo and Alberto Esposito taking extreme umbrage to it. I started thinking how much of what happened to Chris he brought on himself. Part of me wanted to let him wallow in it. He made his choices, stupid though they were. Brian deserved to get away, however. He didn't have a role in all of this. He simply didn't win the lottery when it came to brothers.

I took all the plates and put them in the sink, then chucked the remaining fries. Gabriella sipped her soda. I sat on the couch again. "What brings you back to town?" I said.

"You," she said.

"Me?"

"Dad and I talk at least once a week," Gabriella said. "He told me what happened, that you came to him about Esposito." She chuckled. "And he told me you were a private investigator." Gabriella smiled and shoved me in the arm again. "You? A private investigator?"

"I'm getting to use what I know," I said, "and what I learned in China. I'm helping people."

"That sounds like your parents talking."

"Maybe a little," I said. "Maybe they're rubbing off on me."

"You've always been a good person, C.T.," said Gabriella. "I know you don't like to admit it, but you have."

"Thanks." I gave her a small smile.

Gabriella put her head on my shoulder. I put my arm around her. "You know," she said, "I always wanted you to put your arm around me when we were in high school."

"I know," I said. "However, I didn't want your father to have me drawn and quartered."

"I remember." Gabriella looked up at me. Her green eyes appeared bottomless. "You assumed you would break my heart."

"I was a teenager. Relationships weren't my thing. They're still not, really."

"Mine, either." She sighed. "I know I'll be able to convince my dad to pass the business to me on day."

"He'd be a fool not to," I said, wondering what brought on the rough segue.

"I'm not going to lie, C.T. When I first decided to come here, I figured I would seduce you." She paused. "Actually, I didn't think I would need to. We've always been attracted to one another." I bobbed my head in agreement. "Then I remembered you're working as a private eye. If I do take over one day, I don't want a complicated relationship with you."

"Me, either." It was for the best, really. My conscience barked at me over Bobbi. Even with that door shut, I didn't need Gabriella complicating things. Gloria and I were in a good place. I don't think either of us knew exactly where the place was, but we both liked it. It could even lead to something better.

"I brought an overnight bag, though," she said. "Would you mind if I stayed here?"

"Not at all," I said.

I set Gabriella up in the guest bedroom. A few minutes later, she turned in for the night, and so did I. As I lay in bed, I kept seeing Gloria sitting at my table and also propped up on an elbow in the bed, grinning at me.

My conscience confirmed I made the right choice. Now I wanted it to let me sleep.

* * *

I DREAMED of running with Bobbi Lane. We sprinted on the trail near her apartment. She took off at a pace I couldn't match and got ahead of me. I ran into a wooded area of the trail and looked for her. I called her. She didn't answer. I slowed to a walk and looked around. Somewhere above me, I heard branches and leaves rustling violently.

Just after I dodged out of the way, something landed on the trail. I looked down. It was Anna Blair's body. She had been shot five times in the torso. Her shirt had turned red with blood. I stared up in the tree. Bobbi Lane sat on a sturdy tree branch. She looked down at me and laughed.

I woke up and oriented myself. My bedroom. I could feel my heart beating fast in my chest. I took a few deep breaths. The door opened. Gabriella rubbed sleep from her eyes as she looked at me. "You OK?" she mumbled in a drowsy haze.

"Yeah," I said. "Just a bad dream."

"You yelled loud enough to wake the neighbors."

"Sorry."

Gabriella went back to the guest bedroom. The nightmare left me wide awake. I spent a while staring at the ceiling, then tossing and turning, then staring at the ceiling some more. I kept seeing Anna Blair's body as if it were projected above me onto the white paint. I shut my eyes and rolled over.

It took a while, but I finally got back to sleep.

* * *

I slept late the next morning but still felt groggy as I came downstairs. Gabriella sat in the kitchen, drinking a coffee and looking at her phone. She grinned at me. Even in frumpy pajamas and no makeup, her beauty couldn't be denied.

"Finally," she said.

"Yeah, yeah," I said as I made a cup of coffee. "Rough night."

"Must have been. It's almost lunchtime."

I looked at the clock on the Keurig: ten minutes to noon. "Jesus," I said. "I haven't slept this late since college."

"I've been waiting patiently for you to cook me breakfast for like, two hours now."

"How about we fast-forward to lunch?"

I raided the fridge, emerging with the ingredients for a chicken stir fry. Gabriella, no doubt motivated by hunger, helped me chop the vegetables. I multi-tasked by setting the rice to boil as I managed everything in the skillet. A few minutes later, we each enjoyed a plate of chicken stir fry atop a bed of brown rice.

"Mind if I do a little work?" Gabriella said. She took a small MacBook Air out of her bag. One single bag held her clothes, makeup, and a laptop. She was the anti-Gloria.

"Only if you don't mind me working, too," I said, banishing the thoughts of comparing Gloria and Gabriella. I already knew who won.

We ate in silence while we focused on our computers. Out of habit, I checked a few online haunts for Chris Sellers. I hoped he capitalized on a free moment to send a message asking for help. No such luck. I went back to my trace program on Brian's burner. No activity.

"What's that?" Gabriella said from behind me when I closed the program. I didn't even notice her get up from the table.

How much could I tell her? She would be the last person who would work with Esposito. However, she owed Chris Sellers no loyalty. He made his choice. If he survived, he would owe her, and I knew Gabriella would call in the debt at some point. "A cell phone tracker," I said. In the end, I didn't think Gabriella knowing would be a problem. If something made life more complicated for Esposito, she'd probably consider it a win.

"Whose phone are you tracking?" she said.

"I gave Chris' younger brother a burner."

"Is it online?"

"It has been," I said, "here and there. I can't pin it down to a specific place yet."

"Has he called you?"

"He's texted once. Didn't know where he was. I told him to keep the phone hidden and keep himself safe."

"Do you think you can find him?" Gabriella said.

"I do." I frowned.

"What?"

"I'm concerned about getting him out," I said. "Even if I find where he is, Esposito could have a dozen goons there."

Gabriella smirked. "They don't really like being called goons," she said.

"Then they shouldn't act so goonish."

She chuckled and shook her head. "How many people could you get?"

"Counting me?" I said. "Probably three." I figured Rich would be in. Maybe Paul King. I might even ask Gonzalez, though he'd most likely want to bring a bunch of cops.

"You're not going to send the police?" said Gabriella.

"I want to guarantee Chris and Brian's safety," I said. "If the police get wind of a hostage situation, they'll roll a SWAT team in there and who knows what will happen?" I shook my head. "It needs to be a smaller team."

Gabriella pondered this. "I might be able to get you a man," she said.

"Really?" I said. "One of your father's men?"

"He used to be. He and Dad . . . disagreed on some things. He did a lot of good work, though, so Dad let him walk away."

"You think he'll come out of retirement for you?"

"I never said he was retired," Gabriella said.

I smiled at her moral ambiguity. For all I knew, the man she talked about could have been working for her in her absence. Gabriella was as morally gray as I was, but her dark side trended more toward the dangerous. Tony was a fool; his daughter could run his operation better than he could.

"I'll let you know," I said.

"What are you going to do today?" she said.

I shrugged. "Hope for a bolt of inspiration, I guess. You?"

"Can I hang out a while?"

"Sure. Stay as long as you want."

"Thanks." Gabriella grinned. I liked having her as a sounding board. I wouldn't call her and blather about all my cases with her, but while she was here, why not?

In a couple years, she might take over for her father. I doubted I would have her to bounce ideas off once she established herself as the queen of Baltimore organized crime. So long as she didn't ask me to write any ransomware after the coronation, we would get along fine.

AFTER MORE UNPRODUCTIVE time spent looking for Brian and Chris, I ordered dinner. Forty-five minutes later , the doorbell rang. I opened the door, paid for the pizzas, and carried them to the dining room table. I didn't have a big eating area. The first-floor office was a boon for my job, but it made the dining room and kitchen smaller. My table was square and could fit four people so long as they kept their elbows close to their bodies. It was perfect for Gabriella and I to share a pizza. I got two beers out of the fridge as well. Gabriella smiled when I set the beer in front of her.

"An IPA?" she said. "A man after my own heart."

During our teenage years, there were a few times I thought I might have been. "My favorite, too," I said.

We ate the pizza. It had an appropriate level of grease, which is to say holding up a slice and letting it dangle would cause a stray drop or two to escape. Gabriella wanted Italian sausage. I've always hated sausage on pizza, so I got half her way and half with mushrooms and onions.

Between the two of us, we ate a whole large pie and drank two beers each. After dinner, Gabriella plopped on the couch. She grabbed my cable remote and poked around the On Demand options. I carried the last two IPAs from the six-pack into the living room as Gabriella chose some comedy I saw a trailer for months ago.

We watched the movie and drank the last beers. The movie ended up being funnier than I would have expected. After it was over, Gabriella turned off the TV and picked up her phone. While she busied herself with something there, I looked again for signs of life from Brian's burner phone.

Nothing.

Gabriella leaned against me. "I'm glad I got to see you," she said. "It's been way too long."

"It has," I said. "Let's do this more often."

"I'd like to. Let's see how my schedule works out."

"What are you doing, anyway?"

"Traveling. Learning."

"Learning how to take over for your dad?"

"Just because he doesn't want to teach me right now," Gabriella said, "doesn't mean I haven't found mentors. Being my father's daughter opens some doors."

"Be careful," I said. "Just because a door is open doesn't mean you should walk through it."

"It's nice of you to worry about me." Gabriella yawned and stretched, exposing a tan, toned stomach. "Mind if I crash here again?"

"Help yourself."

"I'm not sure whose reputation this arrangement is ruining more," she said.

I chuckled. "Do people even have reputations like that after college?"

"I guess." Gabriella frowned in thought and pursed her lips. "I don't know, really. I guess in certain circles. Like, your friends might warn you about a guy or girl, and word would probably get around an office."

"People meet online a lot nowadays," I said. "Your baggage isn't on display when they decide to swipe left or right."

"I've missed talking to you," Gabriella said.

"Me, too."

"It's a shame I have to hit the road again."

"There's always Skype."

"FaceTime?" she said.

I grimaced. "Do you really think I would own an Apple product?"

"I guess not," Gabriella said with a light laugh.

I enjoyed talking to Gabriella, and I'd miss her when she left. In the years she spent away, I didn't think about her much. Now, seeing her again—combined with Esposito trying to depose her father—made me consider what she'd be like when she ran the show. Tony and I were on good terms, though he got a little frosty when he first heard of my chosen profession.

Now I wondered if Gabriella and I would be on opposite sides of something I was working on. The thought darkened my mood.

CHAPTER 19

THE NEXT DAY, I WOKE UP AT A MORE RESPECTABLE HOUR. I went downstairs and worked on breakfast. A few minutes later, turkey bacon sizzled in a skillet while multigrain bread browned in the toaster.

The aromas of breakfast cooking and coffee brewing roused Gabriella from her slumber. I heard her feet hit the floor upstairs, and she joined me in the kitchen a couple minutes later. "Smells good," she said, padding to the Keurig.

"I think it'll taste good, too," I said. A couple minutes later, I set two plates on the table.

After drinking coffee and eating about a third of her food, Gabriella said, "What are you going to do today?"

"Hope for a break in the case," I said. "I checked a little while ago . . . still no activity on the burner phone."

"You sure you don't want to use my man? He'd be a help."

"We'll be good."

"You and the police?" Gabriella said.

I nodded. "I'm not looking to go in and kill everyone. Esposito and his goons will be arrested."

"And if there's a shootout?"

"Then I have a gun," I said.

Gabriella looked at me for a few seconds. "This suits you," she said.

"Making breakfast?" I said. "I know my way around the kitchen."

"Being a PI."

"You think so?"

"Don't you?" she said. "It's your job."

"I'm taking to it more than I thought I would," I said. I finished my mug of coffee. "It's not as easy as I first thought."

"Most things aren't," Gabriella said.

I got up and refreshed both our cups. When I sat back down, I said, "Why do you say this job suits me?"

"It lets you use what you're good at," Gabriella said. "Part of that is your interesting moral fiber." She grinned. "And part of it is your willingness to go into who knows where with a gun to save someone you barely know. A lot of people, even people in your job, wouldn't do that. They'd just call the cops and watch from afar. You want to be involved."

"I think people expect it of me," I said.

"No, I think you expect it of yourself," said Gabriella.

I didn't say anything. She continued. "Come on, C.T., I've known you too long. I know you always used to say you didn't want to work. Despite that, I think you've found what suits you."

"Thanks, I think," I said. Gabriella smiled and went back to her breakfast. "What about when you find what suits you?"

"What suits me?" she said.

"Your father's job."

Gabriella snorted. "You know what he thinks about a woman doing the job."

"I do," I said, "and I also know what he thinks of his daughter. You've always been the apple of his eye." Gabriella's cheeks colored. "Whenever he decides he's had enough, I know he's going to turn things over to you."

"Maybe he will," Gabriella said in a quiet voice.

"I'll try to stay out of your way," I said.

"Might be a good idea," Gabriella said with a grin. I figured it would be. When I started working, I made sure to tell Tony Rizzo as a courtesy. He was a little frosty when he learned of my job, but he'd warmed back up. I hoped things didn't frost over with Gabriella when she took the reins.

After Gabriella left, I got back to work. I checked for any signs of life or movement from Brian Sellers' burner phone. Nothing. I checked for interesting traffic on Esposito's router. Also nothing. While I researched other ways I might be able to find Brian, I kept monitoring the phone. At long last, it came alive as a red dot blipped on my screen.

The dot was moving.

Whoever had Brian took him farther into northern Baltimore County. I didn't have much of a relationship with the BCPD. Gonzalez and I hadn't worked together much. I didn't know anyone there like I knew Rich or even Paul King. Still, in the interests of not going into a building guns blazing by myself, I reached out.

"I was wondering when I'd hear from you," Gonzalez said.

"You solved a mystery today," I said. "Put it on your whiteboard."

"We track all that shit electronically now. What do you have?"

"Your people have anything on Esposito or the Sellers brothers?"

"Nothing," Gonzalez said. "You got anything."

"I do," I said. "He's on the move."

"Where?"

"Right now, they're driving deep into the north of the county."

"And you're tracking this from a burner phone?"

"Yes," I said. "And you're probably thinking the same thing I am: what if Esposito and his goons found the phone? They could be driving the phone somewhere to see if we're tracking it and lead us into a trap."

"Crossed my mind," Gonzalez said.

"We can't just twiddle our thumbs. If we get an actual location, we have to check it out."

"You're pretty big on this 'we' shit."

I rolled my eyes. "You're not cutting me out," I said.

"Don't need to," Gonzalez said. "We'll just get the information from you."

"I'm not telling you where they are unless I'm part of the group looking for them."

"Now hold on—"

"No, *you* hold on," I broke in. "You'd barely have a handful of shit without me. You want my info; you cut me in. Or I save it to my extremely encrypted hard drive, and your techies will retire before they break my crypto."

Gonzalez sighed into the receiver. If he were Rich, I would have pictured his reddened face and steam spewing from his ears. I didn't know Gonzalez well, but I liked the visual, so I went with it. After a moment, Gonzalez said, "You're a civilian. I can't guarantee your safety."

"I don't need you to," I said. "I'm a big boy, and I know the risks."

Another pause. "Fine," Gonzalez said. "Let me know when you have a location." He hung up.

I made another call.

"That's in the county," Rich said after I explained the situation.

"Geography may have bored me, but I passed it," I said.

"Did you call Gonzalez?"

"Yes."

"And?" said Rich.

"And he's waiting for a location," I said.

The information made Rich chuckle. "I know Gonzalez a little," he said. "My guess is he didn't want you coming along."

"It's why I want you to come, too," I said.

"Me?" Rich said. "What will you need me for? Jurisdiction issues aside, Gonzalez will bring plenty of men."

"Jurisdiction issues can be overcome."

I didn't say anything. Neither did Rich. He then broke the silence and said, "You want me there, don't you?"

"I just told you I did," I said.

"No, you want me there because you trust me."

Rich wanted me to admit it. Fine. For once, I wasn't too proud. "With my life," I said.

"OK," he said. "I'll do it."

"I'll talk to Gonzalez."

"Let me do it," Rich said. "I think he'll understand it more coming from me."

"All right," I said. "Oh, you have an extra bulletproof vest?"

"I'm sure I can rustle one up." I pictured Rich rolling his eyes. What would he think when I didn't give it back?

"Thanks," I said. "I'll be in touch when I know something."

We hung up. I watched the red dot and waited for it to settle in one spot.

*   *   *

ABOUT AN HOUR LATER, the red dot representing Brian Sellers' burner phone stopped moving. On a circuitous tour of Baltimore County, it finally settled in the Hereford area near Mount

Carmel and York Roads. I hadn't made many trips to Hereford. The ball would be in Gonzalez's court on this one.

Five minutes passed, and, I got a text from the burner. *They moved us. We're OK but you need to come soon.*

I called Gonzalez and gave him the coordinates. "Looks like a car repair shop," he said.

"Whatever it is, it's where they're holding Brian and Chris," I said. "Brian sent me a text and said we should come soon."

"Your cousin called me. I'm OK with him coming along. Can you meet us at the precinct in forty-five minutes?"

"We'll be there," I said.

Two minutes afterward, I was in the Caprice. I carried my .45 and three spare clips. I also brought a tablet to keep tabs on the burner phone. While I drove toward his house, I called Rich. "It's going down," I said.

"Gonzalez gave me a heads-up," Rich said. "Are you on your way?"

"I am. See you in twenty."

"Try to make it fifteen," Rich said, hanging up.

I almost did. Seventeen minutes later, I swung the Caprice into the driveway of Rich's Victorian in Hamilton. He emerged from the house after a moment, carrying a large duffel bag. "I got you a vest," he said as he walked toward his car. "Get in. I'll drive."

Rich had a blue Camaro with a large and loud V8. It was a proper sports car in all ways except its transmission. As a nod to the knee that needed surgery and got him a medical discharge from the Army, Rich had outfitted the Camaro with an automatic. His knee recovered, but he said he was glad not to have to use a clutch with it. I understood, even if I gave him grief for it.

I got in the passenger's seat. Rich tossed his duffel bag on the back seat and fired up the Camaro. The engine roared to life. Rich backed out of the driveway, and within two minutes, we zoomed up Belair Road at a speed to make the city council blush. "You can keep the vest by the way," Rich said.

"I can?"

"I figured you weren't going to give it back anyway."

"It's not something off the scrap heap, is it?" I said.

"No," said Rich. "Kevlar only lasts so long anyway. This is new. A few months old."

"I'll be sure to play dumb when your generosity leads a city bean counter to my doorstep."

"Leon Sharpe approved it."

"I knew I liked him for a reason," I said.

* * *

WE GOT to the BCPD precinct with a few minutes to spare. "We would have been late if you drove," Rich said with a smirk as we got out.

"I made it to your house in seventeen minutes," I said.

"Something would have happened on the way here, then," he said. "You're always late."

"You two always bicker like this?" Gonzalez said, walking toward us from somewhere in the parking lot. I hadn't seen or heard him, so I jumped. My reaction made him chuckle.

"Only when Rich is wrong," I said. "Which is pretty often."

Rich let my barb go. "We're ready," he told Gonzalez.

"Good. My team is headed to the van now. Come with me."

We followed Gonzalez behind the building. Rows of police cars and obvious "unmarked" vehicles waited to be driven. Behind those were a few regular vans and a couple armored ones the SWAT team would use. To my disappointment, we were ticketed for a regular van.

Gonzalez slid the door open. Three men waited for us inside. "Driver's Reyes," said Gonzalez. He was a compact Hispanic man with a dark complexion and a head full of thick, if short, hair. He nodded to Rich and me. "Those two are Sung and Simpson." A wiry Korean man and a tall white guy built like a linebacker offered us muttered hellos. "They all know the details and what we're there to do."

I looked at my tablet. "They're still at the same location," I said. Rich and I sat in the second row of seats. He handed me the Kevlar vest from his bag, and I put it on.

"How are you tracking them?" Sung said.

"It may be best if I don't answer," I said.

"The kid has a burner," Gonzalez said from the passenger's seat. "Past that, I'm sure whatever's happening is shady."

"But beneficial to the people held captive," I said in my own defense.

Sung and Simpson both shrugged. "I got no complaints," Simpson said.

Reyes fired up the van. We pulled out of the parking lot, got on the Baltimore Beltway, and took it to I-83 North. It then hit me what I was doing. I sat in a van, wearing a Kevlar vest, surrounded by cops, and preparing to assault a car repair shop—all in the name of bringing two people out alive. I experienced a lot in my brief time as a PI and more back in China but nothing like this. I trusted Rich and Gonzalez and by extension Gonzalez's men, but it didn't make me bulletproof. It didn't make me a better shot. It didn't make me fearless.

I took a deep breath and not for the first time in my career, I wondered how I got to this moment.

CHAPTER 20

Reyes pulled into a parking lot about a block from the auto repair shop. We could see the front of the building and the fading neon sign. I expected a goon on patrol but saw no one. A sentry would alert passersby something shady was going down inside. Esposito would be more careful. I checked my tablet. The burner remained stationary.

Gonzalez turned in his seat and looked at me. "Well?" he said.

"It's still there," I said.

"All right. Weapons check." Everyone took out their pistols, gave them a quick inspection, and made sure a round had been chambered. I did the same. I was really going to assault a building. Sensing my apprehension, Rich clapped me on the shoulder. "You'll be fine," he said. "I know you're a good shot. Just be careful. Don't charge in anywhere not clear. Stick to the walls if you can."

"Just like Call of Duty, right?" I said, offering a small smile.

Rich grinned. "More or less."

"You shot anyone before?" Gonzalez said.

"Not yet," I said.

"Think you can?"

"I didn't get into this job to shoot people. But if it comes down to them or me, I'll send flowers."

"That's the spirit," Sung said. "Make sure you get to go home, even if it means the other guy doesn't."

"We done with the pep talks?" Reyes said. "This ain't the homecoming game." He reminded me a bit of Paul King, though King looked more disheveled and would have cursed at least twice there.

"Let's go," said Gonzalez.

Reyes pulled the van back out onto Mt. Carmel Road. The body shop sat immediately before the intersection with York Road on the left near a post office and convenience store. I wondered if anyone in the neighborhood ever reported strange goings-on at the body shop. I also wondered how Esposito came to use it. Eddie's Auto didn't sound like something he would be involved in, and I never saw a record of it in his financials.

Before we pulled into the shop's parking lot, Reyes cut the headlights. He stopped the van alongside the body shop, where it was hidden from windows and doors. Past where we stopped, the parking lot turned into a driveway going to the back of the building. The bays must have been around there.

Gonzalez gave earpieces to me and to Rich. Once we had put them in our ears, he gave us small microphones to clip to our collars. "Channel 12," he said. "Your mikes should already be on it." A tiny dial on the side of the microphone indicated channel 12. "We'll do a comms check once we're outside."

Simpson slid the door open. I heard it open before at the precinct, but now I noticed how quiet it was. Most van doors could be heard 100 feet away. This one whispered. Reyes and Gonzalez opened the front doors slowly to be as quiet as possible, and closed them the same way. Once we were all outside the van, Simpson slid the door shut. It made a little more noise as it closed but it was much quieter than any other van I had seen.

Reyes stayed on the other side of the van at first. "Comms

check," he said at a whisper right into my ear. "Can you hear me in your earpieces?" I said I could as did everyone else.

"Simpson and I will go first," Gonzalez said when Reyes had joined us. Sung handed Simpson a portable ram. He carried it like he might have a small two-by-four. "Sung and Reyes next. Rich, you and C.T. in the back."

"Copy," Rich said.

"Yeah, copy," I said.

We padded toward the building. There had been no sign anyone noticed us yet. I hoped it continued. Of course, the element of surprise would be lost when Simpson battered down the door, but if we kept it until then, I liked our chances. As we closed in on the front door, it hit me again I would soon be assaulting a building with five cops. Of all the things I thought I might do in my life, this would rank near the bottom of the list.

At the front door, we stood two abreast. Gonzalez gave Simpson a wide berth so he could swing the ram. He gripped the handles and gave Gonzalez a short nod. Gonzalez held up three fingers, then two, then one. Simpson drew the battering device back and turned his hips, powering it forward. The blunt head hit the door and blew the lock apart. The door opened into the shop. Simpson dropped the ram, drew his pistol, and followed Gonzalez inside. We were doing this.

"Police," Gonzalez shouted to the room. "Hands where we can see them."

Sung and Reyes went in next. While Gonzalez and Simpson went right, they went left. Rich stepped through, and I followed him. All the lights were on inside. Two goons stood near the two car lifts, their jaws slack, and their brows creased. As Gonzalez yelled again, they raised their hands.

Once I got inside, I saw several closed doors. For a body shop, this building featured a lot of rooms and offices, confirming my hunch it had been repurposed. Rich pointed me to one of the doors, and I followed him. Once we were in position, he looked at me and raised his eyebrows. I nodded. Rich moved beside the door and delivered a hard back kick just above the knob. The lock yielded, and the door opened. Chris Sellers sat at a computer, supervised by a goon whose eyes went wide. As he moved to stand, I walked into the room. "Don't move," I said, my gun pointed at him. Behind me, I heard Rich on my heels.

The goon thought about it. He had a gun in reach on the table. He looked at me, looked at Rich, looked at the gun. "Don't do it," Rich said. After another moment of considering his options, Esposito's lackey scowled and put his hands up. Rich stepped forward to arrest him. He turned the man around, patted him down, then bound his wrists behind him with a zip-tie. Rich directed the goon to a chair where he tied the man's ankles as well.

"Chris, are you OK?" I said.

He nodded. His wide eyes darted around the room.

"Stay in here with him," Rich said. "I think we can handle the rest."

"All right." I sat on the desk, between Chris and Esposito's goon. Chris kept looking around the room. The goon sat and scowled, glaring at me and not caring if I looked back at him.

"Untie me," the man said. "Let's see who's tougher."

"I'd still have a gun, genius," I said.

"Put it down, then."

"I'm not untying you."

He spat at me. "You afraid?" he said.

"Yes," I said. "I'm afraid I might beat you to death. Now sit there and shut up before I find something to gag you with."

"Checking the door on the right," Sung said in my ear. I heard shouting, then gunfire erupted. A moment later, wheels squealed outside. I wondered if someone made off with the police van.

"Sung, you OK?" Gonzalez said.

Sung groaned into his mike. "I'll live," he said. "Vest took it."

"One suspect down," Gonzalez said. "Repeat, one suspect down. Another escaped out the window."

I wanted to rejoin the team, but I also didn't want to leave Chris in the room with the glaring goon. Even with his hands and feet bound, he would get the drop on the shell-shocked Chris.

"We have the younger brother," I heard Rich say in the earpiece. "He's fine."

"They found Brian," I said.

Chris released a deep breath. He stopped looking around all the time. "Can I see him?"

"In time," I said. "There are a few more assholes to round up first."

The bound thug spat at me again. This time, he managed to spit on me, getting his slime on my vest. I put my gun on the table, well out of his reach, and walked closer to where he sat. "What are you gonna do?" he said, glowering up at me. "Fucking cops."

"I'm not a cop," I said. I kicked him, clocking him on the side of the head. He toppled from the chair, landing in an undignified and groaning heap on the floor.

A minute later, Rich came back in. He saw the goon on the floor. "What happened to him?" Rich said.

"He's a spitter," I said. "Must have made the floor slippery."

Rich hauled the groggy jackass to his feet. "Let's go, asshole," he said. As Rich left the room, Sung led Brian in. He and Chris hugged tighter than I had ever seen two men embrace before. Sung walked gingerly into the room.

"You all right?" I said.

"Probably cracked a rib or two," he said. "I'll be OK. Light duty for a while."

I couldn't imagine being so matter-of-fact about getting shot, vest or no vest. "Thanks for coming along," I said. It didn't seem like enough, but I didn't know what else to say.

Sung smiled. "Gonzalez said we had a chance to bust a real prick. Too bad he got away."

"It was Esposito who escaped?" I said. Sung nodded. "Shit."

"That sums it up," Sung said.

Brian Sellers walked to me. He spread his arms to go for a hug, thought better of it, and stuck out his hand. I was glad to shake it. "You had me worried," I said. "I didn't know if the phone was ever coming back online."

"I had to keep it off most of the time," he said. "They watched us pretty close for a while, and I wanted to preserve the battery."

"They never found the phone?"

"Like you said, C.T.: no one searches your junk." Brian reached down the front of his pants and pulled out the phone. He held it out to me. I put up my hand.

"Keep it," I said. "Or at least disinfect it before you give it back."

"What happened to Anna?" Chris said. The good mood fled the room. Brian looked away. I wish I could have, too.

"Did they separate you?" I said.

"Yeah. Esposito said they were letting her go." Chris looked around again. "I was hoping she'd be here."

I took a long, slow breath. Never before did I have to tell someone their loved one died. I'd heard it before, concerning my sister, and being on the receiving end was dreadful. The delivering end didn't feel much better. "There's no easy way to say it," I said, watching all happiness evacuate Chris Sellers' eyes. "She's dead, Chris. Esposito had her killed."

Chris might have collapsed if Brian hadn't grabbed his arm. His expression went blank, and his mouth hung open. I knew he had questions. I wished I knew the answers.

* * *

By the time we arrived back at the precinct, the BCPD issued a BOLO for Esposito. Two goons—one dead, one injured—were taken away by people other than the police. The other three, including Sir Spits-a-Lot, rode in a different van. The usual array of police cars arrived as well. Gonzalez commandeered one of them and took Brian and Chris Sellers away. For a second, I hoped they were going back to the safehouse. Then I remembered they got abducted somewhere near there.

The three arrested goons each sat in separate interrogation rooms. Simpson and Sung, the former animated and the latter mostly sitting, talked to one. Reyes and a cop I didn't know talked to another. The cretin who spat on me sat all by his lonesome in a room. Gonzalez and Rich approached me. "Want to talk to the spitter?" Gonzalez said. He looked at the file he carried. "Name's Ray Fish."

"Sure," I said.

"Let's hope he doesn't slip again," Rich said, smirking.

"Always a danger of spitting so much," I said.

We walked in, Gonzalez first, Rich next, then me. There were only two chairs on the business side of the table. I didn't want to leave and get another one, so I leaned against the one-way mirror. "I got nothing to say," the goon announced before anyone asked him anything.

The announcement drew a large round of indifference from the three of us. Gonzalez and Rich were trained investigators who knew how to interrogate people. I just liked to make people sweat. Give them silence, and nervous people will fill in the gaps by saying more than they should. As much as I like to talk in normal circumstances, I appreciate the value of sitting and keeping quiet when questioning someone.

"I said I ain't saying nothing," he said, not catching on. Normally, I would make my English teachers proud and point out the double negative. Instead, I crossed my arms under my chest. Rich glanced at me. He knew I fought an internal battle on the matter. The struggle is real.

"You pigs listening?" It was all we were doing, in fact, but understanding still eluded this fellow.

After another moment of only silence for a response, the goon said, "I want a lawyer."

"You need one," Gonzalez said. "Kidnapping, assault, attempted murder of police officers. . . ."

"I didn't try to kill nobody!"

"A dumbass double negative means you did," I said, unable to resist this time.

"Fuck off."

"The eloquence continues."

"I want a lawyer," the goon reiterated.

"We'll call one for you," Gonzalez said. "But first, I think we need to have a conversation."

"I ain't saying shit without a lawyer."

"Suit yourself," Rich said.

"Christ, we forgot about the dead girl," Gonzalez said.

"You're right," said Rich. "We did. That adds more charges. Kidnapping, murder, breaking and entering. . . ."

"Hey, I didn't kill no girl," Ray Fish said.

"You're the only one we have in custody," Gonzalez said. "Looks like you're getting all the charges."

"That ain't right!"

"Killing people isn't right, either," Rich said. I liked watching him and Gonzalez work together.

The moron looked between them a couple times, then looked at me. I didn't say anything. Gonzalez and Rich had a good thing going; I didn't want to step on it.

"A lawyer will get me out of here," he said after a moment. He puffed out his chest when he said it. I wondered if he tried to convince us or himself.

"A lawyer will advise you to stay quiet," Gonzalez said.

"Sounds good to me."

"Here's the problem with that, Ray," Rich said. "Unless you tell us who did the things we've talked about, you're getting charged with all of them. And if you have to sit there and be quiet like a good little boy, you can't tell us who we're looking for."

The revelation made our prisoner frown in thought. He stayed silent for a minute. This man had never been employed for his brain power, and it showed. I almost expected smoke to come out of his ears. "Fine," he said after another minute.

"Was it Esposito?" I said. Rich shot a sidelong glance at me.

Fish snorted. "The man don't get his hands dirty," he said. "He has other people do the work."

"Tell us what happened with the girl," Gonzalez said.

"We captured all three of them . . . the broad and the two brothers. Kept them together for a while. Then Esposito said he would let the girl go."

"Did you think he would?" Rich said.

"I doubted it," said Fish. Maybe he wasn't as dumb as he looked. Or acted. "What would be the point? She saw us all. She coulda talked."

"So he had her killed."

"Yeah."

"Who did it?" I said.

Fish sighed. He looked down at the table and didn't look up as he answered. "George," he said. "George Hood."

Gonzalez recorded the name. "We'll look into it," he said. He and Rich stood. "Wait here."

"What about my lawyer?"

"We'll call him."

We left the interrogation room. Gonzalez punched in George Hood, filtered some results, and brought up two pictures on his screen when he finished. "Based on age, it could be either of these two," he said.

"I have an idea to narrow it down," I said.

"Are we going to like this idea?" Rich said.

"I doubt it," I said. "It's why I'll do it myself."

CHAPTER 21

Sometimes, the best course of action is to walk into the lion's den.

Alternatively, driving there in a car you stole from the lion's chief minion is an acceptable plan. Soon, I would need to let Matty's BMW get towed away. For now, however, I focused on what I would do when I arrived at the den. The lion had fled. Some level of chaos could be expected.

I considered letting Rich and/or Gonzalez know about my plan, but they would have tried to talk me out of it. For justifiable reasons, I might add. They might have been able to infer it from our last conversation. If so, they hadn't tried to dissuade me. Esposito could have left an order to have me shot on sight. I wore the vest Rich got for me, but I hoped I wouldn't get to test its bullet resistance.

With Esposito in the wind, I needed a plan to try and find him, and I devised one. It was even a good plan. I depended on whoever had established himself as the alpha of the house giving me a chance to implement it. I took the Loch Raven Boulevard exit and drove toward the Oaks. The viability of my plan would be tested soon.

Before stopping and getting out, I drove by the house. I was in

Matty's car. Its bright orange paintjob would be visible from space, let alone from the residence I scouted. This was a car goons would be used to, however, and the darkened windows would prevent them from seeing me at the wheel. I passed the house once, then turned into the alleys and drove by the back. People who left trash cans and parked cars in places not meant for them made navigating the alleys harder than it should have been. I didn't see anyone camped out at the rear of the house.

On the street again, I parked the orange BMW two houses down from Esposito's. I took a deep breath. Just because saun-tering into the lion's den made for the best plan didn't mean I would enjoy it. Even with the lion absent, a bunch of smaller, vicious cats could still make for a rude welcome. I patted the gun at my side, got out of the car, and walked down the sidewalk.

As I climbed the steps to Esposito's house, the door opened. A man I once saw in passing stared out at me. I noticed the gun in his hand, which he held pointed toward the floor at the moment. "You got a lot of nerve coming here," he said. "What the hell do you want?"

"I want to find your boss," I said, stopping a couple feet from him. The gun made my heart rate climb.

"So do lots of other people," he said, confirming Esposito wasn't in the house.

"Who's in charge here?"

"How do you know it ain't me?"

I decided not to use the uncharitable response I had queued up because of the gun, and since I needed these guys not to hate me, at least for a few minutes. Instead, I said, "Because the man in charge never answers the door."

It must have satisfied this fellow as he nodded once. "You packing?" he said.

"I am."

"Gonna need to take it."

"How many men do you have inside?" I said.

He frowned. "Four. Why?"

"You'll have me outnumbered four to one," I said. "If I start to draw my gun, you have four chances to shoot me before I can. The odds are in your favor."

"So?"

"So I'm not suicidal. I'm keeping the gun."

Now he paused to think. "Fine," he said after a moment, "but I'll be watching you."

"The price of freedom is eternal vigilance," I said.

He led me inside. The house was narrow, as I would expect from a duplex, but deeper than it looked from the outside. Tan carpet not yet trampled down covered the floor. The living room held two sofas, a recliner, and a coffee table, all set opposite a large wall-mounted TV. Two men sat, one on each sofa, watching TV. They regarded me with a mix of hatred and surprise as I entered. "The fuck is he doing here?" one of them said.

"He's going to talk to the man," my escort said.

The other one answered my unasked question with a snort. "The man ain't here."

"Then I guess I'm talking to the man's substitute," I said.

"How do you know that ain't me?" the one on the sofa on the right said. After he asked, he stuffed a few potato chips into his wide mouth. Did all of them ask this question?

"Because you're sitting on a couch, eating chips, and watching a shitty house-flipping show."

"So?" he said around his mouthful of half-chewed chips.

I shook my head.

"Come on," the one leading me said. Then he looked at the other two. "Either of you want to come along?"

They groaned, but both got up and followed us downstairs. I wanted them to. The more, the merrier for what I planned. I got led down a narrow staircase off the kitchen. The basement was converted into a large office. A desk bigger than mine sat near the far wall. Three guest chairs were arranged before it. In a leather chair behind the desk sat Esposito's apparent surrogate--the man I knew as his driver.

"Well, well," he said as I sat in one of his guest chairs. The fellow escorting me and one of the other goons sat, too. "Surprised?"

"I guess I shouldn't be," I said. "Jeeves was the brains behind Bertie Wooster, after all."

The erstwhile driver smiled at the reference. The others self-identified as literary philistines by their confused expressions. We sat in silence for a few seconds. "Driven any nice cars lately?" I said.

"I could ask you the same thing."

I smiled and shrugged. "People who want to keep their cars shouldn't get their asses beaten."

"So I should try to take the car back the same way?" he said.

Now I needed to be careful. The guy behind the desk didn't worry me in a fight, but I was outnumbered four to one by the others, who did worry me to varying degrees. Even if they were just thugs used to ending a fight quickly, there were still four of them and sheer numbers would pose a problem. Never mind they probably all packed guns. "I didn't come here to talk about cars," I said. "I came here to talk about your boss."

The driver leaned back in his chair. It took him almost parallel to the floor before he adjusted and came forward. "He's missing," he said.

"I'm aware."

"No thanks to you."

"I didn't kidnap two people and have a woman shot," I said.

He didn't say anything. There wasn't much to say, really. Esposito's problems were of his own making. As much as this guy wanted to blame me for them, he knew the truth on some level. "You didn't," he said after a moment. "What do you want?"

"I want to find Esposito." The goons surrounding me chuckled. "Did I say something funny?"

"What makes you think you can find him?" was the only answer I got.

"I found Brian and Chris."

The revelation stopped the chuckling. Jovial expressions turned serious and unfriendly in an eyeblink. "Yes, you did," the driver said. "I'm sure you know that you're not the only person looking for Mr. Esposito."

"Of course," I said. "But there's one difference between me and everyone else looking for him."

"Really? What is it?"

"I don't want to kill him."

Now everyone fell silent. "You don't?" I shook my head. "What do you want, then?"

"I want to bring him in."

"You're not a cop," the driver said.

"Thank goodness," I said.

"Why would you want to bring him in?"

"Because he abducted two people and ordered Anna Blair killed." I watched the group for reactions to what I said about Anna. Nothing. Maybe none of these men killed her. Or maybe her killer owned the kind of poker face Lady Gaga would sing about.

"And now you want to bring him to justice?"

"It's more than he'll get if Tony Rizzo's men find him first." The driver looked surprised. "Really? You think Tony doesn't have people looking for your boss?"

The driver sat up and leaned forward. He put his elbows on the desk, rested his chin on his fists, and sighed. "I don't know where he is," he said.

He looked at me the whole time he said it. I didn't see any hint of nervousness. A quick glance at the goons showed similar behavior. He told the truth. "Do you have contact with him?" I said.

"Here and there."

"Good. Tell him to reach out to me when he gets tired of running."

"I don't think he'll like it," the driver said.

"I think he'll like it more than dying," I said.

The driver nodded. "I'll see what I can do."

"All right. Thanks."

He nodded at one of the goons. "Billy will show you out." He was the one escorting me so far. I stood. "We're going to want Matty's car back," the driver said.

"When I'm done with this, you can have it," I said. "I don't like it much, anyway."

Billy and his brutish coworkers—one of whom looked like George Hood—led me upstairs. One of them opened the door for me. I walked out. As soon as I cleared the threshold, the door shut and locked. I survived the lion's den. The absence of the lion might have helped. I walked back to Matty's BMW. Once I got in, I checked my phone.

Five attempted Bluetooth hacks, five successes. If Esposito reached out to anyone in the house, I would know about it.

Now I leaned on the hope he did.

* * *

In an ideal world, I would have five burner phones handy. Then, I could repurpose each into a clone of the ones I hacked. The downside would be carrying a total of six phones. The upside would be not straining the power of my lone unit. I gave Brian Sellers one of my burners and failed to get it back from him, leaving me with one. I could go out and buy four more, but what if Esposito reached back to his old employees while I was busy setting them up? No, keeping everything on my phone was the better option. I hoped it wouldn't be for more than a day or so.

I plugged my cell in and resolved to keep a more watchful eye on its battery level. It would deplete faster while it kept track of the five hacked phones. While I waited for some activity on that front, my stomach rumbled and reminded me I hadn't eaten much. I ate breakfast with Gabriella earlier and a snack en route to Esposito's—it's always better to eat in someone else's car—but nothing else. While I considered lunch options, my phone rang. I looked; it was mine and not one of the cloned ones.

"I was wondering if you were up for a late lunch," Gloria said.

"As a matter of fact, I'm starving," I said.

"Good. You want to come up here? I'll order something."

I said her offer sounded good. Leaving from my house or Gloria's would make little difference unless Esposito set up shop in downtown Baltimore. Since Tony Rizzo's people were looking for him, it struck me as unlikely. Still, I wanted to be ready to go at a moment's notice. In addition to my usual overnight items, I packed the bullet-resistant vest, a gun, and three spare clips.

Gloria owned a posh house in Brooklandville. It was one of many posh houses in the area, and all told, probably around the middle of the pack. Even the smallest house in the neighborhood could have fit mine twice over with space for a sunroom. Hedges and shrubs framed Gloria's driveway. Her red Mercedes rocket was in the garage. I parked Matty's BMW to the side of the wide driveway. If I'd brought the Caprice, the neighborhood watch would have been waiting to tar and feather me as I left.

After she answered the door, Gloria pushed me up against it and gave me an aggressive kiss. "I haven't seen you in a while."

"It's been an interesting few days," I said.

Gloria ordered Japanese. A tray of sushi sat between two steaming entrees. "I got you shrimp and chicken," she said. "Whenever we go to these places, it's what you order."

I smiled. She remembered. Gloria and I went out for Japanese a few times, always sitting at the tables surrounding the cook for the full experience. I couldn't begin to say what she ordered. Filet mignon peeked out from her takeout box, surrounded by fried rice, vegetables, and lo mein noodles. True to form, Gloria transferred her food to a proper plate once we sat down. I kept mine in the box. She used a knife and fork. I opted for chopsticks.

"Did you ever find the older brother?" she said after a few minutes of eating.

I nodded. "It took a while. His girlfriend didn't make it, though."

"They killed her?"

"Yes."

Gloria's eyes widened. "That's terrible," she said. "Couldn't they just let her go?"

"Apparently not," I said.

"Did you catch the man in charge . . . what's his name? Esposito?"

"Good memory," I said with a grin.

"I listen when you talk."

I could tell from the food spread, though the sushi turned out to be California roll. Not bad but disappointing. I remembered Gloria liked it. "He's run away," I said. "We've rounded up some of his crew."

"What about the rest of them?" said Gloria.

"They're hanging out at his house. It's kind of weird. I think they're waiting for him to come back, or at least to contact them."

"You think he will?"

"I'm counting on it," I said. Then I talked about my cell phone hacks.

"What are you going to do if he does call his men?" Gloria said.

"Attempt to find him," I said. "I tried tracking his former phone number. No activity. He probably got rid of it when he disappeared."

"Be careful, C.T." Gloria frowned in what I hoped was concern. "This man is scared and running. He could be dangerous."

"Don't want to have to learn someone else's Japanese order?" I said with a sly smile.

"I'm serious," Gloria said. "I know you say your job isn't dangerous very often, but there are times it is." She grabbed my hand from across the table and squeezed. I squeezed back. Then we both looked at our clenched hands, realized what we were doing, and pulled back. Neither of us tried to cover it by talking. I didn't know if denial made the moment more awkward or less. Gloria resumed eating her steak. I ate one more piece of California roll, which would be my last, before diving back into my entrée.

When we finished eating, I cleared away the plates, containers, and utensils. A very nice stainless steel sink sat amid Gloria's granite countertops. She also owned a flat-top stove I might have knifed someone to own, as well as a fridge at least double the size of mine. If this kitchen were mine, I would cook at least two meals in it every day. I wondered if Gloria cooked in it twice a month. The rare times she tried to cook or help cook in my kitchen ended with the smoke alarm going off, or the contents of the blender painting my wall and countertop.

Gloria said she wanted to find a series to stream. We settled in on her very comfortable couch and agreed on *Justified*. I already viewed the first season but didn't mind watching it again.

After a couple episodes, Gloria changed out of her normal clothes into sweatpants and a tank top. Both hugged her in just the right places. Everything Gloria owned seemed to be made just for her, even if she bought it off the rack. As I admired the way the tank top clung to her braless breasts, I wondered how she pulled her fashion achievement off.

We got a few more episodes in before Gloria got tired. Tired of watching TV, at least. Despite her yawns, I barely got in her bed before she climbed atop me. Not like I intended to complain. She said it had been a while, and it was true, and the interlude must have made it even better than usual. As we lay together afterwards, I thought about the last few weeks. Bobbi Lane entered my life, and it was fun, but our involvement would never resume. Gabriella showed up at my door, and I spurned her after wanting her for fourteen years.

When it came down to it, none of them were Gloria. She and I did not have a conventional relationship, but we cared about each other on some level. She worried about me when my cases went pear-shaped. I supported her recent interest in fundraising. For now, I felt happy the way things were with Gloria. I wondered if the nature of our association would ever change.

I chided myself for thinking such serious things as I drifted off to sleep.

* * *

EVEN AT GLORIA'S HOUSE, I woke up before she did. I went downstairs into her palatial kitchen and nosed around to see what lurked for breakfast. It looked a lot like my pantry and fridge when I neglected to go shopping for a few days. I resolved if I ever had a kitchen like this, I would keep it well-stocked. Or more accurately, pay someone else to do it. If I could afford a place like this, I could afford to have someone do my grocery shopping.

The highlights of Gloria's refrigerator and pantry included eggs of indeterminate freshness, very soft sourdough bread, and an unopened pack of provolone cheese. And coffee. She did get the beans right. I started a pot brewing while I cracked the eggs and hoped for the best. They turned out to be fresh. I fried four, added cheese toward the end, and toasted four pieces of sourdough. At the end, I produced two egg sandwiches to shame any McMuffin or diner product.

Gloria came into the kitchen as I finished. She wore small sleeping shorts and a clingy tank top almost causing me to over-pour a mug of coffee. I set everything on the table. Gloria smiled as I sat. "Thanks for cooking," she said. "I was just going to pick something up."

"I was concerned you wouldn't have enough in the kitchen," I said. I ate a bite of the sandwich. The sourdough toasted perfectly: crunchy on the outside but retaining softness away from the crust.

Gloria nodded. "I know. I cook so little I don't keep much on hand." She paused. "The stuff I have, I usually get in case you stay over. I know you like to make breakfast in the morning."

I didn't have an answer, so I took another bite of my sandwich and drank coffee. Gloria kept a key to my house. I didn't have a key to hers, but she stayed the night at my place far more often than I did at hers. Still, buying things for the rare times I slept over struck me as venturing past the bounds of our relationship of convenience.

Was it changing? Did either of us want it to? I didn't push for it, and neither did Gloria, but things have a way of evolving over time. I wondered how this would evolve and how we would deal with it if it did. Gloria ate her egg sandwich and drank her coffee, too. Maybe similar thoughts ran through her head. I liked her. I knew she felt the same about me. Worse things happened.

"Anything from your phone?" She broke the silence a minute later.

"Nothing yet," I said. "Some texts between the lackeys but nothing indicating they know where Esposito is. And nothing from him."

"What are you going to do if he doesn't text?"

It seemed an eventuality he would. "I don't know. If it comes to it, I think I'll let the police handle it. They can devote more people to finding him."

"Wow," Gloria said with a smile. "Turning something over to the police. You're getting soft."

"I did what I was hired to do," I said. "Brian wanted his older brother located and returned. Mission accomplished."

"So why are you keeping at this?"

"Because Esposito is an asshole," I said. "He killed a woman for spite and convenience. He needs to pay for it."

"I'm sure you'll make him pay," said Gloria.

"I'll do my damnedest," I said.

* * *

I LEFT Gloria's house close to lunchtime. All remained quiet on the Esposito front through the afternoon. I went back and checked his router. My added route no longer existed. It lasted longer than I expected, and the one good piece of info I got from it justified the work. I passed the time by running, having lunch, and reacquainting myself with some video games. Afternoon yielded to evening. I made a turkey burger and a Caesar salad for dinner. I almost finished eating it when my phone went crazy.

Esposito reached out. *I'm going crazy out here.*

A reply came in from one of the goons. *Good 2 hear from u boss*

I'm going to need more supplies soon. Don't want to go out and get them and don't want to be left here alone. The message meant someone stayed with him. Made sense. Esposito was a wanted man with some degree of paranoia. Expecting him to be in hiding by himself would be unreasonable.

Dont know where u r. how do we find u??

Talk to Danny tomorrow. He'll tell you.

ok

I waited a few more minutes but nothing else came across.

Finally, Esposito made contact. And his asshole brother knew where he was.

I grabbed the keys to Matty's BMW. I needed to visit Danny Esposito.

CHAPTER 22

Earlier in the case, I looked into Danny Esposito's information and found his home address. I didn't know if I would need it, but data is always good to have. He lived in Perry Hall in the county about ten minutes from Alberto's house. I considered Danny might be housing his brother, but the police would have visited him and searched the house. Unless his house hid a secret room somewhere—a paranoia indulgence I respect with the hidden closet in my second bedroom—his brother was probably somewhere else.

I pulled onto Danny's street. Medium-sized single-family homes, each made from one of four different cookie cutters, lined both sides of the road. Individuality in these communities was always in short supply and manifested itself in unusual shutter colors or a tacky boat in the driveway. As I drove down the street, I felt glad I didn't live in the suburbs.

Danny Esposito's house, like all the smaller models, boasted of a one-car garage and a short driveway. The larger residences had two-car garages and sat back about ten feet farther from the road. I parked in front of the house past Danny's. No car sat in his driveway, yet there was the garage. Two lights shone from the first floor. I would take my chances he was home.

I couldn't be as reckless as usual here. It was early enough for people to be awake and nosy, and there were enough houses on the street for the odds of a nosy neighbor to approach one hundred percent. I walked up to Danny's porch, used the knocker to bang on the door, and covered the peephole with my thumb. A few seconds later I heard footsteps move toward the door, then stop. Danny would be looking through the peephole, seeing nothing, and getting curious.

Sure enough, two locks disengaged, and the door opened about a foot. Danny's head appeared. "Hello, Danny," I said. He frowned. I surged forward as he tried to close the door.

I slammed into the door shoulder-first. The force of it staggered Danny back into the living room. The door flew open. I walked in and closed it behind me. By then, Danny recovered. Instead of doing anything useful, he stood there and glared at me. "What are you doing here?" he said.

"Danny, you're so rude to your guests," I said.

"You're no guest. Why shouldn't I call the cops?"

"Because I know you know where your brother is," I said. His glare softened for an instant, confirming it. "If you call the cops, I'll make sure they know, too."

Danny kept glaring at me. At least he was consistent. "I guess you came here to find out where he is," he said.

"I did," I said.

"I'm not telling you."

"Why not?"

"You're gonna kill him," Danny said.

"Actually," I said, "I think I'm the only person looking for your brother who doesn't want to kill him."

My reasonable response softened his glare again. "Really?"

"Really."

With the glare gone, Danny just stood there looking at me.

The whole thing was kind of pathetic. "We should probably talk," I suggested.

"Right," said Danny. "Yes. In here."

He led me into his living room. Tan laminate flooring covered every room in view. A few rugs were spread out in the living room, mostly under things like his boxy black coffee table. It didn't go with anything else in the room. The furniture was about two shades darker than the flooring. Danny's plain entertainment center was white. The coffee table stood out for the wrong reasons. Danny noticed me looking at it. "You like the coffee table?" he said.

"It's, um . . . very modern," I said. I tried to play it down the middle. If I insulted Danny's ugly coffee table, he could refuse to help me in a fit of pique. If I sounded like I liked it, he might offer me the hideous thing.

Danny nodded, then said, "Yeah, I like it." Bullet dodged.

"Where's your brother, Danny?" I said.

"You promise you're not going to kill him?"

"I can't promise."

"You said you didn't want to," Danny said, frowning.

"I don't," I said. "But if he pulls a gun on me, I'm not going to stand there and be a handsome target."

Danny pondered my words a moment. "OK," he said, "I guess that's fair."

"It's a lot more fair than he'll get from Tony Rizzo's men."

"A house our mother owned," Danny said, "is where he is."

"I'm surprised the police haven't found him," I said.

"It's not in her name. Her grandmother left her the house. I don't think our mom did much with it. Before she died, she set up a trust. It's not named after her or any of us, but the trust owns the house. Alberto's always had a key."

"Where do I find it?" I said.

"I'll write the address down," Danny said.

He jotted it and passed it to me. I looked at it. "Where the hell is this?" I said.

"Southern Maryland."

"At least I'll have a scenic drive."

"You want me to call my brother?" Danny said. "Tell him you're coming?"

"No," I said.

"Why not?"

"Because your brother is an asshole, Danny. You can grimace all you want. It's true, and you know it. He also doesn't like me and is likely to have me shot on sight."

"Maybe I'll call him anyway," Danny said, crossing his arms under his chest.

"You could," I said. "I could stop you, but I won't. I don't think you should make the call, though."

"Yeah? Why's that?"

"Because if your brother does have me shot on sight, I can't bring him in alive. But I promise you one thing: before I bleed out, I'll tell Tony Rizzo where he is."

Danny uncrossed his arms and sat back on the couch. He stared at me, then recrossed his arms. Then uncrossed them again. "Fine," he said after his bout of posture indecision, "I won't call him."

"Good," I said. "Thanks for the address."

"Yeah."

I left Danny sitting on the couch. He'd crossed his arms under his chest again.

* * *

AFTER I LEFT Danny's house, I stopped at home to pick up the bullet-resistant vest to wear under my shirt. Just because Danny said he wouldn't call ahead didn't mean he would keep his word.

He couldn't decide on where to keep his arms while he sat on the couch. I couldn't trust him to reach a decision on calling his brother. Even if he didn't call, the goon Esposito would have with him could be of the trigger-happy sort.

From Federal Hill, there were several ways of getting to southern Maryland. I headed south, picked up the Baltimore Beltway briefly, then took I-97 to Route 3. Past the Route 50 interchange, Route 3 continued as Route 301. I stayed on 301 for what seemed like an interminable distance before it merged with Route 5. How people drove across the country, I would never know. Navigating halfway across my own state was enough for me. Around the city of Waldorf, Route 5 split off from 301, and I took it south. I stayed on Route 5 past its weird interchange with Route 235 and drove into Leonardtown. It was not a big town. Maybe Leonard was not an important man.

Traffic thinned a lot as I got farther into the sticks. Not many other cars traversed the streets of Leonardtown. I found Washington Street and drove past some local businesses, including the county courthouse. The car behind me turned off there as I found the long driveway leading to the residence I wanted. It was a plain white structure, set off from both the road and the houses nearby. I noticed a lot of space between them in general here, a hallmark of more remote areas like this.

I cut the BMW's headlights as I turned into the driveway. It was paved and smooth. My approach wouldn't be silent but a lot quieter than driving over gravel would have been. I saw a couple of lights through the windows on both levels. Blinds were drawn upstairs but open on the first floor. I followed the driveway to the side, where it got twice as wide. Esposito's car, with his absurd MISTER E license plate—way to be inconspicuous—sat ahead of me and perpendicular to the driveway.

I killed the engine. No signs of activity from inside. If someone had noticed me, I saw no indication of it. I presumed someone did, however, so I didn't want to make any sudden movements and goad a goon into shooting me. The vest wouldn't stop everything and didn't protect my head. I opened the door a few inches at a time and stepped out of the car. Then I closed it at the same rate. It made little noise. I patted my side. The gun was there, should I need it.

I turned to make sure no one snuck up behind me. Score one for the good guy. Now I wanted to get to the front of the house unseen. Once there, I needed to figure out a way inside. Ringing the bell and picking the lock both struck me as poor plans. They gave anyone inside ample chances to shoot me. Picking the lock could make me seem like an assassin come to take out Esposito. Ditto going in through a window. If I had to, I would ring the bell. It was the least awful of my options.

I took out my gun and padded a few steps along the driveway to the front. I walked over the grass. As I got closer, I saw my options for getting in drastically reduced. A man holding a pistol stood on the porch. A few steps closer, and I saw him well enough under the porch light to recognize him. He was a member of Esposito's crew but not one I knew by name. He wore a t-shirt tight across the chest, covered by a windbreaker zipped about a quarter of the way. "You're a long way from home," he said.

"Just out for a drive," I said. I slowed my pace but took another couple steps.

"That's far enough," the goon said. He didn't point his gun at me. Still, I could hear my elevated pulse in my ears. "What are you doing here?"

"I came to take your boss in," I said.

"Can't let you do that."

"You haven't heard the rest of my offer yet."

The goon frowned. "Fine," he said. "Let's hear it."

"You know your boss isn't a popular guy right now," I said. "He knows it, too. I'm not the only person out looking for him.

But I am the only person who wants to take him out of here alive."

"But you still want to take him in."

"'Alive' is the key word. Maybe your boss would rather deal with Tony Rizzo and his men. Good luck getting this kind of promise from them."

"Boss doesn't want to go anywhere," the goon said.

I said, "How does he think this is going to end? Anyone but me comes here, and your boss is leaving in a body bag. You are, too, by the way."

"Maybe nobody else will come for him."

"I found him. It wasn't difficult. I'm brilliant, sure, so it didn't take me long, but I'm sure someone else will figure it out."

The logic made the man on the porch think. After a moment, he shook his head. "Can't let you take the boss," he said, "alive or otherwise. Get out of here."

"Can't," I said.

He raised his gun.

I raised mine.

We were about ten yards apart. From this range, I peppered the valuable spots on many a paper target. I presumed the man on the porch was a capable shot, too. But how capable?

"How good are you with a pistol?" I said.

"Good enough."

"You're going to need to be a whole lot better. See, I'm wearing a vest. So if you want to put me down, you've got to make a head shot. All I have to do is go for center mass."

"How do you know I got no vest?" he said.

"Not under that silly T-shirt," I said.

The goon raised the gun a touch more. He was aligning it with my head. He'd have to be a good shot to hit me. And I just gave him something to worry about, which would muck with his breathing and pulse. I assigned him a ten percent chance to hit me. I had about a 100 percent chance to hit him.

"I'm going to need you to leave," he said.

"Can't," I said again.

He held the gun on me. I did the same. It grew heavy. We couldn't have this standoff forever. Then the goon surprised me by setting his gun down on the porch.

"Toss yours, too," he said. "We'll settle this the old-fashioned way."

"Fair enough," I said. I tossed the gun about fifteen feet to my left. It landed with a soft plop in the grass.

"It'll be fair enough when you take that vest off," he said.

"Kick your gun away, then," I said. "You could pick it up and shoot me."

He nodded and kicked the gun toward the far end of the porch. I couldn't see it move but heard it slide across the wood and thud into something at the end. I took my windbreaker off, tossed it aside, then undid the bullet-resistant vest and tossed it atop the jacket.

"Now it's fair," the goon said. He ran down the stairs toward me. I took a defensive stance.

Clear of the stairs, he kept running. He stopped a few feet short and launched a kick at my face. His weight stayed back, and his balance remained good. It was a strike he practiced many times before. This guy was not the typical one-punch brute. I saw the kick coming and leaned away. He followed up with a series of punches, each of which I blocked. I tried for a wristlock on his last punch, but he wriggled free before I could cinch it in.

More punches followed. I blunted them all. After blocking a right with my right forearm, I turned my arm, stepped forward, and drove my elbow into my opponent's face. I aimed for his nose, but he twisted enough at the last instant to take the blow on his cheekbone. It still staggered him a step. While the goon's hands instinctively went up, I planted my foot and kicked him hard in the stomach. He doubled over but covered his face. I stepped beside him and pushed him backward over my leg. He tumbled to the ground.

I like to think myself above putting the boot to a foe while he's down. The reality is fair fights are for suckers and competitions. I kicked his ribs, then his back as he rolled away. I launched another to only glance off his back as he moved and got into a crouch. When he did, I spied the knife in his hand just before it flashed out at me. I dodged as best I could but still felt the blade bite into me. I glanced down at my shirt and saw a small tear. Could have been worse.

While I learned how to fight people with knives, it's never been something I cared for. A skilled opponent is at least predictable. The average person with a knife has a much lower skill level, but their moves are wild and unpredictable. They only need to get lucky and nick an artery once, and it's all over. I backed away as the goon got to his feet, swinging the knife in a wide arc to keep me at bay. No worries there.

I needed a weapon to make this fairer again. When I tossed my gun, I threw it to my left. The fight took us—or maybe my opponent steered us—to the right. My gun was too far away and so was his. Enough trees filled the yard for me to find a stick. It would be better than nothing.

He came at me with the knife, slashing at my chest. I stepped to the side and shoved him away. The goon stumbled forward. I looked around my immediate area for a good-sized stick or discarded baseball bat. Five feet to my right, a stick at least as wide as my thumb and about two feet long lay in the grass. I sprinted, grabbed it, and held it before me as my opponent came forward with the knife again.

Blocking it with the stick would be too difficult. Instead, I would need to avoid the blade or hinder the arm, then retaliate with the stick. I settled for avoiding the first few stabs. They were short and quick, though, and I found no chance to respond. After a third stab, I saw my opponent shift his grip on the hilt. He did a backhanded slash, which I stepped to the rear and my right to avoid. The blade missed gutting me by less than an inch.

The attack gave me an opening, and I took it. I smashed the goon behind the knee with the stick. His leg crumpled and forced him down on one knee. Before he could bring the knife around again, I whacked his hand. He didn't drop the knife. I whacked it again. The knife fell to the grass. He tried to curl up on defense, but I was quicker. I clubbed him in the back of the head with the stick. He fell forward and groaned.

I walloped him in the skull again when he tried to get up. Then again. And some more until he stopped moving. Blood trickled from his head. The stick finally broke. I nudged my fallen foe with my foot. He didn't move or make a sound. I knelt behind him and felt for a pulse. Not strong, but it was there. Once I corralled Esposito, I would summon an ambulance for this fellow. In the meantime, I retrieved my gun and put the vest and jacket back on. The slash across my midsection barked when I tightened the vest. Stitches were probably in my future. For now, I felt good enough to plow ahead.

I searched the fallen goon and found a set of keys. Gun in one hand and keys in the other, I walked up the four steps to the porch. Esposito was inside. He could have a gun and feel cornered. Feeling cornered might compel him to use said gun. I promised to bring him in alive if possible. If he gave me the chance, I would. If required to shoot him, I would do that, too.

The door stared back at me. One way or another, this whole mess would end soon.

* * *

I TRIED THE DOOR. Smarter than the average goon, he left it locked. I crouched to the left of the door. With my gun in my right hand, I finagled the key into the deadbolt with my left. Being right-handed made this a challenge. I got the deadbolt unlocked and started working on the main lock. The keys nearly tumbled from my grip at one point. Doing this in front of the door would have been easier, but then it also would have been easier for Esposito to shoot through the panels. Life is all about tradeoffs.

After a minute of fumbling, I got the lock undone. I felt like the stereotypical teenage boy fumbling to get his first girlfriend's bra unhooked. Those challenges never plagued me in my youth. I opened the door while crouching beside it, raised my gun, and waited. No bullets. I swung into the doorway. No one waited. As far as I could tell, the house was empty.

I stood and walked inside. A shabby living room greeted me. The furniture needed to be replaced a generation ago. Incinerating the carpet would have been a mercy. An empty pizza box sat on the coffee table, completing the disheveled look. Books and magazines lay about, amid a lot of empty soda and beer bottles. The TV played national news. I found the remote and turned it off. Esposito already knew I was here.

The dining room and kitchen were deserted. Neither looked better than the living room. The entire house was outdated. If someone younger than seventy were to buy it, it would need a complete revamp. I poked around more. Even the coat closet was empty of all but a couple of light jackets.

I ventured upstairs, gun barrel leading the way. As I got near the top, I could see light emitting from under one door. It could have been a decoy, but I doubted Esposito was so subtle. "Esposito, I'm coming up," I said, stopping a couple steps shy of the top. No reply. "I took care of your goon. I'm not here to kill you."

"Go away," came a reply from the bedroom.

"I'm here to take you in," I said. "You won't get the same courtesy from Tony Rizzo's crew."

"What are you saying?"

"I'm saying you can come with me, or I can tell Tony where you are."

"Yeah?" Esposito said. "What if I just shoot you?"

"You're welcome to try," I said, "but you should know I have a gun. If you come out with your own, my promise to take you in alive goes out the window."

"You're going to arrest me?"

"I'm going to drive you to the people who can," I said.

"What if I don't go quietly?" Esposito said.

"Ask your goon how well it went for him," I said. "Though you might want to wait until he wakes up."

No reply came. I waited on the stairs. Esposito had a lot to think about. Whatever empire he thought he would build crumbled around him. Defiance wouldn't help him. If Tony's men found him, the best he could hope for would be a quick death. If he came out of the bedroom guns blazing, I would shoot him. If he surrendered, he would go to jail, and the county would build a case against him to keep him there for a long time. He didn't have a good option. I hoped he decided against taking the easy way out in suicide by PI.

"All right," Esposito said a minute later. "I'll go quietly."

"You have a gun?" I said.

"Of course I have a fucking gun."

"Hold it out the door. Two fingers. Then toss it away."

I crouched behind the wooden banister as much as I could. Between the posts and being a couple steps down, I didn't think Esposito would have an easy shot. He would need to find me first. I could see the bedroom door and knew where to fire. I was ready. The door opened. Esposito did what I told him, holding the pistol out with a two-finger grip. He tossed it into the hallway.

"Come out slowly," I said. "Keep your hands up."

"I know the drill," Esposito grumbled. He walked from the room. His eyes had circles under them, and he needed a shave several days ago. I walked to the top of the stairs.

"Turn around," I said.

Esposito glared at me. "Make me," he said, in another little act of defiance.

"OK," I said. I kicked him in the side of the thigh. When his body bent toward me, I used my free hand and shoved him hard into the wall. His head dented the drywall.

"Jesus Christ," he said.

"You asked for it," I said. I took a zip tie out of my pocket and bound Esposito's hands behind his back.

He turned around and looked at me. His eyes showed no fire, and his eyelids looked heavy. This was a defeated man. "You're really gonna take me in?" he said.

"I'm not a killer," I said.

Esposito nodded. I led him downstairs. "You need anything for the ride?" I said as we walked into the living room.

"No," he said.

Once through, I opened the front door. The goon still lay unconscious in the yard. "He ain't dead, is he?" Esposito said.

"He wasn't when I came into the house," I said. I took out my phone and dialed 911 to get an ambulance. While it rang, I led Esposito onto the porch and down the steps. The 911 operator picked up. I asked for an ambulance.

As I did, I heard a loud bang, like a gunshot. Out of the corner of my eye, I saw Esposito's head burst. He toppled over as I dropped to the ground. My heart raced. At the end of the drive-way, I saw a car speed away. It looked an awful lot like the car I saw turning into the courthouse.

Someone followed me here.

I glanced at Esposito. The upper right part of his head was

missing above his eye. Blood and gray bits covered the walkway and the left side of my windbreaker. Probably my face, too, but I didn't want to check. I stayed in the grass. The car and shooter were gone. My pulse slowed, and my breathing became more normal. From the grass near me, I heard the 911 operator.

"Sir?" she said as I picked up my phone, "is everything all right?"

My hand shook from adrenaline as I held the phone. "I think I need more than an ambulance," I said.

CHAPTER 23

THE ST. MARY'S COUNTY SHERIFF'S DEPUTIES HAD THEIR share of questions for me. After the coroner's men took Esposito away, the paramedics checked me out. The cut measured about five inches long but wasn't deep. A round of wound cleaning and staples later, the medics took Esposito's goon away in the ambulance. I was left alone with the deputies. I had wiped as much blood and other fun biological matter off myself and my clothes as I could. Now I dealt with their questions, some at the scene and some at the sheriff's office.

They knew soon I didn't shoot anyone. Their people determined I had no gunshot residue on my body, my gun hadn't been fired in a while, and the bullet they dug out of Esposito would never fit into it anyway. I answered their questions as best I could. No, I didn't know who the shooter was. No, I hadn't noticed someone following me. Yes, it's true I may not be the best person at knowing if I'm being followed. Yes, I went there to take Esposito in alive.

One question stumped me, however: why didn't I call for an ambulance before going into the house? If I had, Detective Rollo pointed out, Esposito may still be alive. I conceded his point. The paramedics, perhaps accompanied by deputies, may well have scared off the shooter. I pointed out the goon was breathing and stable when I went into the house, thus not in need of urgent medical help. I also pointed out the brazenness of the shooter. He may have been undeterred by first responders and would still have enjoyed a significant head start on any pursuit.

In the end, St. Mary's County talked to Gonzalez and Leon Sharpe. I heard neither was happy to be awoken with questions about me, but both vouched for me. It was nearly two in the morning when I got dropped off at the crime scene and got into the BMW. I felt glad the cops hadn't asked for its registration. A couple still processed the scene. Yellow tape marked off the area where Esposito fell and covered the front door of the house.

I drove home. With the late hour and my lead foot, I made it in ninety minutes. I formulated my own set of questions about what happened, and I worked most of them out on the drive. Tomorrow, I would try to get answers if my quarry were still in town.

* * *

THE ANSWERS CAME TO ME. They were what I expected. After I ate breakfast, a car pulled up in front of my house. I looked out my front window. The car was dark, German, and appeared fast. It looked exactly like the car following me into St. Mary's County and sped away after Esposito got shot. Gabriella Rizzo stepped out of the passenger's door and came up my walkway. She gave me a small wave as the car drove away. I opened the door. "Good morning, C.T." Her smile and the morning sun playing on her skin made her look gorgeous.

"Good morning," I said, opening the door wider. Gabriella walked in and sat on my couch. I locked up and went back to the window. The car didn't come back.

"Jonah isn't returning until I call him," Gabriella said.

"Jonah?" I said. "Sounds like a nice Italian name."

Gabriella smiled. "Every now and then, Dad will hire a non-Italian."

"I presume he's the man you were telling me about earlier."

"He is."

"And now he works for you," I said.

"He does," Gabriella said with a nod. "He'd been with Dad over twenty years. I didn't want him getting away."

"So now he's your bodyguard?"

"More or less." Gabriella shrugged. "I don't know I've needed him for that but it's nice having him around."

"And sometimes, you find a way for him to use his particular set of skills," I said.

"That's a good way of putting it."

I walked into the kitchen and grabbed two IPAs from my replenished stock. Gabriella took one with a smile. "Jonah followed me," I said.

"He said you were pretty easy to tail," Gabriella said.

"He didn't follow me of his own volition."

"No," she said, "he didn't. I knew you would find Esposito eventually."

"And you wanted him dead," I said.

"He was trying to take over from my father," Gabriella said. "If he lived, he would regroup and try again."

I drank some of the beer. This was earlier than I liked to start drinking, but the current conversation offered a good excuse. "Your father didn't have people trying to find him?" I said.

"Sure," Gabriella said, "but his men are brutes. They have no subtlety. They may as well ask questions with their fists. If they can't beat an answer out of someone, they're not going to learn anything."

I nodded. Her explanation made sense based on what I had

seen of Tony's men. "And you had Jonah shadow me instead," I said.

"It seemed like the better move," Gabriella said. She took a long pull of the beer. "Following my father's goons wouldn't have done much."

"They don't like being called goons," I pointed out.

Gabriella smiled. "Then they shouldn't act so goonish," she said.

"What if Esposito would have forced me to shoot him?" I said.

"Then Jonah would have come home," Gabriella said. "I told him he wasn't to do anything to you."

If Gabriella took over for her father, I wondered how long Jonah would honor her order.

"Are you OK, C.T.?" she said. "I wasn't going to let anything happen to you."

"I'm fine."

"You understand why I did it?"

I nodded. "You did what you felt you had to do," I said.

Gabriella smirked. "That's not much of an endorsement."

"You are who you are, Gabriella," I said. "You're your father's daughter."

She nodded. "I am," she said. "But I'm still your friend, if you'll let me be."

Having Gabriella in my corner would be a giant perk. At some point, she would take over her father's operation, despite his current attitude on the matter. Tony and I had a pretty good relationship based on the fact he had been friends with my parents forever. But Tony and I weren't friends. He didn't come to my house, sit on my couch, and drink beers. I didn't know how often Gabriella would once she was running things, or if she would at all. Still, I would rather have her as a friend than an enemy—or even a frenemy.

"I'd like to be," I said.

"Good," Gabriella said with a genuine smile.

We finished our beers. Gabriella called Jonah to pick her up. We shared a long embrace, and she left. Halfway to the car, she looked back over her shoulder and gave a small wave.

Whenever she came back, I knew it would be interesting. And interesting wasn't always a good thing.

* * *

Later in the day, I drove Matty's BMW back to Esposito's house. I didn't know where else to take it. I also didn't know what kind of reception I would get, so I asked Joey to come with me. Billy answered the door when I knocked. He glared at me. "You got some nerve showing up here," he said.

"I didn't know someone would shoot your boss," I said. "He was alive when I brought him out of the house."

He didn't have an answer, so he kept glaring. I held out the car keys. "I said I would bring these back when I finished."

Billy held out his hand. I dropped the keys into it.

"You'd better be telling the truth," he said.

"I am," I said. "If you'd like to drive down and talk to the St. Mary's County Sheriff, I can give you a point of contact."

He shook his head. "Fuck off," he said, closing the door in my face.

"These guys don't get paid for their manners," Joey said.

* * *

Later in the evening with Gloria at my house, I got the call I had been expecting. "Coningsby, what a mess," my mother said.

"You don't know the half of it," I said. I decided not to tell her anything about Gabriella Rizzo. It would open a thread of conversation I had no interest in exploring.

"Your father and I heard you were OK," she said. "Richard told us." I heard a little peevishness in her tone.

"I'm sure he gave you all the details," I said.

"It would be nice to hear them from you sometimes, dear."

"I'll try and work on it," I said.

"Please do," my mother said.

"I did find the missing brother, at least."

"Yes, dear," she said. "The younger brother was very happy to talk about the job you did."

"I wish I had done it a little better."

"You got a family back together, Coningsby," said my mother. "That's important. It's worth doing."

"I know," I said. "I just wish this hadn't been such a problematic case."

"The easy ones would only bore you, dear."

My mother knew me well. "True," I said.

"Your father and I have transferred the usual amount to your account," she said.

"Thanks, Mom."

"You're doing good work, Coningsby. I wish it weren't so dangerous sometimes."

"Like you said, Mom, the easy ones would bore me."

"Very well, dear," she said. "We're proud of you. Keep it up."

"Thanks," I said.

"Just got paid?" Gloria said once I hung up.

"Yep," I said.

"Where are you taking me?" she said with a smile, then kissed me.

"How about upstairs?"

"You always know what to say to a girl," said Gloria.

"It's a gift," I said.

END of Novel #2

Dear reader,

Thanks for coming along on this adventure.

C.T. got to use all his skills, and still not everything worked out.

His next case will challenge him even more. What looks pretty straightforward leads to the worst criminals C.T. has come across yet. And not everything is what it seems at first blush.

Read *The Workers of Iniquity* today!

THE END

Do you like free books? You can get the prequel novella to the C.T. Ferguson mystery series for free. This is unavailable for sale and is exclusive to my readers. Just go here to get your book!

If you enjoyed this novel, I hope you'll leave a review. Even a short writeup makes a difference. Reviews help independent authors get their books discovered by more readers and qualify for promotions. To leave a review, go to the book's sales page, select a star rating, and enter your comments. If you read this book on a tablet or phone, your reading app will likely prompt you to leave a review at the end.

The C.T. Ferguson Crime Novels:

1. The Reluctant Detective
2. The Unknown Devil
3. The Workers of Iniquity
4. Already Guilty
5. Daughters and Sons
6. A March from Innocence
7. Inside Cut

8. The Next Girl

While this is the suggested reading sequence, the books can be enjoyed in whatever order you happen upon them.

Connect with me:
For the many ways of finding and reaching me online, please go here. I'm always happy to talk to readers.

This is a work of fiction. Characters and places are either fictitious or used in a fictitious manner.

"Self-publishing" is something of a misnomer. This book would not have been possible without the contributions of many people.

- The cover design team at 100 Covers.
- My editor extraordinaire, Chase Nottingham.
- My wonderful advance reader team, the Fell Street Irregulars.